# Murdered Under the Pools

## A Kay Lytle Mystery - Book 2

G. G. Rodriguez

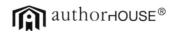

*AuthorHouse™ LLC*
*1663 Liberty Drive*
*Bloomington, IN 47403*
*www.authorhouse.com*
*Phone: 1-800-839-8640*

*Published by AuthorHouse 6/24/2013*

*ISBN: 978-1-4567-3716-0 (e)*
*ISBN: 978-1-4567-3717-7 (hc)*
*ISBN: 978-1-4567-3718-4 (sc)*

*Library of Congress Control Number: 2011901221*

# Contents

# I DEDICATE THIS BOOK TO:

God - The Father Almighty
My Cousins – Dennis and Lisa Corley
My Sister-In-Law - Norma Ramos
My Dearest Friends - Pearl Stockum
Ted and Sue Barker
And
My Proofreader – Nancy Carpenter

# ACKNOWLEDGMENT

I was disappointed and embarrassed when my first book, <u>Murder Under The Pool – A Kay Lytle Mystery</u> was published with grammar and spelling mistakes which were not edited. I apologize to anyone that bought my first book and had a difficult time understanding the story line due to those errors. It was like reading a jigsaw puzzle. I want to thank everyone who purchased the book and encouraged me to write this sequel. A librarian in Timpson, Texas, read my book and claimed it was the worst book he ever read. My publisher consoled me by saying that I would receive both good and bad reviews and not to let the bad reviews discourage me. My sister said the mistakes gave the book levity. She enjoyed reading it and encouraged me to keep writing. My precious friend, Pearl, bought ten unedited editions and made me sign everyone one of them in our Church parking lot for her family. Thanks to the support from the Peace Lutheran Choir Director, singers, and some of my closest friends, I was persuaded to complete the second book about Kay and her dangerous crusade to find her murdering husband, Leonard. My friend, Nancy, proofread the second book, so hopefully I have rectified this book of any embarrassing blunders (minimum errors) and the story will be easier to read and entertaining.

My husband has been my biggest supporter because he is the villain in the story and loves being the desperado: however, he is the bravest man I have ever met and nothing like the character in the story. I want to take the time to thank him. I would like to thank my precious friend, Donna, whose main source of communication is reading because she is 90% deaf. While she bravely battled liver cancer with weekly chemotherapies and an abundance of medicines, she has never stopped persuading me to write another book. Her love for God, family, and friends (in that order) has encouraged me daily to keep writing about Kay's adventures.

# A TIP-TOP LANDING

# CHAPTER I

The flight home started out to be a long and uneventful trip for Kay who was concerned about her Mother and Mr. Hughes' health issues. She could not understand why Mr. Blackstone's pen had reappeared in her purse the moment the plane flew over the area where Leonard's parachute was found. She wondered if he had survived the fall, especially since he had an injured kidney from the stab wound her Mother had afflicted on him at their last encounter. As she sat quietly reading her Bible, Officer Cox thought she was a little bit too quiet.

Officer Cox asked, "Do you really believe those stories in that book?"

"Of course I do," Kay smiled as she lowered the book. "If I did not think it was true, I would not waste my time to read it every day. Are you going to tell me, that after all we have been through, you do not believe someone is watching over us?"

"I think we have been very lucky," said Officer Cox.

"Luck, had nothing to do with it," argued Kay. "I believe we are being watched, even now. Have you ever read the Bible?"

"I read it when I used to go to Church until I realized that it was nothing but a good story book," said Officer Cox.

"You are very wrong. The Bible is the history of events that occurred over two thousand years ago," continued Kay. "It is divided into several sections: Psalms, which are songs written by David and Solomon to give thanks and praises; and Proverbs, which are words of wisdom and rules from Solomon; and the Scriptures, which are the words of God and the history seen by those that were there."

"Whatever!" alleged Officer Cox. "I do not believe it, end of story."

"No, this is not the end of the story," argued Kay. "Were you there when the civil war was fought? Were you?"

"No, Kay," answered Officer Cox.

"Then how do you know it happened?" asked Kay.

"I know where you are going with this, but it will not work," argued Officer Cox. "I have seen so many fake money hungry religious leaders in this world who have committed some execrable crimes. They said they were holy people. Explain that."

"Get back to the original question, 'Were you there?'" asked Kay.

"I told you no. I would be over a hundred years old," answered Officer Cox.

"There were people present during that time that recorded those events in the history books, along with the discovery of America, the holy wars over seas, and the Black plague," explained Kay. "The Bible is one of the oldest history books ever written. There were people who lived during that time and wrote the events on anything available to record the history of their times so their children and others would know what had happen during that time period. I know some of the recorded information has been lost over the years due to floods, fires, and wars, but there were those that safeguarded the facts and saved some of the documents to pass the history on to their families and friends for generations. The stories may seem contradicting because everyone sees events happening differently and they record their versions."

"That is all fine and dandy," argued Officer Cox. "That book reads that the creator is going to return. Explain that, Kay. It has been years and still no sign of him."

"Officer Cox," scolded Kay. "You must have been sleeping during your church services."

"You can not answer me, can you?" laughed Officer Cox. "And no, I was not sleeping."

"I did not say I could not explain it," said Kay. "This is how I see it. When you look up into the sky to see the sun, you have been taught it is there to keep us warm, it provides light, and it is the center of our galaxy. However, when there is a storm, the clouds cover the sun which makes it appear to be missing. When the storm is over, the clouds move away and the sun reappears in the sky. It never left, neither has God. God will make a formal appearance at the appropriate time; when the storm is over."

"Your family seems to be genuinely religious," said Officer Cox. "You go to church, you visit your sick friends, and I know how caring you are from working with you. So how do you explain Leonard? He killed your father, my friends, and destroyed your life!"

"Leonard is evil," growled Kay. "I saw what I thought was a good man but I was blinded from the truth. It was not God's fault that my father died. Leonard killed him and your friends. Officer Cox, have you ever heard of 'Free Will'? God gives each of us 'Free Will'. How you use it is your decision. I made a mistake when I married Leonard. Millions of people are fooled every day by being blinded from the truth. You selected a career that would help others by serving in the army and becoming a policeman. Leonard chose to live on the dark side. Good and bad things happen to everybody, but those who believe, know that God is there to help them through everything."

"We could argue the rest of the trip, Kay," said Officer Cox. "But it would not solve anything or change the way either one of us believe. You believe one way and I...."

Kay turned away from Officer Cox and opened the Book to finish what she was reading in the Bible.

"Kay," said Officer Cox as he watched her lower the book again. "I did not mean to make you angry. Everyone believes differently. Some people even believe in angels."

"And what is wrong with angels?" asked Kay.

By the look on Kay's face, Officer Cox knew he was touching a delicate subject. He said, "Nothing, I am sorry I even mentioned it. Go back and finish your reading."

Kay glanced at Mr. Blackstone's pen and commented, "Angels are everywhere."

A defeated Officer Cox shut his mouth and glared out the window.

As he stared out the window, he got a whiff of cologne that perfumed the air around him as in the past.

Kay closed her small white Bible and placed it in her purse. She could smell the man's cologne, too. She knew something was amiss. She had not seen Pilot Ed or the stewardess, Ms Sandy Stone, since they had taken off. Pilot Ed was suppose to bring them something to eat.

Office Cox noticed Kay unfastening her seat belt.

Officer Cox asked, "Where are you going? You do not have to change seats. I am sorry if I made you mad. Please, sit down."

"Something is wrong," Kay alarmed Officer Cox. "Neither Pilot Ed nor Sandy have returned to see if we needed anything. When we left the airport, he asked if we wanted something to eat or drink. Remember? He has not returned to check on us so I am going to check on him."

"Kay, you are letting your over-active imagination get away with you at twenty thousand feet," alleged Officer Cox. "They are probably eating the sack lunches that they purchased from the young boy at the gate when we first arrived at the airport. If you want me to, I will go and check on them, but you stay there."

"Thank you," smiled Kay.

Officer Cox had some intense thoughts of his own about the two frequent fliers. He was imagining Pilot Ed and the beautiful Ms Stone having an intimate moment in flight and he hated to interrupt them but Kay was insistent. She knew when she smelled that special cologne that something had to be wrong with either the plane or the pilot. Officer Cox knocked on the door of the cockpit but Pilot Ed did not respond. Officer Cox felt uneasy about breaking in on a romantic interlude, but when he saw Kay coming, he knew he'd better act fast. The door was unlocked so he entered the cockpit to find Pilot Ed and Ms Sandy Stone unconscious. Officer Cox hurried to Sandy who had white foam oozing out of her mouth. Pilot Ed's head was resting on the control panel. The same white foam was bubbling out of his mouth, too. He was able to set the plane on automatic pilot before he had passed out. From Officer Cox's observation, they had decided to eat the sack lunches and were poisoned. He checked their pulses and vital signs to see if either one of them were alive. There was vomit on the floor and foam on the control panel. It looked as if Pilot Ed was going to warn them about the lunches because he was holding the microphone in his hand to make his final announcement. Officer Cox collected the remaining lunch residue, returned it to the small brown paper lunch bag it came in, and put it in his coat pocket. He started to move Pilot Ed out of the way so he could pilot the plane when he felt a hand on his back. He jerked around to spy Kay trying to look over his shoulder.

"Oh my goodness," gasped Kay. "Are they both dead?"

"Kay," said Officer Cox. "Yes, they are both dead. I need you to return to your seat, fasten your seat belt, and stay calm."

"CALM," yelled Kay. "My pilot and Stewardess are dead. I know I can not fly this plane and I know you can not fly this plane. How can I stay calm? How did they die?"

"I am not sure but I think something poisonous was packed in the sack lunches," answered Officer Cox. "Right now, I am more concerned about getting us on the ground."

Officer Cox and Kay moved the bodies into the passenger area and laid them in the aisle. They both returned to the cockpit of the plane. Officer Cox sat in the control seat and attempted to alert the nearest control tower by sending out a distress signal.

"May Day," said Officer Cox. "I have a serious situation up here. Our Pilot and crew are dead. I need to make an emergency landing. Can anyone hear me? May Day."

The static finally cleared and there was a voice on the radio.

"This is the control tower in Colorado Spring. My name is Brice Green. What is your name?" asked the controller.

"I am Officer David Cox," he answered. "We were scheduled to land at Cortland Airport, but our flight crew was murdered and I need to make an emergency landing in an unpopulated area because I am not a professional pilot. Can you help us?"

"See if there is a flight instruction manual on board. Is there someone with you that can look for it?" asked Mr. Green.

"Yes, the owner of the plane is with me," he answered very nervously.

Looking at Kay, he asked, "Would you look around the cockpit area for the flight instruction manual. It would help me to know which gauges on the control panel I will need to use in order to land this plane."

Kay began to look in some of the compartments in the cockpit to see if there was a flight manual. She located it and handed the book to Officer Cox.

"We have it," Officer Cox reported to the controller.

"Turn to the section marked "landings," requested the controller. "It should have pictures of the gauges and control levers you will be using to land the plane. Are you sitting at the control panel?"

"Yes," said Officer Cox.

"Grab the yoke (the control steering device) with both hands," commanded Mr. Green. "Take a look at the gauges. There is an altimeter to the right side of the yoke. It measures the altitude. Can you tell me how high you are?"

Officer Cox studied the gauges. He spotted the altimeter located above the fuel gauge.

He reported, "The altimeter is at twenty thousand feet. I noticed the fuel pressure gauge is at the half way point. Will we have enough fuel to land?"

"What is your speed?" asked Mr. Green. "The air speed gauge should be below the fuel gauge. Do you see it?"

"Yes. The speed is 250kph. " answered Officer Cox. "Will we have enough fuel to land?"

"You should be able to land," said Mr. Green. "I need you to take the plane out of automatic pilot. There is a switch to the left of the yoke. Do you see it?"

"Yes," said Officer Cox as he switched the automatic pilot to the off position.

As soon as the automatic pilot was turned off, the plane began to take a nose dive toward the ground. Officer Cox was not prepared to lose control of the plane so quickly. He pulled the yoke toward him to level the plane out. This plane was nothing like the planes he had flown in Viet Nam. Kay was holding the armrest so tightly that her hands squeezed their impressions into the leather. She thought she was going to break the armrest off the seat. She wanted to say something to Officer Cox but she was scared speechless. Sweat was beading on Officer Cox's brow and running down the sides of his face. Faster and faster the plane plummeted towards the ground. They could hear the flight controller's voice over the radio asking what was happening and yelling out flight instructions. Officer Cox continued to pull back on the yoke until finally, he was able to get control, leveled the airplane, and answered Mr. Green.

"We are flying at nine thousand feet now, sir," exhaled Officer Cox. "I have control. What do I do next?"

From the celebration noises coming from the other end of the radio, Officer Cox could tell the control tower people were relieved and happy he had gotten control of the plane.

"You need to keep your directional compass gauges at latitude and longitude **38n50**, **104w49**, to Colorado Springs, Colorado. Your estimated time of arrival (ETA) should be fifteen minutes. We are preparing a runway for your arrival. I will need you to circle the landing strip twice before attempting to land. Are we clear with this?" asked Mr. Green.

"Yes sir," answered Officer Cox as he turned to look at Kay. "How are you doing?"

Kay was totally amazed that he could get the airplane to fly straight again. She had already visualized them crashing into a mountain and exploding in flames. She was able to paste a frightened smile on her face for Officer Cox as she used the sleeve of her blouse to wipe the sweat off his face. She realized he was as scared as she was.

"If you know any prayers or have any angel friends that could help us out of this situation, I think this would be the appropriate time to ask them for some help," said Officer Cox.

Kay was praying. She thought jumping out of a burning plane over the mountains in Black Hawk, Colorado was scary until now. She closed her eyes to say another prayer for Officer Cox.

"Give him strength, Lord," she silently prayed. "Please keep him safe."

"I never dreamed I would be flying again," said Officer Cox to break the silence. "It is harder than I thought but I was told it was like riding a bike. Once you have flown an airplane, you can fly anything.

"So, when we were flying out of control, nose-diving towards the ground," Kay sarcastically questioned. "Is that how you used to fly in Viet Nam?"

"I think I liked you better when you were reading your Bible," he remarked. "You could give me a little support here."

"I am sorry," moaned Kay. "But we still have to land in Colorado

Springs. If you get this plane safely on the ground, I will give you a raise."

"Officer Cox, you are nearing the runway. Do you have a visual?" asked Mr. Green.

"No, I do not see it," answered Officer Cox.

"I see it," yelled Kay. "Look, it is directly in front of us. It is that tiny cleared area."

"You have got to be kidding," groaned Officer Cox. "You want me to land on that?'

"Son, you can do it," encouraged Mr. Green. "I want you to stay focused. Lower your landing gear. The landing gear levers are between the seats. Once the wheels have locked into position, I want you to decrease your speed."

Officer Cox had no problem locating the landing gear levers. He and Kay listened to the wheels as they lowered beneath the plane and locked into place. There was a green light on the control panel to indicate that the landing gear was locked. Then he decreased the flight speed to 190kph as instructed.

"It is done, sir," confirmed Officer Cox.

"I want you to fly over the landing strip first before you try to land," tutored Mr. Green. "How much gas do you have?"

"The indicator is two notches in front of the "E" on the gauge," reported Officer Cox.

"That is plenty of fuel to get you down to the ground," inspired Mr. Green. "I want you to fly over the landing strip and make a mental note on how to approach it when you come around the second time."

As Officer Cox circled over the landing strip, he noticed several emergency response vehicles lining the sides of the landing area which gave him an uneasy feeling inside. He was glad to see them waiting but he was hoping he would not need them.

"Kay," whined Officer Cox, thinking this might be the only opportunity to tell her how he felt about her. "I want to tell you something."

"What is it, big boy," Kay bitingly said "Please do not tell me that you can not see the landing strip again."

"I can see it," smiled Officer Cox. "I want to tell you that.."

Mr. Green interrupted him saying, "You are doing a fine job, son.

Now line the plane's wings even with the two red blinking lights on the opposite sides of the runway. Once the plane is in line with these lights, I want you to open the fuel compartment and dump the fuel out. Empty the compartment completely."

"Why do you want me to dump the fuel?" asked a concerned Officer Cox. "We are going to need it to land."

"There is too much fuel in the plane," instructed Mr. Green. "The tanks need to be emptied if you hit the runway at an angle or crash. Since the tanks are empty, the plane will not explode."

"Explode," shrieked Kay.

"It will be all right, Kay," reassured Officer Cox. "I can do this. There is not going to be any explosion today. Mr. Green, we are coming in."

Officer Cox lowered the plane's right and left rudders and then continued to decrease the air speed as he approached the runway. He lined the plane's wings parallel with the lights on both sides of the runway. He decreased the plane speed again and pushed forward on the yoke. Finally, the plane touched the ground but it kept moving forward until he used the brake foot paddles in an attempt to stop the plane before they ran out of runway. He pushed the brake paddles completely to the bottom of the floor of the plane to force it to stop.

Suddenly, the front disc brake locked on the front wheel causing the plane to start to tip over. The two dead bodies that were placed on the floor in the passenger area, slid down the aisle to the cockpit's door, covering it and causing it to jam. The emergency response rescue crew followed the plane to the end of the runway. The plane finally came to a stop but was balancing on the tip (nose) of the plane and the front tire. The rear end of the plane was pointing straight up into the air, aiming towards the sky. Officer Cox released his seat belt while he was clutching the yoke he climbed out of his seat and tried to open the door which was blocked by the two bodies. Kay stared at the ground and watched the rescuers running towards the front of the plane. Officer Cox tried kicking the door but was unsuccessful in opening it. He removed his gun (covering Kay's face with his arm) and shot out the window. The emergency crew rescuers were running to the plane carrying fire hoses and stretchers, while others were preparing to catch Kay and Officer Cox.

"Kay," said Officer Cox. "I am going to release your seat belt. I want you to grab my arm before I release it and hold on tight. Then I am going to lower you to the men outside."

When Officer Cox released Kay's belt, she fell forward, towards the control panel but Officer Cox grabbed her in time to keep her from falling out of the broken window to the ground. The rescuers were ready to catch Kay when Officer Cox lowered her petit body out the window. Once Kay was safe, Officer Cox used the seat belts to lower himself out the window.

Then he dropped on the airbag below him. All of the rescuers applauded Officer Cox for his courageous tip-top landing. Several men patted him on the back and yelled, "Well done."

Officer Cox glared at Kay as they walked towards the airport terminal. He knew she was going to say something sarcastic about his unusual landing technique.

"I know you want to say something," he moaned. "So get it over with. Just open your mouth and say it."

"Is this how they landed planes in Viet Nam?" asked Kay.

"Yes," replied Officer Cox. "Is there a problem?"

"No, there is not a problem," smiled Kay as she gave Officer Cox a huge bear hug. "You are wonderful. Thank you for getting us here. By the way, what were you going to say before we landed?"

"I wanted to know how big of a raise you were going to give me," he lied as he helped her into the rescue vehicle.

He could not tell her what he was really thinking, but he hoped there would be another opportunity to express his compassionate feelings of love to her.

There was a man standing in front of the airport control tower waiting for the rescue team to bring Officer Cox and Kay to the front for questioning.

"You must be Mr. Green," smiled Officer Cox.

"Yes. I am pleased to meet you," greeted Mr. Green. "That was one outstanding landing, until the plane tipped. When was the last time you flew a plane?"

"Viet Nam," answered Officer Cox as both men shook hands.

"Why didn't you empty the fuel tank?" questioned Mr. Green.

"I knew I could land it," said Officer Cox.

"That was taking a big gamble, but you did. Who is this with you?" asked Mr. Green.

"This is Kay Lytle, sir," introduced Officer Cox. "She is the owner of the plane."

"I am pleased to meet you, Miss," smiled Mr. Green. "I think I saw you in the paper about a week ago? You were rescued off the side of a mountain near Black Hawk, Colorado. If I remember the article well, you were hanging from an American flag decorated parachute."

"That was me," confessed Kay. "My husband was trying to kill us."

"I remember that article," said Mr. Green. "It read that your husband's body was never found. Are they still looking for him?"

"Yes, I hope so," said Kay. "Although, I believe he was responsible for the poisoning of my pilot and crew."

Officer Cox had the same feeling, but he was not letting Kay know about it. He asked Mr. Green if he could speak to the airport security guards. He and Kay were taken to the security office at the airport. Officer Cox was interested in finding the young boy who had sold the bag lunches to them at the gate when they had arrived at the airport to board their plane to return home. If they could find the boy, they might be able to locate Leonard. Once in the security office, the security guard in charge had some questions of his own that he wanted answered before he would let Officer Cox ask any of his questions. After the airport security personnel had interrogated Kay and Officer Cox and they had verified their story about the lunches, poison, and emergency landing (and they were satisfied with their answers), they allowed Officer Cox to ask his questions. He wanted the security people to acquire the video from the private airport's security station to see if the hidden cameras had captured the boy's image while he was selling the lunches at the side gate. He furnished them with the half eaten lunch which he had salvaged from the plane, so they could analyze it. Then he made a call to Lieutenant Gorman to give him an up-date on the situation in Colorado.

While Officer Cox was busy with the security personnel, Kay watched as a huge tow truck go down the runway to the plane. A man climbed into a basket connected to a cherry picker crane which lifted him to the tail of the plane where he attached and secured a chain to the rear end of the plane, then waved a signal at another man below to move him away from the plane so the tow truck could gently lower the tail end to the ground. Once the plane was leveled, a team of men unlocked the plane's door and entered. A few minutes later, a man waved for the paramedics to bring the stretchers aboard. Kay could not watch as they removed Pilot Ed and Ms Stone from the airplane. She remembered how excited Pilot Ed was when he got to fly this new airplane. Since she had only known both of these people for a short period of time, she realized that she did not know any personal information about them. All she knew was that they had been employed by Mr. Blackstone. She would have to go through all the personnel files of the company when she returned back to Cortland so she could notify their next of kin or their emergency contact person. She was hoping that the human resource department with the company would help her contact the two families. She turned away from the windows and walked slowly back to the security office to be with Officer Cox. She asked the receptionist in the security office if she could use the telephone to call her Mother. The receptionist pointed to a telephone that was on a table in the waiting room for visitors.

Kay telephoned her Mother at the hospital to inform her that she was going to be late returning home. She did not tell her about the deaths or the unique airplane landing performed by Officer Cox because she did not want her to worry. Most of the information would be reported in the morning paper. She was not accusing Leonard for the deaths of her flight crew, but she had a gut feeling that he did it. She did tell her mother that Leonard's body was still missing. Her mother was hoping some wild animal had eaten him. She asked her Mother if she could talk to Carolyn. While she was talking to Carolyn, she spotted Officer Cox waving at her from the receptionist's desk to follow him. She wanted to tell Carolyn about everything that had happened and to keep the newspaper away from her mother, but she had to end the conversation and hurried over to Officer Cox to see what he wanted.

"There is a group of reporters at the airport entrance that heard about the airplane crew and they want a front page story. We can not say anything to them. If they approach you, it is important that you keep walking," ordered Officer Cox. "If you say anything to them, it might incriminate you."

"I will not say anything to them," agreed Kay. "Where are we going from here?"

"We are going to get a room at the hotel across the street so I can be near the airport while the security people are investigating the flight crew's deaths. They are retrieving the video tapes from the other airport to see if that boy is on them. Once we acquire a good picture of the boy off the video, we will have a composite drawing of him constructed and start passing it around the area surrounding the airport to see if anyone can identify him," answered Officer Cox. "The police lab in town is going to analyze the remaining lunch residue to detect the type of poison used to kill Pilot Ed and Ms. Stone. Once they have identified the poison used, we might be able to locate where it was purchased and who purchased it.

"That sounds like a good plan to me," smiled Kay as she thought to herself, "nothing but police talk."

As they started across the street to the nearby Hotel, there were several News Reporters waiting outside the door of the main airport terminal.

There was one lady, who was standing on the right side of the reporters, waiting for Kay.

"Mrs. Morgan," yelled the Lady. "I need to talk with you."

It had been quite some time since Kay had been called Mrs. Morgan. She spotted the lady waving from behind the reporters and motioning for them to come in that direction. Kay noticed that the lady was alone and did not have a camera. There was something alluring about her that made Kay want to find out what she needed.

"Officer Cox, I want to talk to that lady that is standing behind the reporters, please," requested Kay.

"What lady?" asked Officer Cox who was pushing the reporters out of Kay's path so they could get to a nearby awaiting taxi.

"Follow me," ordered Kay.

Officer Cox did not like the idea of running over to meet a stranger after two fellow employees had been killed. He thought this was a crazy idea but he followed Kay to the lady who was standing by a white Ford SUV which was parked next to the curb with the doors opened for them to climb in. Officer Cox made a mental note of the license plate before he got into the car. The lady hurried to the driver side and told them to buckle up. When all the doors were shut, she stepped on the gas and hurried out of the airport parking lot.

"My name is Janet Cross," introduced the Lady. "I read an article about you in the news paper several days ago. There was a picture of you and your ex-husband above the article which told about him trying to kill you and bury you under a swimming pool. The man looks like my sister's ex-husband. Would you look at this wedding picture of my sister and her husband and tell me if it is the same person?"

Janet handed Kay an eight by twelve framed wedding picture of her beautiful sister.

The moment she saw the picture, Kay recognized Leonard, wearing a black tuxedo and standing beside the blushing bride. Although his hair was a tint lighter and he had shed a few pounds, she knew he was Leonard.

"Yes, this is my ex-husband," verified Kay as she handed the picture to Officer Cox. "When did they get married? Do you know where he is?"

"He arrived in town four years ago to go to college here," answered Janet. "My sister met him in her Psychology class. She said it was love at first sight. Within a month of their meeting, they ran off to Las Vegas to get married. My family was furious. My father never liked the man from the first day my sister brought him home. He said his name was Tom Morgan and was studying to be a psychologist. My father's wedding gift to my sister was a home in Colorado Springs near Seven Falls."

"After five months into their marriage, my sister (who's name was Kaylyn but we called her Kay) began to act differently towards us and stopped visiting us as often. When I would go to visit her, she seemed paranoid. My parents became concerned so they hired a private investigator to follow Tom each time he left the house. While he was away from the house, mother and I paid my sister an unexpected visit to find out what was going on with her. We knocked on the front door several times but there was no answer. So we nonchalantly strolled around the side of the house and went through the side gate to the back yard. We thought my sister might be back there, unable to hear our knocks. My sister was no where in site; however, there was a beautiful swimming pool in the back yard that was newly constructed. When we returned home we tried calling my sister. My father went to the college to see if he could talk to her there. The college attendance assistant said she had dropped out of all her classes about a month ago and she did not return. My sister would never drop out of school because she wanted to be a psychologist and work with handicapped children. We contacted the police and met them at my sister's home. Tom was very cooperative. He allowed the police to search the house while he explained that Kay had gone on a school project with her psychology class out of town and would not be back for several months. We knew that was a lie because we were told she had dropped out of school. Tom showed us an airline ticket receipt to Panama which was dated three days earlier. He said he thought she had told us where she was going and when she was leaving. He apologized on her behalf for neglecting to tell us about the trip and causing us to worry."

"I know my sister would never leave without telling us. My father had the private investigator check with the airlines to see if a lady fitting Kay's description had bought the ticket and taken the flight. After he had investigated the airlines and examined the security tapes, he reported that a woman that fit Kay's description was spotted boarding the jet. We never saw my sister again," cried Janet.

Kay patted Janet on the shoulder to console her. She asked,"Did you try to contact her in Panama?"

"Yes," cried Janet. "My brother and I flew down there with several pictures of my sister but everyone at the airport there said she was not seen getting off the plane. None of the local people or police had ever seen her. We stayed there several days searching for her in the schools, hotels, and local hospitals. We called Mom and Dad every day to see if she had returned, but there was no word of her. My Father knew there was foul play committed so he put a hold on all my sister's assets and thought it would be a good idea to freeze her bank account so Tom could not withdrawal any of her money. However, it was too late because Tom had taken large amounts of money out of her accounts and had listed their home with a neighborhood realtor for sale, two months before my sister had vanished.

The new owners had paid Tom in cash for the house plus they had a deed which was signed by both my sister and him. Everything was handled legally. Then Tom disappeared, without a trace, with all of my sister's money, jewelry, and her car which was found two days later at the bottom of Grand Lake. "

"That is terrible," comforted Kay.

Janet continued, "When I saw the pictures of you and him in the paper and read the article, I thought you might be able to help my family get some closure," said Janet. "I hurried to the airport to talk with you but your plane had taken off. As I was driving home, I heard on my radio that you were going to make an emergency landing in Colorado Springs which would give me a second chance to talk to you so I hurried to this airport to meet you."

"What can I do?" asked Kay.

"Do you think Tom could have buried my sister under their pool like he did to you?" asked Janet.

"Why not go to your sister's home and ask the new owners if you can excavate the pool to see if she is buried there?" asked Kay.

"I went there after reading your article and I did ask them if I could have the pool hollowed out to see if my sister was buried there but they told me no. I told them I would pay for everything but they still would not let me do it. So I was thinking if you would go with me to the police and enlighten them about your story and identify Tom as Leonard, your ex-husband, then we could get a search warrant and have my sister's body exhumed from under the pool," begged Janet. "I will pay for your next flight out and your hotel rooms if you would please help my family."

Kay looked at Officer Cox who had been quiet through the entire story. She knew she needed to get home to bury Mr. Blackstone, who was her best friend and she had to check on her mother, Carolyn, and her other responsibilities. She knew they were tired after surviving a tiptop landing, but she thought delaying her trip home for one more day would not hurt them if they could help this family. Besides, it might give the police the time they needed to locate that boy from the airport and they could question him about Leonard.

"I would like to help her," Kay said looking at Officer Cox with her big doe eyes.

"There is a man out there trying to kill you," argued Officer Cox. "If he can kill your flight crew without being on the plane, he can get to you, too."

"He does not know where we are," insisted Kay as she looked at the mountains and trees in front of her as they traveled north down the highway. "In fact, I do not know where we are. I think it would be a good idea to help these people. It might bring Leonard, Tom, or whoever he is out of hiding."

Officer Cox knew that was a possibility so he agreed to stay and help.

Janet drove the car to a police station located downtown in Colorado Springs. She introduced Officer Cox and Kay to one of the policeman that was handling her sister's case. After talking with Kay, the officer was able to get a search warrant for Janet's sister's home. Janet called her parents and asked them to meet them at the house. The new owners of the home did not want anything to do with the police, Janet, or the construction workers that had followed them to the house; however, with the legal search warrant that was signed by a local judge, they had to let everyone in the back yard to excavate their beautiful pool. Janet's parents arrived after the construction workers had started digging. Janet introduced her parents to Kay and Officer Cox and asked Kay to explain how this man had destroyed her life. Kay could see the sorrow in this family's eyes. She could not help but think how this could have been her family excavating her pool for her body. Kay thought how lucky Janet was to have both of her parents. She remembered as she told this family what Leonard had done to her father and how he had planned to kill her mother with drugs to make it appear to be a heart attack. If she had not escaped from her bomb shelter tomb, both her parents would have perished.

After working for six hours, it was at five o'clock in the afternoon on a cool mid-September day when one of the workers was able to break through an area of ground underneath the pool. Something wrapped in a shower curtain was uncovered which released the horrible smell of decay. Janet's mother fainted when she watched as they attempted to pull her beloved daughter from beneath the swimming pool. Janet and her father cried uncontrollably as they tried to revive Mrs. Cross who was lying on the ground fifty feet from the burial sight. Kay ran inside the house to fetch a wet towel for the woman's face. As she was returning with the wet towel, she could smell that familiar man's cologne which was her warning signal for danger. She hurried to the family's side and handed the towel to Janet.

"Officer Cox," Kay whispered. "Something bad is going to happen. We need to get this family out of the back yard away from the pool area."

"What is going to happen?" asked a paramedic who had rushed to the family to render aide.

"I do not know, but I smell something that is making me very uncomfortable," said Kay.

"Everyone can smell that," said Officer Cox.

"Not that horrible smell, the cologne smell," said Kay. "We need to get away from the pool."

As Kaylyn's body was being excavated from underneath the pool, a construction worker noticed a wire that was tied to the body which anchored it to the pool. He tried several times unsuccessfully to untie the wire. Two more workers and a policeman hustled over to the area to help him cut the wire. Officer Cox was intensely watching as the workers and policeman tried to remove the wire from the body when he realized he had seen that same scene when he was on one of his tours of duties stationed in Viet Nam. The Vietnamese would partially bury a United States Soldier's body and then tie a wire around it which they would connect to a bomb. While the medics were uncovering the body, they would disturb the wire and trip (detonate) the bomb.

"DO NOT TOUCH THAT!" he yelled as he pushed Kay to the ground next to the family, lying his body on top of theirs trying to cover all of them from harm. "**IT IS A BOMB!**"

# THE ONE-EYED DOCTOR

# CHAPTER II

When the policeman attempted to remove the wire which had become entangled with the bottom part of the body, the bomb was detonated. They heard Officer Cox's yells but it exploded before they could flee to safety. Pieces of the swimming pool's ceramic tiles, cement, and dirt flew through the air, covering everyone that was in the backyard. Many of the windows in the house, facing the backyard, were broken from the airborne debris and the blast from the explosion. Some of the neighbor's back windows were broken and part of the fence that separated the yards went down with the blast. The three workers and the policeman that were trying to remove the wire were killed instantly. Their bodies, along with Kaylyn's body, were blown into pieces and were scattered across the lawn. Janet's family, Kay, Officer Cox, and the other workers were far enough away from the pool causing them to only receive some minor abrasions and small surface injures from the flying debris. The owners of the house were watching from the second story windows when the explosion occurred but the windows did not shatter, they cracked.

A policeman, standing guard in the front of the house, was interrupted by the explosion while he was talking on the patrol car radio. He spotted some of the debris flying through the air so he immediately called for more emergency assistance. Officer Cox, who was covered with dirt, was assisting the seriously injured workers while Kay helped Janet and her family to the front of the house.

"You are bleeding, Kay," gasped Janet pointing at Kay's arm.

Kay looked at both of her arms until she spotted the blood oozing from a small laceration above her left elbow that looked worse than it was. A young paramedic rushed over to help her and asked her to sit on the ground so he could assess the seriousness of the wound.

Caring people from all over the neighborhood dashed over to see what had happened and render aide if needed. Some of the neighbors were bringing medical supplies, towels, and sheets to wrap those who were in shock or bleeding. The sounds of sirens filled the night as fire trucks and ambulances rushed the obliterated area to provide help. The paramedic told Kay that she would need to go to the hospital for some stitches. He and another paramedic tried to assist Kay to a near by parked ambulance. Kay thought they were making too much out of nothing, even if there was blood covering the left sleeve of her blouse.

"I need to tell Officer Cox where you are taking me so he can come get me," resisted Kay. "Besides, there are other seriously injured people here that need you more than I do."

"We will have someone at the hospital call the Officer for you," said the persistent paramedic.

"I would rather go with my friends," ordered Kay as she pulled her arm away from the paramedic. She could smell that man's cologne again and it was not coming from either one of those paramedics.

She frantically yelled at the paramedic, "Help those other injured people and leave me alone. Officer Cox, where are you?"

Officer Cox, who had been busy carrying some of the injured workers to the front lawn, had not noticed that Kay was out of sight until he spotted Janet helping her parents into their family car. He thought that he heard her call out his name, but there were lots of people running around crying and screaming.

"Janet," he yelled as he hurried to the car. "Where is Kay?'

"A paramedic said she needed some stitches in her arm," answered Janet. "They are taking her to the hospital in an ambulance."

"What ambulance?" demanded Officer Cox. "What hospital?"

Janet pointed toward a man who was opening the back door of an unmarked emergency vehicle, while another man was dragging Kay toward it. He could tell that Kay was being forced to go with them and was fighting to free herself. Officer Cox pulled his gun and fired a shot into the ground to get their attention. Everyone in hearing distance of the shot fell to the ground and the screaming began again. Some of the other officers that were helping in the front yard pulled their guns and ran to assist Officer Cox. The ambulance driver raised his tattooed hands into the air as if he was being arrested. The other paramedic released Kay's arm, causing her to fall to the ground, and raised his hands into the air but he kept walking towards the vehicle. One of the Colorado Springs officers yelled at the men to drop to the ground, but instead, both men darted to the vehicle, jumped in and fled the scene.

Officer Cox fired several shots at the fleeing vehicle but was unsuccessful in stopping it. Two other officers jumped into a patrol car and pursued the two fugitive paramedics. With all the confusion, everyone assumed that the men were with the emergency team and had no reason to think anything else while they were helping Kay.

Officer Cox hurried to Kay's side and helped her up from the ground.

"I think I remember telling you not to go off with strangers," scolded Officer Cox.

"I told them that I did not want to go," said Kay. "Honest, I did. Who were those men? What do they want with me?"

"Let me look at your arm," he demanded as he returned his gun to the holster. He could see the blood but after examining the small cut, he knew she did not need hospitalization. He stuck a sterile 'Curad' band aide across the top of it to keep it clean. He was hoping the pursuing policemen would be able to get a license number to track the car or be able to stop those men so he could interrogate them at the police station.

Kay and the officers walked to Janet's car. Officer Cox asked Janet if they could use her car until they had another flight out of Colorado. Janet's mother invited Officer Cox and Kay to stay at their home while they were in town for as long as they wanted.

"My home, is your home, child," she said as she gave Kay a hug. "Thank you for helping us. Now Kaylyn can rest in peace."

Officer Cox explained that if they stayed with them it would be putting their lives in danger.

Janet handed Officer Cox the keys to her car and said, "You can keep it for as long as you need it."

"How do you get to the police station from here?" asked Officer Cox.

"You can follow me, sir," said a policeman that was standing behind him. "I am going there to make my report. It is not far."

Kay thanked Janet and her family for being helpful. She and Officer Cox followed the fellow officer to the police station to find out if the two phony paramedics had been apprehended.

The police station was five miles from the exploding crime scene. Once inside, Officer Cox identified himself to the officers on duty. He wanted to know if the two men driving the ambulance had been apprehended. The dispatcher on duty said that the weirdest thing had happened during the chase. While the officers were in pursuit of the fleeing vehicle, the vehicle lost control at the top of the hill on Highway 25, a few miles west of 21st Street. The unmarked ambulance flipped three times before it burst into flames and continued to fall to the bottom of the gorge. One man was thrown from the vehicle, which the pursuing officers were able to rescue. The other man went down with the car and burned to death. The officers are taking the rescued man to the local hospital in Colorado Springs where he will be questioned and identified.

"How do you get to the hospital?" asked Officer Cox. "I need to ask him some questions, too."

The dispatcher wrote the directions to the hospital on the back of a card that had the police station telephone number on the opposite side. He told Officer Cox that the weather was getting awful and snow flurries were expected to fall all night. Officer Cox was not concerned with snow. He escorted Kay to Janet's car and they drove to the hospital.

At the hospital Officer Cox asked one of the candy striper volunteers, who was working in the nurse's station at the emergency room, for information on the man that was brought in by the police. She pointed to a door down the hallway and told Officer Cox that the men were in that area.

Officer Cox asked Kay to stay at the nurse's station while he went to question the bogus paramedic.

"If anyone tries to take you anywhere, call me," ordered Officer Cox. "I should not be long. While I am doing this, would you get the directions to the airport? I remember seeing a Hotel near there and we can get a room."

"Rooms," Kay corrected him. "Be careful."

Officer Cox smiled at Kay and hurried down the hall to the emergency room area where two officers were standing guard near a bed where the hurt fake paramedic was being treated.

"May I talk to this man?" asked Officer Cox as he showed the two officers his identification. "You can call the station to verify that I do have permission from your commanding officer to question this man."

"You will need to check with the doctor to see if he is able to answer any questions, sir," said one of the guarding officers. "However, I will call this in to follow protocol. Will you give me a minute?"

"Yes," answered Officer Cox. "I will talk to the doctors while you make the call."

One doctor was wrapping the man's head while another doctor was inserting an intravenous needle into one of the veins in the man's handcuffed arm. The needle was connected to a bottle of fluid by a long tube that was hanging from a post on wheels for easy mobility. There was a nurse next to the doctor assisting with the patient. The patient experienced a minor head injury from the car accident, along with some gashes and bruises that needed to be bandaged. He watched as the doctors treated his injuries and asked if he could make a telephone call.

"You are lucky to be alive," remarked one of the doctors. "I understand that you were thrown from the car as it was flipping."

"It was an ambulance, doc," smarted off the man. "I need to make a telephone call."

The guarding officer returned to tell Officer Cox that he could question the detainee.

"May I have a word with this patient?" asked Officer Cox, flashing his badge. "It will not take me long."

"He may have a concussion, sir," said the Doctor. "I would like to keep him overnight."

"That will have to be someone else's decision," said Officer Cox. "I just want to question him."

The doctors nodded with approval as they stepped outside to let Officer Cox get near the man to do his questioning and to give the other officers more space for the interrogating; however, the nurse stayed behind to administer any type of medical aide if needed.

"What is your name?" asked Officer Cox.

"What is it to you?" remarked the man. "I want to make a phone call. I know I am allowed to have one telephone call."

"Why were you at Cheyenne Blvd today? Who told you to kidnap that lady?" asked Officer Cox.

"I want to make a call. I know my rights," he said ignoring the questions.

"LOOK, Mister," yelled Officer Cox. "I can pin three cases of murder on you right now. One of the victims was a fellow officer who was killed in the line of duty. You will not last one day in prison if you are even able to get into a prison. Now, answer my questions and I might see if I can get a lighter sentence for you. Are you going to talk or not?"

"I did not kill anyone, sir," said the prisoner who was looking at the two other mad officers standing near his bed that were nodding their heads in agreement with Officer Cox's statement. "This man paid us to drive up in the ambulance to pick up that woman. He said he was making a movie and he wanted us to play the part of paramedics. He paid us one hundred dollars each and promised us another hundred dollars when we called him on the radio to let him know we had the girl."

Officer Cox handed the man a picture of Leonard and asked, "Is this the man."

The prisoner looked at the picture then returned it to Officer Cox as he replied, "It sort of looks like him, but this man has only one eye and wore a black patch over the missing eye. He had a scar on his face above his brow and his hair was longer. It could be the same guy."

"Do you know where that man could be?" asked Officer Cox.

"No," said the prisoner. "He gave us a number to call when we had completed the scene."

"If you thought you were in a movie, why did you flee from the police? Were you thinking that they were actors, too? Why did you run?" asked one of the guarding officers.

"When I saw the fear in that girl's eyes and heard that gun fired, I knew that this was a set up," said the man. "We only wanted to get out of there to find that man who had paid us so we could bring him in to explain what we were doing. We tried to radio him several times, but we never could reach him. The next thing I heard was a shot through the driver's side window and my best friend's brains were splattered all over the inside of the car and on my body. I tried to stop the ambulance but lost control and it began to roll. You did not have to kill him. We were not going to hurt anyone."

The two guarding policemen looked at Officer Cox and said, "We did not fire one shot at those boys during that chase."

"YOU LAIRS," yelled the prisoner. "You police people stick together. No one will ever know you shot and killed him because the fire destroyed any kind of evidence that would prove you shot him."

"You said the shot came from the side window," Officer Cox alleged. "The officers were behind you which would have made it impossible to shoot at you through the side window. Someone else killed your friend and did not want you to talk to us. Can I have the telephone number that you were supposed to call?"

"Yes," said the frighten prisoner. "It is in my back pocket. My name is Jeff Turner. Are you going to help me? Is he going to try to kill me, too?"

Officer Cox and the policemen could tell that Jeff was telling the truth. They assured him that there would be a guard by the door all night and they would represent him in a court of law in his defense to prove he was a pawn used to kidnap Kay. He would probably get a lesser sentence or be released. Jeff felt relieved to know they were going to help him and he closed his eyes to rest. Officer Cox could see that Jeff was tired and asked the policemen to step into the hall so he could inform them of how dangerous Leonard was and what he was capable of doing. He wanted them to be on the alert at all times because Leonard had nothing to lose and he would kill anyone who got in his way. He asked them not to let anyone in the room without checking for some identification.

While they were talking, a doctor stepped into Jeff's room. He asked the nurse to get a mild sedative to calm the patient so he could rest more peacefully. Jeff's eyes were still closed when the doctor entered the room. He never saw the doctor stick a hypodermic needle full of Phenol Guanidinium Thiocycanate, the same poison used to try to kill Kay, into the side of the intravenous tube leading into Jeff's arm. He dropped the hypodermic needle on the floor when the nurse returned faster than he had predicted with a tray that had the tranquilizer and a small cup of water on it. The doctor thanked her and he left the room, leaving the syringe under the hospital bed. Jeff thought he recognized the doctor's voice and opened his eyes to see who the nurse was talking to, but he only was able to see the back of the doctor's head and white coat as he closed the door to leave. The nurse administered the sleeping pill to Jeff and she watched as he finished the water. As she was taking the cup from his hand, he began to go into convulsions. The nurse pressed the emergency button on the speaker to get some help into the room. The two doctors, that had greeted the other emergency room physician coming out of the room, rushed into the room to save Jeff. The officers were distressed because they had only questioned the boy for a few minutes and it did not seem like Jeff was injured badly enough to go into convulsions. The doctors asked the police to leave the room so they could do their job. As Officer Cox turned to leave the room, he spotted the empty syringe on the floor under the bed. He stooped down to retrieve the syringe and put it in his coat pocket. One of the policemen asked him what he had found, but Officer Cox was thinking of only one person, Kay. He could smell a man's cologne that was very familiar. It was the same fragrance he had smelled on the airplane when he found the pilot and Miss Stone dead. He knew he had to get to Kay.

Kay was talking to the candy striper volunteer and telling her about the explosion that had occurred on Cheyenne Blvd. when she heard the emergency alarm sound off and heard a nurse calling for doctor assistance. A doctor passed Kay, while she was standing at the nurse's station, smiled, and went down the fire escape stairway.

She remarked to the nurse that it must be hard being a doctor with one eye. The candy striper was going to say something but Officer Cox rushed up and told Kay that they needed to leave. Kay had seen that look in his eyes before so she thanked the volunteer for the directions to the airport and hotel as she hurried off with Officer Cox.

"What happened?" Kay asked as she got into Janet's car.

"He is in the hospital," said Officer Cox as he drove madly out of the parking lot, checking his rear view mirror to see if they were being followed. "I think he was impersonation a doctor. I did not see him but I knew he was there because he left a calling card with his finger prints on it. I found this empty syringe on the floor under the bed in Jeff's room. I think there is poison in it."

"Who is Jeff?' asked Kay. "Please, slow down. It is snowing and the roads are slick."

"He was the young man that was paid by Leonard to kidnap you," answered Officer Cox as he ran through a red traffic light. "He thought he was being paid to be in a movie until he looked into your eyes. He knew you were not acting when you started screaming. I do not know when he got into Jeff's room because I was telling the policemen to be on guard to watch for Leonard. I should have never left the boy. He was a good kid. I can tell a good kid from a bad one, and he did not deserve to die like that. When I went into that hospital room and smelled that man's cologne, I knew Leonard had been there and I needed to get to you."

"Died? Jeff is dead?" questioned Kay. "I thought you were going to question him. How did he die?"

"I think the poison in this syringe killed him. In the morning I am going to take this to the police station to have it analyzed. I did get a little information from Jeff. When he looked at the picture of Leonard, he said that his appearance was different."

"Different in what way?" asked Kay. "Did he dye his hair again?"

"No," answered Officer Cox. "Jeff said he had a scar above his brow and was wearing a patch over one of his eyes. He must have lost an eye when he fell out of the plane."

Kay got cold chills as her face turned white when she looked at Officer Cox and asked, "Was it a black patch?"

"Yes," answered Officer Cox.

"He passed me while I was talking at the nurse's station. He could have taken me at that time but the alarm went off as he was passing so he went down the fire escape stairway. Oh NO, he is alive," cried Kay.

# THE SNITCH

# CHAPTER III

The snow started coming down thicker and harder until it was almost impossible for Officer Cox to see to navigate the car on the road. He must have missed one of his turns in his hurry to get away from the hospital because he seemed to be getting farther away from the city and civilization as the snow covered road started becoming narrower. He could see nothing but night and snow in the rear view mirror.

Out of nowhere, Kay spotted a service station's flickering lights on the left side of the road and told Officer Cox to stop because she needed a quick break. He did not realize they were running low on fuel so he turned into the service station to fill the gas tank and ask for some directions to any nearby hotel to get out of the weather.

Inside the station, Kay asked the clerk where the ladies room was located. The clerk smiled and said it was in the back of the store to the right of the soda machines. Officer Cox stood guard in front of the door while Kay vomited in the toilet. She could not believe Leonard was alive and he had walked right pass her in the hospital. The more she thought of him, the more she vomited. After she washed her face, she stepped out of the ladies room feeling tired and hungry. Officer Cox handed Kay his gun and asked her to stand watch while he used the restroom. When he had finished, he replaced the gun in his holster and paid the clerk for the gas. Kay asked the clerk if there was any place to eat that would be opened and near by.

Kay whined, "We have not eaten all day and the snow seems to be getting worse."

"There is a small hotel located half a mile from here that offers a hot breakfast in the morning. The owner of this station also owns the hotel. You might want to buy some hotdogs while you are here. I have been told that they are delicious. It is always a good idea to have something in your car to eat and drink when you are in Colorado. You never know when the weather is going to get worse," alleged the clerk as he looked up from his reading material. "There are no stores or restaurants beyond that hotel. I would suggest that you stay there and leave after breakfast. By then, the road should be cleared enough to get to the airport."

"What are you reading?" asked Kay.

"The Word," smiled the clerk. "I never get tired of reading or hearing The Word. You look like someone who reads and believes The Word."

"I read the Bible every day. Is that what The Word is?" asked Kay.

"Yes, but we call it The Word," said the Clerk.

After Officer Cox had filled the car, he returned to the inside of the station to see why it was taking Kay longer than it should to get directions. He did not notice that he had dropped one of his gloves on the ground when he entered the store to get Kay.

"Help me pick out something to eat. The clerk told me that there is a hotel up the road that serves a hot breakfast in the morning; however, everything beyond that point is closed," informed Kay.

"No, I said there was nothing beyond that point," repeated the gray headed clerk. "It is important to leave the hotel the same way you arrived. You will see your route clearer in the morning. This storm will not last long."

Kay bought some drinks, bags of chips, two hotdogs, and a few candy bars for the night's meal. Officer Cox added four more hotdogs to the groceries.

"I think there is a man following us," warned Officer Cox. "He is very dangerous. Here is a picture of him but he wears a black patch over one of his eyes. If he comes here, he will hurt you because he does not like snitches. It would be best to keep the door locked after we leave."

"Thank you for your concerns. I was keeping the store open for you," smiled the clerk. "When you leave, I will leave, too."

Kay paid the clerk and thanked him for all his help.

"Have a blessed night, sir," smiled Kay.

"I always do," returned the Clerk. "You have a safe trip and keep reading The Word."

"What is The Word," asked Officer Cox as they walked to the car.

"The Word is the Bible," answered Kay. "He was reading the Bible when we arrived. When he was talking to me, I felt reassured that everything was going to be all right tonight. There was a certain kind of serenity about him. Did you feel it?"

"All I know is, I am tired and hungry and I want to get out of this snow," he groaned.

The moment they left the service station's flickering lights disappeared in the falling snow. There was a hotel, named Emily's, located on the same side of the road as the service station which had a shining vacancy sign posted in the front window. Officer Cox drove under the covered parking area that was in front of the hotel registration entrance door. He and Kay grabbed their luggage, their groceries, and entered the beautiful carved door of the hotel.

The hotel was beautiful with a huge fire place next to the registration desk that had a warm inviting fire burning several large rotten logs. At the desk, Kay asked to have two rooms that were connected.

"There is one suite remaining," advised the desk clerk. "It has a sofa in one room, a wet bar, and a lovely king size bed in the sleeping area. It is a non-smoking room located on the first floor. Room numbered seven."

"That will be fine, sir," said Officer Cox looking at Kay. "I will sleep on the sofa."

Kay handed the clerk her credit card, signed the ledger, and asked when breakfast would be served.

"Breakfast is ready at six o'clock, Miss," answered the clerk as he returned the credit card and pointed to the dining area of the hotel. "It is complimentary with any suite."

"Will it be acceptable if I leave my car under that cover?" asked Officer Cox. "If not, I will move it. I could not see any parking areas due to the snow when I drove up."

"It will be fine, sir. I know you will be our last customers for the night. I hope both of you will sleep well," said the Desk Clerk as he changed the vacancy sign to read "no" vacancy.

Kay and Officer Cox slowly walked to their room. Kay was extremely tired and hungry and the smell of the hotdogs was making her stomach growl. The suite was very large with a desk and two chairs in the sleeping area which they decided to use as a table to eat on. They wasted no time spreading the groceries on the desk for their mid-night street food feast. Officer Cox had eaten half of one of his hotdogs before Kay could open a bag of chips or apply mustard to her hotdog.

"Is it good?" asked Kay looking at the starving Officer Cox. "I would offer you some of this mustard but it looks like you do not need any."

"These are good hotdogs," replied Officer Cox talking with his mouth full. "I think we should have bought six more."

Kay wrapped a napkin around the bottom of the warm cooked frankfurter, added some pickle relish to the top, and bit into the juicy hotdog that popped when her teeth penetrated the skin casing causing warm juices to run down the sides of her face. It was a delicious frankfurter. She grabbed for another napkin to try to wipe off the juices that were dripping down both sides of her chin. She tried to keep it from dripping onto the table and her clothes. Officer Cox laughed at her attempts to be a sophisticated lady eating a street vender's hotdog.

"It is supposed to be messy," he laughed. "The messier it is, the better it taste."

"Do not talk with your mouth full," she smiled as she took another bite.

"That man knows a good hotdog," Officer Cox said. "We are going to have to buy some more of these to eat on the airplane on the way home. I think I will buy some foil to wrap them in so we can have a good lunch."

"That is a great idea," agreed Kay with her mouth full. "We can take some home to Mom. She will never believe how good these frankfurters are until she samples them for herself."

"We will have to buy Carolyn one, too," said Officer Cox.

"I am not trying to change the subject; but when we were at the store you told that clerk that Leonard did not like a snitch. What did you mean?" asked Kay.

"He killed that young man in the hospital so we would not find out his location," said Officer Cox as he wiped his mouth. "That is what you call an informant, a snitch. Years ago, they were called Stool Pigeons or Moles in prison. Times change and so do names."

"So you think Leonard would have killed that clerk because he saw him," asked Kay.

"That is right," he answered. "Do you want that last hotdog?"

Kay did not realize she was eating the hotdogs as fast as Officer Cox was consuming them. The food was delicious and the conversation relaxing. Kay handed the last hotdog to the street food eating king along with a bag of chips. In three bites, that hotdog was history.

"I am not trying to change the subject again but the holiday season is almost here and I was wondering," asked Kay. "Are you going to spend the holidays with me, us, - I mean, my family or are you going to take a leave of absence and spend the holidays with your family?"

"It is almost October, Kay. We are a month away from Thanksgiving and two months from Christmas. Are you asking me to spend the holidays with you?" responded Officer Cox. "Or are you interested in finding out about my family?"

Kay was wondering if Officer Cox had a family because he had never mentioned anything about his mother, father, ex-wife, or children. She knew he was not married because he lived in that apartment near the lake. She was being inquisitive (or snooping into his personal life).

"I am sorry for prying," she apologized. "I would like you to be with us at Christmas. I feel safe when you are around while Leonard is out there, somewhere, waiting to hurt me and my Mother. If you do not have any other plans, please stay and share Christmas with us."

Officer Cox was astounded, "Let me think about it. Right now, I think we need to get some rest. You can use the restroom while I clean up our mid-night picnic."

Kay could see that she had touched a sensitive subject so she lowered her head as she left the table to take a bath. She did not mean to pry but with the holiday season one month away, she was concerned about him having a lonely holiday.

As she reached the bathroom door, Officer Cox said, "Lock the door."

She nodded her head "yes" and closed the door. Officer Cox heard the lock fasten.

Once Kay had finished bathing and she had dressed for the night, she yelled, "It is your turn."

The snow continued to fall all night. Kay listened to the wind blustering against the hotel's windows while Officer Cox was taking his shower. Her bed was warm, soft, and comfortable. Poor Officer Cox was going to sleep on a sofa that was shorter than he was long. She listened as Officer Cox turned off the shower, pushed the shower curtain to the side, and slipped on the cold, wet restroom floor.

"Are you all right?" yelled Kay.

"Just fine, thank you," growled Officer Cox.

He exited the bathroom, walked towards the uninviting sofa which Kay had covered with an extra sheet and blanket that she had found at the top of the closet, and he grabbed a pillow from Kay's bed. He hung his clothes on the chair in front of the desk before he retired to the sofa.

"I am sorry we got lost," he apologized. "We probably would be home by now if I had not rushed out of the hospital trying to play hero. If Leonard was going to do something to you at the hospital, he would have done it at that time. I am thinking he has something else planned. Did you notice that there is not a phone in this room?"

"No," answered Kay, half asleep. "I did notice that there is no television in this room. The reception must be extremely bad up here especially during snow storms like this one. Why would you have a television when you can not get a signal or a clear picture? Maybe that is why they do not have telephones in the rooms."

"I think it is weird that there is no telephone in the room," studied Officer Cox as he covered himself with the blanket. "What if we were hungry or thirsty or needed another blanket?"

"We are none of those things and we have another blanket, so go to sleep," yawned Kay. "We can ask the clerk in the morning. Good night."

The sofa may have looked short but it fit Officer Cox like a glove. His feet reach the arm rest and his head sank into the soft pillow on the other arm rest. It was as if the sofa was made to order by the way his body fit from one end to the other.

The storm continued to blast against the hotel windows, making a howling noise as it blew through the trees. Snow covered the front part of the car as it blew against it, making it impossible to see from the road.

Slowly, a car made a u-turn in the parking lot, driving beyond their car, never seeing it. It slowly drove out of the parking lot back towards the main highway. Neither Officer Cox nor Kay heard or saw the car as it left the parking lot because they were both sound asleep.

Officer Cox was awakened to the smell of fresh coffee. Little by little he opened his eyes to discover a cup of coffee on the table in front of him. He knew that where there was coffee, there was breakfast.

Kay was in the bathroom putting on some make-up when she heard Officer Cox yawning and starting to move around.

"You can have the bed if you want to try to get some more rest," she said. "I am up and ready for another day. I slept like a dead person."

"Believe it or not, this sofa is the most comfortable sofa I have ever slept on. I do not think I woke up once. I do not remember when I have ever slept that sound in my life. There had to be something in those hotdogs." said Officer Cox.

"I think we were overly tired," said Kay as she put the last touches on her face. "You can have the bathroom now. I am finished."

"To be honest, I hate to leave this sofa," yawned Officer Cox. "I think I have become a part of it. What time is it?"

"It is seven o'clock," smiled Kay.

"Why so early? I feel like I could sleep a week on this couch," stretched Officer Cox.

"I can not sleep another wink. We have to get to the airport, find out about our flight, return this car to Janet, and I have to contact the relatives of Pilot Ed and Ms Stone so they can prepare their funerals. Did you ever find out what kind of poison killed them?" asked Kay.

"No. I was planning on calling the CSPD when we arrived at the airport, but we got lost in that storm and this room does not have a telephone. You are right. The sooner we get out of here we can take care of business," said Officer Cox as he jumped to his feet to go to the bathroom. He grabbed his clothes that he had worn the day before that were hanging on the chair in front of the desk they had used as a dinning table.

Kay did not see what Officer Cox was wearing when he went to bed since the lights were out. She was too tired to care about any fashion statement parading in front of her or anything else that might be going on around her; however, now that she was rested, refreshed, and the room was brightly lit, she could not help but notice his purple and white pin-striped, baggy silk pajama bottoms being held up around his waist by his black leather belt. As her eyes moved up his body, she noticed his holster was draped around his uncovered, muscular left shoulder and it hung down to his six pack rib area. The gun bounced up and down off his masculine crest as he walked to the bathroom.

As she watched her Greek God of a Policeman walk, she thought to herself, "So this is my protector. If anyone tried to hurt me, this well buffed, half dressed, Army hero would take them out with one shot. Just the sight of those pajama bottoms would frighten the worst of intruders. I can read it now, woman saved by the purple pin-striped crusader. His motto would be 'have gun, will use it'. No wonder Caroline flirts with him all the time. Now I know what to get him for Christmas, a good pair of pajamas that fit around the waist."

Kay's thoughts were interrupted when Officer Cox splashed the cold water on his face to shave and let out a manly yell.

"Did we use all the hot water last night? There are no telephones, no televisions, no reception, and no hot water. What kind of a Motel is this? I will have to complain to the manager when I see him this morning," growled Officer Cox.

"Oh, stop your whimpering, you big baby," scolded Kay. "We are warm and dry and safe. What side of the sofa did you wake up on? I thought you slept wonderful. Did something happen between the sofa and bathroom that I missed? Let me reminded you that this Motel has a hot breakfast waiting for you in the lobby. Does that make the place a little better?"

"Yes, I can see all things bright and wonderful now, Kay," he muttered. "Did you check to see if this place has a Bible? It does not have anything else. I bet you there is not a Bible in this room?"

"Sorry to disappoint you, but there is a Bible in this room located in the right night stand and I have already read it, while you were asleep," she boasted.

"What time did you wake up?" he asked.

"I think it was five o'clock. Long enough to get dressed, read the Bible, and get you a cup of coffee," Kay answered. "Now, will you stop talking to me and get dressed so we can go eat, pay the bill, and leave. It has stopped snowing and I would like to get on the first flight back to Cortland if it is possible."

"I bet this place is a great place to do some serious snow boarding," Officer Cox said as he pointed out the window while he walked back to the sofa to get his shoes. "I would like to come back here on my vacation, if I get a vacation, and stay for a week. That snow is calling my name."

"It is not the snow calling our names, it is me and we need to leave," whispered Kay.

"My shoes are on and my bags are packed. We can leave now," smiled Officer Cox as he looked out the window at the snow covered mountains, and trees enhanced by the vast sapphire sky that framed the entire picture. "But I am finding it hard to leave this great place. This is what I think heaven should look like."

"Heaven," said Kay. "I thought you did not believe in places like that."

"I had a weak moment," he alleged as he picked up their bags. "I want to make one more stop at the Gas Station to get some of those hot dogs to take with me on the plane."

They walked to the front desk to return the key. Since there was no one at the desk, they continued to the restaurant to eat breakfast. It was a buffet style breakfast with open seating so Officer Cox and Kay picked a table near the exit door so they could see their luggage and anyone who entered the breakfast area that might pose a threat. On the buffet, there were several round shaped hot breads with butter and jams, hot and cold cereals accompanied by fresh fruits and nuts, soft boiled eggs, coffee, milk, and juices. They both noticed that they were the only guest attending breakfast. After they had eaten, they returned the key to the unattended front desk, walked through the lobby to the car, loaded the luggage into the trunk, and drove through the snow covered parking area towards the services station. There was only one way to go from the Hotel to the service station because there was a deep cliff drop off in the other direction.

After they had driven for ten minutes, Officer Cox stopped the car and stared at the snow covered forest and said, "This is the way we came, but where is the service station. I know we stopped here because I have a full tank of gas."

"Maybe we drove further than you think," assumed Kay. "It might be up the next hill. When it is dark everything seems different."

"What does that mean?" asked Officer Cox.

"We were under a lot of stress yesterday," answered Kay. "I was not looking at my watch or noticing how far we drove to get to the hotel. So keep driving and when we see it, we can stop. I would like some of those hot dogs to take to Mother and Carolyn, too."

"Kay, I am sure that gas station was here," alleged Officer Cox. "I am trained to know where I am and what my surroundings are at all times. I know this is the place. Stay in the car while I go look at something."

Officer Cox left Kay in the car and walked over to the field near the forest to look down the road towards the Hotel. The snow cracked under his feet as he walked slowly, looking in both directions for anything that resembled a gas station. He stood there for several minutes, scratching his head in wonderment. As he started back to the car, he noticed something on the ground near the edge of the road. His eyes widened as he moved closer to recognize his lost glove. He kneeled down, picked up his glove, and put it in his pocket.

As he looked up at the sky, he whispered, "Thank you." Then he returned to the car.

"What did you find?" asked Kay.

"Nothing," he answered. "You are right. It must be down the road. We need to get to the airport before it starts snowing again."

"What about the hot dogs?" Kay solicited.

Officer Cox did not say anything as he continued to drive a short distance down the country road towards Interstate 25 to get to the Colorado Springs Airport. Once he reached the ramp to Interstate 25, he spotted a highway sign to lead him in the direction to the airport. They both noticed several cars, located five miles from the ramp, that had slid in the snow, and driven off the side of the Interstate, and were stuck in the snow. There were people standing near the cars watching as wreckers attempted to pull the cars out of the snow and back onto the Interstate Highway.

"That is strange," committed Kay. "We were only fifteen minutes from this highway. If we had not stayed at that hotel last night, that could have been us. I hope no one was hurt."

Officer Cox shook his head in agreement with Kay and continued to drive.

Once again there were a group of News Reporters waiting for Kay and Officer Cox outside the airport entrance, but since they did not know what type of car they were driving, they were unable to detect them as Officer Cox drove into the covered parking lot.

"That is how Leonard knew when we were flying home. Those reporters told him our every move when they reported the first plane crash on the television and in the papers," Officer Cox assumed. "He was able to have that boy at the gate with those poison sack lunches which Pilot Ed bought. His plan failed when you and I did not eat the lunches. Due to these reporting snitches, he has been one step ahead of us wherever we go. Whatever you do, do not say anything to those reporters. We are going to have to find a camouflaged pathway or some sort of diversion to get passed them after we park so we can get to our flight. Once we leave this car in the parking lot they will know we are here. If Leonard obtains the information on the flight we are taking, he will try to hurt you and possibly destroy the entire plane, killing everyone. He is probably in the lobby stalking the ticket counters and waiting for our arrival. Do you have any ideas how we could get passed these people?"

Kay could not believe her ears. This was the second time he had asked her for her opinion.

"I do not know if this will work, but you could call the police station from a near by gas station and tell them that we are going to fly out of a smaller private airport, like Gunnison Crested Butte Regional airport. My family used to use that airport when we would fly here to ski. Golden Colorado has a small airport, but I do not know what the name of it is and it is closer. You could tell them that we are not going to use the City of Colorado Springs Municipal Airport because we think Leonard will be there. It would be a good idea if you would tell them to have the airport security check everyone's ID that is standing around waiting on departing flights in order to catch Leonard if he is here. I know the reporters are equipped with police scanners and they listen to them all the time. They will leave the airport to follow us, with Leonard tagging alone for the kill. It might work, but then again, it might not," Kay schemed.

Officer Cox was amazed at Kay's ability to come up with a structured proposal within seconds. He made a U-turn in the parking area, left the airport, and drove to the nearest Circle K convenience store.

While he was on the telephone with the police department, he asked what type of poison was used to kill Pilot Ed and Ms Stone. The officer informed him that the sandwiches were lined with common drain cleaner that could be purchased at any local grocery store and Phenol Guanidinium Thiocycanate. Officer Cox explained his situation and his plan to the commanding officer on duty, which was impressed and agreed to broadcast the idea over the radio and to send some officers to the airport to look for Leonard. He also notified the airport security of the situation and faxed them a copy of Leonard's picture with a black eye patch added to his face. The policeman asked Officer Cox what had happened to them last night because there were several officers at the airport waiting for their arrival to get them on a plane home. Officer Cox elucidated to him that they had made a wrong turn from the hospital and with the snow storm impairing their vision to drive; they decided to stay at a hotel called 'Emily's' located off the road north of Interstate 25 near a service station that was owned by the same person.

"That is odd," remarked the policeman. "I do not remember ever seeing a hotel or service station in that locality. What was the name of the place again?"

"The sign was covered with snow, but I am sure it is on the receipt. I think it was called Emily's," answered Officer Cox. "This place is next to a deep cliff. It serves a small breakfast buffet in the morning in a restaurant that over looks the snow covered cliffs and mountains. The service stations sales the best frankfurters I have ever eaten. We were lucky to spot the flashing lights of the station when we did, because the car was almost out of gas and the station was closing. He stayed open for us long enough to get gas and something to eat."

"I will have to check out that place. It must be new in the area," said the policeman.

The conversation ended with a bewildered Officer Cox wondering why these policemen had not heard of this restaurant, hotel, or service station when it is a fact that most policemen know where all the best places to eat are located.

He returned to the car, informed Kay that the plan was being initiated, and he drove back to the Colorado Springs Municipal Airport. There were no reporters waiting for their arrival at the entrance of the airport when they returned to the parking lot for the second time. They were able to walk to the ticket counter, purchase their tickets, and board the airplane for their trip home without any questions or delays.

"That was a good plan, Kay," smiled Officer Cox. "Now we can sit back and relax. Do you have the receipt to the hotel where we stayed?"

"Yes, it is in my carry-on bag," answered Kay. "Why?"

"When I was telling the Colorado Policeman where we had stayed, he said he had never heard of the place," alleged Officer Cox. "All the signs were covered with snow so I never got the name of the place. Besides, I would like to go back to do some snow boarding in that area."

Kay unzipped all the compartments of her purple carry-on bag but she could not find the receipt to the hotel or for the service station purchases.

"I must have packed it away in my luggage," she explained. "I can not find it anywhere in here."

"It is going to be a long flight home, Kay," said Officer Cox. "Tell me what you read today from the Book."

"The Bible?" she asked surprised. "Officer Cox, you are scaring me. First you mentioned Heaven and now you want to know about the Bible. What happened to you in that place? Did you see a spirit or something? You are the same Officer Cox that I hired to protect me or are you some alien man?"

"Kay, Kay, calm down," he said as he comforted her. "It is me. I was trying to make conversation with you. If you do not want to tell me what you read today, that is fine. I will go to sleep."

"Oh, no you are not," she ordered. "Something happened to you on this trip that caused you to get religion and I want you to do some talking."

"I will tell you this," said Officer Cox. "If you do not find the receipt to the hotel or the service station, I will start reading your book. Other than that, I have nothing to say."

Kay was puzzled as she watched Officer Cox close his eyes to take a nap on the way home.

# FAMILY TIES

# CHAPTER IV

Kay watched as Officer Cox slept during their flight home. She kept thinking about the day that Leonard stormed into Mr. Hughes' office and shot everyone, except Carolyn who was hiding in the ladies restroom. She could not understand how Leonard had discovered that she was going to Mr. Hughes' office that day. There were only four people that knew where she was going that day, her mother, who was not going to say anything, Office Cox, Carolyn, and herself. Even Mr. Hughes did not know she was going to show up that morning to handle Mr. Blackstone's paperwork.

She continued to ponder the events that had happened in the last three days. She remembered that Mr. Blackstone had investigated Carolyn before she was hired to take care of her Mother. She hated to think anything evil of Carolyn, but she seemed like the only person that could have had access to a telephone to call Leonard or someone that knew him.

"Officer Cox," she whispered as she shook him awake from his power nap. "How do you think Leonard found out I was going to see Mr. Hughes? Someone had to tell him. I have been thinking, what if Carolyn innocently called someone from your home to inform them of her condition and what she was doing. None of us were able to talk on the telephone while we were in the safe house. She could have called a family member that she thought might be worried about her from your home. Is there a possibility that the family member she called might have known Leonard and they told him where we were planning to go? Can you shine some light on these questions?"

"You woke me up for this?" Officer Cox yawned. "You could have waited until we reached the airport before you decided to wake me. Let me see, you are thinking Carolyn called someone. When could she have made the call? We have been together everyday except when we were kidnapped by Leonard and we fell out of the plane in Colorado."

"I have been thinking about it," said Kay.

"There you go again, Ms Sherlock Holmes," laughed Officer Cox. "I think we need a vacation from all the stress that Leonard has gifted us with, if you want to call it a gift.

"Stop laughing," scolded Kay. "I am serious. I think Carolyn made the call from your up-stairs bedroom while I was in the bathroom getting dressed. She had plenty of time to tell someone, a brother, sister, or parent, that she was fine and going with me to Mr. Hughes' office."

Officer Cox did stop laughing and became more interested in what she was saying, because he realized Kay was on to something. He thought to himself, "There was no other way Leonard could have known where they would be unless it came from a call made by Carolyn."

"I do not believe Carolyn would intentionally hurt my family or friends," continued Kay. "If she spoke to someone, we need to find that person and we need to find out if they know where Leonard is hiding. Officer Cox, are you listening to me?"

Officer Cox was definitely listening to Kay's babbling and he knew she was on to something. If Carolyn did call someone that had tipped off Leonard to their location, then that person knew where her mother was staying and that Mr. Hughes was not killed from the gun shot. He needed to get in contact with Lieutenant Gorman as soon as possible so he could ask him to apprehend Carolyn for some questioning and to put some guards at his home to protect Mrs. Lytle.

Kay babbled on, "If Carolyn calls that person again to tell them we are on this plane to Cortland, they might call Leonard and tell him that we have outmaneuvered him. We may have outsmarted Leonard this time but when he gets something on his mind, he will stop at nothing to pursue what he wants. After we question Carolyn, and I get Mr. Blackstone's affairs in order, I want to return to Blackhawk. Everyone knows he is alive now due to the recent plane crash and the murders of Pilot Ed and Ms. Stone. We need to do some major brain storming to figure out a way to catch him before he has an opportunity to hurt us again."

Officer Cox could see how determined Kay was on finding and having Leonard apprehended. He wanted Leonard captured as much as Kay wanted it and he wanted him taken out of her life completely. In his entire police career, he had never known a man as dangerous as Leonard. He had read about people like him in police reports, but he had never encountered anyone as devious.

Kay continued with her babbling, "I think we should ask several of the pool contractors if we could see their construction records of all the pools that were installed five years before Janet Cross' sister was murdered and see if he murdered any other ladies under their pools. He may have some sort of perverted murder pattern that could lead us to him and help solve some of the missing ladies' cases in that area."

Officer Cox looked at Kay as if he had been roused from a trance, "What did you say? Go back to the part about Janet's sister."

"I knew you were not listening to me," whined Kay.

"Yes, I was," he pleaded. "The part you said about looking at some old construction records is a good idea. I need to jump on that right now while it is fresh on my mind. Do you think I can use the phone on this plane?"

He pushed the button on the arm rest to call the stewardess.

"May I help you or is there a problem, sir?" the stewardess asked as she approached the now standing Officer Cox.

"No, there is no problem," Officer Cox answered as he secretly showed the stewardess his badge. "I need to make an emergency telephone call to the Cortland police station. May I use the telephone on the plane?"

"Yes, sir," answered the stewardess eagerly to assist the officer. "Please follow me."

Officer Cox left his seat to follow the stewardess to the employee service area where an airplane telephone (from air to ground) was located. He looked through his array of business cards to get a hold of the number to the Colorado Springs Police Station. The stewardess returned to the area where Kay was seated with a chocolate candy bar.

"The gentleman said this was your favorite type candy bar," the stewardess said as she handed the candy to Kay. "I like to eat them, also."

"Thank you," replied Kay taking the Germany made, hazelnut candy bar from the stewardess. "Chocolate and hazelnuts were made for each other. These candy bars are very hard to find in Cortland. Was he able to make the call?"

"He should be able to call anyone on the ground from that telephone," the stewardess responded with a smile.

She and Kay chatted while Officer Cox made one telephone call to the Colorado Springs Police Department and another call to Cortland to talk to Lieutenant Gorman. He asked the Lieutenant to put a guard on Mr. Hughes, Marie, and Carolyn and to tell them not to telephone anyone until he and Kay returned. He told him he would explain everything when they arrived.

When the stewardess spied Officer Cox returning to his seat, she ended her conversation with Kay.

She said as she winked at Officer Cox, "If you need anything else, buzz me."

"Thank you," smiled Officer Cox, who was surprised by her flirtation.

The stewardess strolled down the center of the plane to see if she could assist any of the other passengers. Officer Cox fastened his seat belt and asked Kay if he could have a piece of the candy bar. He had remembered seeing some of those candy bars at Kay's home and wanted to taste one until Kay had informed him that Leonard might have put poison in them. Now was his opportunity to try one without fear of poison.

"I knew this candy was not for me," Kay smiled as she handed him the unwrapped chocolate. "How did you know it was one of my favorites?"

"Do you remember that first day at your home when I was making myself a sandwich masterpiece in your kitchen and you told me to throw it away due to poison?" he asked.

"Yes," answered Kay thinking back on how he hated to part with his double decked handheld meal. "It was the biggest sandwich I had ever seen."

"I remembered seeing these candy bars on the shelf next to the cookies you would not let me eat and I wanted to try one," smiled Officer Cox as he opened the chocolate hazelnut temptation. "Now I can."

"You were right," laughed Kay as she watched her hungry protector devour the chocolate sensation. "It is one of my favorite candy bars. My father used to order those candies once a month from Germany and have them delivered to my house. By the way, she was flirting with you."

"Who?" asked Officer Cox as if he did not know who she was talking about.

"You know who," laughed Kay. "I saw her wink at you and you smiled at her."

"I was being polite," he grinned.

She stopped talking for a moment as she remembered a happy memory of her father and being with him at one of the company picnics. There was a young man (Allen Green) at that picnic that had flirted and danced with her. The memory of that happier time in her life brought some tears to her eyes. She turned her face away from Officer Cox, who was devouring the Germany delicacy, so he could not see her cry. She wiped away the tears to regain her composure so she could ask him about the telephone call.

"Did I say something that caused you to spring from your seat to make that call?" she asked. "Who did you call?"

"You sure are a curious sleuth. I know you thought I was not listening to you, but there are times when you say something that could be beneficial to solving this case," he alleged. "You said something about looking at the pool company's construction records that dated back several years to see if any of those owners went missing. I was thinking that Leonard might have used this technique to kill other wealthy ladies in the area or state, but he disappeared when Janet's family started investigating him. I telephoned the Colorado Spring's Police Department and asked them to fax some of the old pool construction records to Cortland so I could review them. While I had the lieutenant on the line, I asked him to telephone Janet so she would know where to find her car. Next, I telephoned Lieutenant Gorman and asked him to put a guard on your mother, Mr. Hughes, and Carolyn. If Carolyn did telephone someone from my home, Leonard knows where I live and will possibly try to hurt your family again."

"You were listening to me," smiled Kay. "I have another idea."

"Wait a second, young lady," he laughed. "We need to get home first and then we can talk about your other ideas. Deal?"

"It is a deal," Kay smiled and winked at Officer Cox. "I think we make a good team."

Officer Cox was surprised when she winked at him.

He said, "I think I will get some more 'zees' before we land. Wake me when we get to Cortland."

A man, sitting across the aisle from Kay, dropped a magazine he was reading that fell next to Kay's feet. Kay bent over to retrieve the bartender magazine to return it to the man. As she handed him the magazine on bartenders, she noticed the man had several animal tattoos covering his left arm, a snake tattoo was on his neck, and there were four eye brow piercings above his left eye.

"Thank you," he said as he put his right tattooed hand out to shake Kay's hand. "My name is Mike Lambie."

"Hello," smiled Kay as she stared at his right hand that had a different snake on each finger. The body of the snakes continued up his arm until they reached his neck to form one large snake. She wondered if she should give him her real name or lie. She decided to lie, "my name is Katy."

"Nice to meet you, Katy," said Mike as he shook her hand. "Do you live in Cortland?"

"No, I am just visiting some friends and relatives," she fibbed again. "How about you? Do you live in Cortland?"

"No, it is a stop over and then I catch a connecting flight to Vegas," Mike whispered. "That place is too weird for me. I am passing through to continue on to Vegas where there is a real life happening. I am going to enter the bartenders' competition at the Desert Palms Hotel. That place is rocking. Are you going to Vegas, too?"

"No," she answered. "I will be staying and visiting some friends. So, you are a bartender from Colorado Springs?"

"Not just a bartender, I am a drink specialist and artist," Mike bragged. "The competition is not until next week but I thought I would scope out the local talent and check out their moves, if you know what I mean, to get the edge on them in the competition."

"Well, good luck to you," Kay smiled as she was hoping Officer Cox would rescue her from this one sided conversation.

"I noticed you were staring at my tattoos," Mike whispered as he pointed at his left arm.

"I am sorry," apologized Kay for being rude. "I did not realize you had noticed me staring. My mother would have had a seizure if I had a tattoo printed on my body. You have so many. Did it hurt getting them?"

"The first one hurt but the rest were a piece of cake. I know what you mean about mothers," smiled Mike. "My parents had a heart attack the first time they saw mine. My father said, 'No self respecting man would have a tattoo. Anyone that is someone does not have tattoos. Boys that have tattoos live at home and do drugs.' Yep! That is what my father use to tell me. I bet your parents were the same."

"Yes, they were," smiled Kay now hoping Officer Cox would stay asleep because the conversation had gotten interesting.

"Well, I proved him wrong," Mike alleged. "I have a job as a bartending specialist and I live with two of my buddies from high school. If I win this competition, the first thing I am going to do with the money is open my own bar."

"How much money will you win?" asked Kay.

"A big whopping ten thousand dollars," smiled Mike.

"You are going to need more than that amount of money to open your own bar," explained Kay. "You will need to rent or purchase a building, get furniture, apply for an alcohol beverage permit to sell and serve liquor, purchase paper or glass containers to serve your drinks in, and ten thousand dollars is a drop in the bucket to start a business like that. There is insurance to think about that will cover your establishment and your customers."

"I know that," Mike acknowledged. "I plan on getting a small business loan from the bank to cover any other expenses."

"You are going to need to have some sort of collateral to cover that loan," explained Kay. "Do you have that?"

"Sure I have collateral," alleged Mike. "Besides, my father knows some people at the bank. He can pull some strings and sign the papers for me."

"When you walk in that bank with all those piercings above your eyes and all those tattoos exposed, you are going to see that those people are not going to want to loan you any money. They want someone who they can depend on to get their money returned with interest. They will look at you and assume that you think having a tattoo is more important than paying your bills. If I am not mistaken, tattoos are expensive. Most people will want to know why you put so much money into those tattoos instead of the bank, investing."

"You sound like my father," argued Mike. "I can get my money without using the bank."

"Yes you can and prison is not half full," scolded Kay.

"What is that suppose to mean? Who are you anyway?" angrily whispered Mike.

"I am a curious sleuth that is sticking my nose into your business," apologized Kay. "I am sorry. Your bar is going to be fine because you have foresight and ambition."

"You really think so?" timidly smiled Mike.

"Yes, I do," said Kay. "I have a friend that is an attorney and if you would like his advice, I will give you his number. I also have a friend that is in construction work that could help you with your building."

"Thanks Katy," smiled Mike as he handed Kay his magazine. "You are all right. You can write their numbers on my magazine. If there is any thing that I can do for you, you can count on me. I thought this was going to be a boring flight. I wish you were going to Vegas. I know some great places I could show you. What kind of movies do you like?"

"Thank you Mike," Kay smiled as she scribbled the numbers of her friends on his magazine cover with the pen Mr. Blackstone had given her. "I like the old time western movies. You could recognize the good guys from the bad guys."

"No joke," laughed Mike. "I like those good old cowboy movies myself. Who is your favorite actor?"

"I know I am going to sound corny," alleged Kay. "I love John Wayne. He was tall, strong, and represented everything good in the movies. Who is your favorite?"

"You are going to laugh at me," supposed Mike.

"No I am not. Please tell me," begged Kay. "You did not laugh at me."

"I like Clayton Moore. Would you believe me if I told you I met him once in a hardware store? He was bigger than life to me and he shook my hand. He said, 'live by the law and it will protect you.' I will never forget that day," said Mike as he tore a piece of paper from one of the pages of the magazine and wrote his telephone number on it before he handed it to Kay, "if you ever need me."

"My favorite is Roy," said Officer Cox who was awakened when he heard the sound of the landing gear being lowered on the plane and the stewardess ordering everyone to fasten their seat belts for the landing.

"Mine, too," said one of the passengers sitting in front of Kay. "Roy and John were the best, but I had a place in my heart for Mr. Clayton Moore."

"We should have taken a poll," laughed Kay.

"Young man," continued the old gray haired lady as she leaned back in her seat to talk to Mike. "She is right about the people in the bank. When you go, wear a long sleeve shirt and take those ugly piercings off of your face. I know it is popular with the young people today, but it is not professional. The Bank people can and will intimidate you by looking professional and acting more educated than you are so when you walk into that bank to get your money, dress for success. You can put your piercings back on when you go out to party."

"Are you one of her friends?" asked Mike looking at Kay as if she knew everyone on the plane.

"No," smiled the old lady, who was dressed in a professional black suit, as she turned back to face forward. "I work at the bank in Cortland. Good luck getting your loan."

"Thank you," said Mike as he fastened his seat belt.

The Cortland Airport was in view from the airplane's windows. Once the plane was on the ground, Kay and Officer Cox departed the airport heading towards the hospital in a rental car to check on Mr. Hughes. Kay was dreading returning to that hospital where Mr. Blackstone had died. That was the last place she had seen Mr. Blackstone alive, before she left on that wonderful trip to the Bahamas. She was thinking of her friend, Mr. Blackstone, and how ashamed of herself she was for thinking Carolyn would do any thing to hurt her family, especially after all they had experienced together. As soon as Officer Cox parked the rental car in the covered garage, Kay could feel a lump growing in her throat. She wanted to scream, cry, or hit something. Officer Cox was not aware of the anxiety that was building inside Kay as he exited the car to open Kay's door. The minute Officer Cox opened her door; she burst out screaming and crying. Officer Cox did not know what to think. He thought everything was going fine. The flight was successful and the food was good. He knelt in the parking lot next to Kay.

"Kay," said Officer Cox noticing some people coming over to see what was wrong. "We are home now and everything is going to be fine. I promise. Please stop crying."

"Can I help," asked a concerned man behind the couple. "I am a doctor."

Other people behind the doctor were whispering," Is she all right? Should I call the police?"

"She is having a stress attack," answered Officer Cox. "I am a policeman. Please step back and give us some air."

Kay's face was buried in her hands as she wept. Officer Cox unfastened her seat belt. He gently patted her on the back.

"There are a lot of people out here, Kay," whispered Officer Cox. "I think we should go in now. Your mother is waiting. If you will stop crying I promise I will spend Christmas with you."

"Can you give me a minute?" asked Kay as she wiped her face on a handkerchief someone in the crowd had handed her.

Officer Cox stepped aside and closed the car door. He explained to the concerned rescuers that Kay was having an anxiety attack due to one of her friends dying at the hospital and two others dying in a plane crash. One lady said her father had died at that hospital and she knew how Kay felt. Once the crowd was assured that she was going to be fine, they strolled away from the car to give Kay some privacy to clean up her face. She slowly opened the car door, stepped out of the car, and started to walk with Officer Cox towards the place that had taken her dearest friend and was housing her mother and Mr. Hughes.

"Do I look like I have been crying?" asked Kay. "Mother always knows when I am crying. She will be worried."

Officer Cox examined Kay's appearance. She had on a light blue sweater, some blue jeans that fit perfectly, and white tennis shoes. Her hair was pulled back with a white plastic hair clip. There were a few strands of her hair hanging down around her face. Her eyes were slightly puffy and there was a small red spot, possibly a pimple, next to her mouth.

"You look beautiful," said Officer Cox.

"Oh yes!" Kay said embarrassed. "A real beauty queen. Sorry I asked."

"Really, you look nice," smiled Officer Cox.

"Come on, funny man," replied Kay as she picked up her pace walking into the hospital. "We have some work to do."

"What did I say wrong," he asked, following with his arms up in the air. "Ok, you look like a dog."

"I knew it," said Kay inspecting her clothes. "Should I go home to change?"

Officer Cox softly pushed her from the back, "Get in that hospital before I have an anxiety attack of my own."

Kay asked at the information desk which room Mr. Hughes was staying in. After a few kind words from the information nurse (who was one of the ladies in the parking lot that came to Kay's rescue), the two continued to Mr. Hughes' room on the second floor.

There were two guards stationed outside the hospital room that Mr. Hughes was occupying and they were told to ask for some sort of picture identification before they would allow anyone to enter his room. The guards recognized Officer Cox but they followed their orders and asked both him and Kay for their identification before they opened the door for them.

Kay and Officer Cox walked in on Doctor Peterson as he was prescribing some medication for Mr. Hughes' head injury. Marie was sitting next to the bed. She was so excited to see Kay. She hurried to greet her with a hug.

"Kay, you have been crying?" Marie asked, "Did they find Leonard's body?"

"I told you she would know I was crying," Kay remarked before answering Marie, "They have not found him as far as we know. They said they would notify me once he was apprehended."

"That means, he is still alive," Marie glared furiously at Officer Cox. "I told you to shoot him. Now we have to relive the nightmares all over again. I knew that was why the Lieutenant had placed those guards outside the door."

Kay said, "Yes, mother, he is still alive. He already tried to kill us while we were in Colorado. The reporters inadvertently tipped him off to our location when we were returning home. Talking about tipped off, where is Carolyn?"

"Carolyn was picked up by Lieutenant Gorman and taken to the police station for questioning after he had received a call from Officer Cox. Lieutenant Gorman said he was going to take her to lunch; however, when she did not return, I called the station and he said that you would explain everything to me when you arrived," answered Marie, not knowing why Officer Cox had called from the airplane to have her detained.

"So that is why you called from the plane," frowned Kay towards Officer Cox. "You must have thought it, too. Is that why you had Carolyn arrested?"

"You were the one who gave me the idea," defended Officer Cox. "I did not have her arrested. She is being held for questioning. I like her, too."

"I know, but I did not call anyone. I just told you," argued Kay. "I did not want her arrested."

"Now children," scolded Marie. "Do I have to put both of you in the corner for time out? She is with the Lieutenant. She will be fine."

Doctor Peterson and Mr. Hughes begin to laugh.

Doctor Peterson smiled, "Laughter is a good thing to have around here. Welcome home, Kay. We have missed you."

Kay poked Officer Cox in the arm, and then she walked over to Mr. Hughes' bed side. Mr. Hughes smiled and kissed her on the check.

"Mr. Hughes," she apologized. "I am so sorry you were shot. You are lucky that bullet did not kill you."

"That is what everyone here has been telling me," smiled Mr. Hughes. "I was lucky Carolyn was there to call for help. Not to mention, her being a nurse. She saved my life."

"I am glad she was there, also." Kay continued as she glared at Officer Cox. "Would you like to stay at our house until you can get back on your feet? Mom, Carolyn, and I will take good care of you."

"I know you will, sweetie," said Mr. Hughes. "However, I think your house, like my office, is going to need some professional cleaning. My office has quite a bit of blood on the walls and furniture."

"I forgot about that," said Kay. "I was hoping it was cleaned by now. Since Leonard is alive, I do not think my house or Officer Cox's home will be a safe place to stay."

"Why would Officer Cox's house be unsafe?" asked Marie.

"That is why Carolyn is in jail," said Kay. "It is my fault."

"You are not making any sense at all," scolded Marie. "Sit down sweetie, and tell me why Carolyn is in jail."

"I told (or suggested to) Officer Cox that someone had to inform Leonard where we were staying the day Mr. Hughes was shot. No one knew but you, Officer Cox, Carolyn, and me," explained Kay as she sat on the edge of the chair next to her mother. "Even Mr. Hughes did not know where we were or when I was going to show up at his office to sign those papers."

"I still do not understand why Carolyn was arrested," questioned Marie.

"Mother, the only one that could have made a telephone call was Carolyn," said Kay.

"Who did she call and when did she call? We were always together," asked Marie.

"I shared my idea with Officer Cox that I thought she made a call from his up-stairs guest bedroom while I was in the bathroom getting dressed," continued Kay as she glared at guiltless Officer Cox again. "I think she might have called a relative to tell them that she was fine."

"You think she is one of Leonard's relatives, like Roxie?" asked Marie.

"No, I think she called one of her relatives that might have known Leonard and they told him where we were going, hypothetically speaking," said Kay.

"I thought I would have Lieutenant Gorman hold her until we returned so she could not accidentally leak out any more information about us. I am going to the station right now to question her," interrupted Officer Cox. "I would like Kay to stay here with you while I am at the station."

"In your dreams, big boy," reprimanded Kay. "She is my best friend.

I got her in jail and I am going to get her out of jail. I am going with you."

"I figured you would say that," said Officer Cox. "If you will excuse us, we are going to find out if Carolyn made any calls."

"Mother, I will be back as soon as I can. Hopefully Carolyn will be with me," said Kay. "Officer Cox, what are you doing?"

Officer Cox was looking down the hallway for Officer Rodriguez.

Officer Cox turned and answered. "I was looking for Officer Rodriguez. Did Lieutenant Gorman assign him to guard you, Mrs. Lytle?"

"Yes," replied Marie.

"Where is he?" asked Officer Cox.

"He went to grab us something to eat. I do not know what is taking him so long to return," said Marie.

"When he returns, will you ask him to call me?" requested Officer Cox.

"I will do that for you. Please be careful," smiled Marie patting him on the back. "Take care of my girls."

"Hello," said Kay waving her hands. "I am trying to get your attention. It looks like Mr. Hughes has something to say."

Mr. Hughes smiled, "I know you are in a hurry to help Carolyn but I want you to know that you are welcome to stay at my home. It is clean, empty, and I have five bedrooms that you can pick from. Everyone would have their own private room. I would not have to pack any of my clothes to leave and I like sleeping in my own bed. My keys are here in the drawer next to the bed. Take them and have several made for everyone."

"That sounds great, Mr. Hughes," agreed Office Cox. "When can we move in?"

"Wait a minute, big boy," Kay stared. "I have not agreed to that."

"It is a wonderful idea, Kay," Marie added. "We would be at a location where Leonard could not find us. Plus, I would like to sleep in a bed without two other ladies stealing my covers."

"I did not steal your covers, Mother," argued Kay.

"Then it is settled," said Mr. Hughes. "Take my keys and have duplicates made for all of you."

Doctor Peterson thought it was a good idea for Mr. Hughes to sleep where he would be the most comfortable and safe. He also thought it would be good to have Carolyn there for both Mr. Hughes and Marie (even though Marie did not need Carolyn to assist her any more). After all, Carolyn was a registered nurse.

"May I say something before I go?" ordered Doctor Peterson.

He was so quiet, that everyone in the room had forgotten he was even there.

"What?" Kay, Officer Cox, and Marie asked simultaneously.

"I think Mr. Hughes has a good idea," Doctor Peterson alleged. "There is safety in numbers. With all of you there, he will have someone with him day and night without having to hire outside help, possibly hiring another one of Leonard's friends."

Kay was out voted. It was decided that they would move in with Mr. Hughes until he was well and their home was cleaned. While Kay was getting advice on how to help Mr. Hughes from Doctor Peterson, Officer Cox asked Marie how she knew Kay had been crying.

"Kay gets a tiny red spot that looks like a pimple near the corner of her mouth when she is crying," answered Marie, pointing at Kay's mouth. "It happens every time."

Officer Cox remembered seeing it when they were walking into the hospital.

Officer Rodriguez arrived with the food as Officer Cox and Kay were leaving to pack their bags again and move into Mr. Hughes' home. Officer Cox up-dated Officer Rodriguez on the situation with Carolyn and told him that Leonard was still alive and to be on the alert at all times. Finally, Kay had to pull Officer Cox away from the mouth watering Spanish type meals that Officer Rodriguez had purchased. She thanked Officer Rodriguez for getting her mother something to eat.

Kay stopped by the information booth on the way to the car to thank the receptionist for her concerns during her anxiety attack in the parking lot. Officer Cox drove the car to the hospital entrance door to pick her up. Kay noticed that he was not driving in the direction of his home.

"Where are you going? Never mind, I already know. You are going to the nearest restaurant. Your stomach alarm must have alerted your brain that it is past your lunch time," smarted Kay.

"Nope," laughed Officer Cox. "All though that is a good idea. I am going to the police station first so we can talk to Carolyn. Have you already forgotten about her?"

"No, I have not forgotten about her, big guy," said Kay. "I thought that since your home is closer to the hospital than the police station, we would get our stuff first."

"It would be better to have Carolyn with us so she can get her stuff, also," replied Officer Cox. "Besides you planted the idea in my head while we were on the airplane coming home. You were right before so I want to handle this first."

"So," flaunted Kay. "You are saying that I am right sometimes."

"You have your moments," confessed Officer Cox.

"Is this one of them?" asked Kay.

"Could be," answered Officer Cox.

"I knew it. You have to be hungry to say that I am right," laughed Kay. "Let's go talk to Carolyn. By the way, thank you."

On the way to the police station, Officer Cox picked up an order to go from their favorite seafood restaurant that was near the florist where Kay used to order Mr. Blackstone's flowers. Kay remembered having several meals with Mr. Blackstone at that place. He laughed at her because she could not remember what she had eaten. Officer Cox snacked on some French fries while he continued to drive to the police station. By the time they reached the police station, all his fries were eaten and he had dropped some tartar sauce in his lap.

"Kay, would you mind if we ate the remainder of our meal in the car?" asked Officer Cox. "I would like to talk to you about Carolyn in private before we go in there and question her."

"I think that is a good idea, messy man," laughed Kay as she handed him another napkin. "What about Carolyn?"

"Have you decided what you are going to ask her?" integrated Officer Cox.

"I think so," said Kay. "First, I want to know if she made any telephone calls from your home and to whom. Then, I want to know what she said to them. I want to know if she gave them our location. Then I want to know where that person is that she talked to. How is that for a starter? "

"That sounds like a plan to me. I am sure Lieutenant Gorman has made a back ground check and has the information available. He will know if she knew Leonard or anyone connected to him. If she does not know Leonard, then we need to focus on who she talked to that does know Leonard. I think you and I know Carolyn well enough to say she is not a snitch," responded Officer Cox.

"Well, I am ready," said Kay. "Snitch or not, I want to find out what she does know. This information may lead us to Leonard."

Kay and Officer Cox finished their parking lot lunch. Officer Cox was still chewing the last bite of his crunchy fish sandwich when they entered the police station. They were greeted by some of Officer Cox's associates as they walked through the station to Lieutenant Gorman's office. Kay was surprised when the Lieutenant gave her a welcome home hug. She was asked to have a seat while he greeted Officer Cox with a hand shake and a soft pat on the back.

"Welcome back," greeted Lieutenant Gorman. "You both look rested after destroying thousand of dollars of city property, crashing an airplane, and sky diving over the Colorado Rockies."

"What city property?" asked Officer Cox.

"Two police cars were shot to pieces and one airport barrier gate was destroyed in that get-away chase with Leonard."

"Hey, Leonard did all that damage, not us," argued Officer Cox. "If you would have put more guards on the man, he would have never escaped from the hospital."

"Do not try to pin any of this on me, Officer Cox," launched Lieutenant Gorman.

"If my eyes were blue, if, if, if....," interrupted Kay. "The only person at fault is Leonard and we have to find him before he destroys another friendship, family, and more city property. Where is Carolyn?"

"Here I am, Kay," smiled Carolyn as she entered into the office.

A surprised Officer Cox sat in the chair next to a bewildered Kay. She thought Lieutenant Gorman would have had her in a locked interrogation room, but instead she was bringing a pitcher of tea to Lieutenant Gorman's office.

"You look surprised to see me," smiled Carolyn as she poured several glasses of ice tea and handed one to the Lieutenant. "We had a luncheon date."

"She does not know?" asked Officer Cox looking at Lieutenant Gorman. "You did not tell her?"

"I thought it would be best if it came from you," answered Lieutenant Gorman.

"What came from you?" asked a puzzled Carolyn.

"I was asked to bring you here, Carolyn," replied the Lieutenant.

"I do not understand," pleaded Carolyn. "I thought this was a luncheon date."

"Please have a seat," said Officer Cox. "The Lieutenant was only doing what I asked him to do. Kay and I would like to ask you some questions concerning the day that you went to Mr. Hughes' office."

"What kind of questions?" asked Carolyn.

Officer Cox looked at Kay to let her interrogate Carolyn first since Carolyn was one of her employees.

Kay cleared her voice and looked Carolyn directly into her eyes, "Did you make a call to anyone from Officer Cox's home while I was in the bathroom getting dressed that day?"

Carolyn's eyes widen as she realized what was happening to her, "I can not believe you would think I would hurt you or your family. I thought we were friends. Why would you think I would hurt you or do anything to jeopardize my job?"

Carolyn began to cry. Officer Cox handed her one of his unsoiled napkins. Carolyn wiped her eyes and stared angrily at Kay. Kay knew how up-set Carolyn was becoming because she had sat in that same interrogation hot seat two weeks before Mr. Hughes was shot, knowing she was innocent of murder.

"Would you answer Kay's question?" asked Officer Cox. "I can have the telephone company pull my records to see if any phone calls were made that day."

Carolyn knew by the sound of Officer Cox's voice that she was in some big trouble.

She said, "Yes. I made a telephone call to my brother to let him know that I was doing fine. I had not spoken to him in over a week and I knew he was going to start getting worried and I was afraid he might expose our location so I called him to reassure him that I was safe."

"Does your brother know Leonard?" asked Kay.

"No and yes," answered Carolyn. "He works here at the police station and he has read all the reports on Leonard, but he has never met him. That is why he was worried about me."

"Your brother is a policeman?" responded Officer Cox and Lieutenant Gorman. "Who is he?"

"His name is Officer Dennis Rue," answered Carolyn. "Is he in trouble?"

Lieutenant Gorman left his office, walked to the nearest desk and asked one of the on duty officers to bring Officer Rue to his office. He returned to his office wondering how he could have missed knowing Carolyn had a brother on the force.

"Kay, I am so sorry if I caused all this mess," cried Carolyn. "I would trust my brother with my life. He would never be an informant. Can you forgive me?"

"I told Officer Cox that you were innocent," cried Kay as she hugged Carolyn. "It is his entire fault."

"My fault," Officer Cox rebuked as he threw his hands up into the air. "Why is this my fault?"

"Because it is, that is why?" scolded Kay.

Officer Cox did not want to dispute that answer so he sat back in his chair and watched the ladies cry.

Officer Rue entered the office unaware there was a family crisis about to start. He was greeted by his sister with a hug and she introduced him to Kay and Officer Cox. Lieutenant Gorman asked him to take a seat and said he had some questions to ask him.

The room became very quiet as Lieutenant Gorman began his interrogation, "Officer Rue, you know that it is company policy that any information being released in reference to the arrest of a known felon is punishable by dismissal from the force?"

"Yes sir," answered Officer Rue who was sitting next to Carolyn and holding her hands.

"Did you, at any time come in contact with Leonard Morgan?" he asked.

"No sir," answered the young inexperienced officer.

"Then tell me, how would Leonard know where your sister and Miss Lytle would be going on the day of Mr. Hughes' shooting? Carolyn has already admitted to calling you from Officer Cox's home that morning. Since there were only four persons, other than yourself, that knew where Miss Lytle was going, how is it possible that Leonard got the information if you did not tell him?" asked Lieutenant Gorman.

"I do not know, sir," answered the officer.

"Can you tell me what happened on that day when your sister called you?" asked Officer Cox.

"Yes, sir," replied a very nervous officer who was looking at his sister. "I received the call from my sister at about seven forty five that morning. I remember the time because I had clocked in and brought my time card to my desk. She told me she was fine and not to worry about her. She said Officer Cox was kind enough to let them stay at his home until Kay's home was clean. She said she was going with Kay to Mr. Hughes' office and she would see me later because she was coming to the office to return the Officer's red car. I think she said it was a GTO. I told her to be safe and I would see her later. When I hung up the telephone, Officer Soleman asked me what was going on. Since he knew about the murders, I did not think it would hurt to tell a fellow officer."

"Stop," yelled Kay. "Did you say Officer Soleman?"

"Yes," said Officer Rue. "He sits next to me on the third flood. He said he knew my sister and was concern about her safety."

Kay looked at Officer Cox, both knowing that Lover Boy did not like Kay after he was reprimanded for being out of uniform on duty while at her home. Lieutenant Gorman knew what Kay and Officer Cox were thinking and he called his secretary on his intercom system.

"Ask Officer Soleman to come to my office," demanded Lieutenant Gorman.

"He left the station when you asked me to come to your office, sir," informed Officer Rue. "I saw him go out the front door."

"We have the informant," said Kay. "He did it."

"Kay, we have to look at all the evidence before we can point the finger at Officer Soleman," lectured Lieutenant Gorman. "I will look at the hospital registration log book to see if he went to the hospital because that is the only place he could have talked to Leonard. I do not think he would have used his telephone because that would be too easy to trace. Once I know if he went to the hospital, then I will put out a warrant for his arrest."

Lieutenant Gorman asked his secretary to contact the hospital to review the officers on duty registration log book.

"I know he did," said Carolyn. "He hated us. This was his revenge for messing up his trip to Jamaica. If I had never….."

"Stop that Carolyn," scolded Kay. "You did nothing wrong. He is a bad man just like Leonard. Once we apprehend him, we can get Leonard.

"Leonard is still alive?" asked Carolyn. "I thought he fell out of the plane in the mountains. How could anyone survive that fall?"

"I do not know unless he fell into a lake or deep river," alleged Kay. "I do know that he walks with a cane and he wears a patch over one of his eyes."

"You have seen him?" Carolyn shrieked as she moved closer to her brother. "Oh my gosh, he is going to come back here and kill us."

"Not if we can catch him first," Kay thought to herself.

# THANKSGIVING SURPRISE

## CHAPTER V

After reviewing the security video tapes, the hospital authorities and the security department verified that Officer Soleman had gone to the hospital on the morning that Leonard had escaped from his guarded hospital room. The tapes revealed Officer Soleman walking down the hall towards Leonard's hospital room, nonchalantly chatting with the guard assigned outside the prisoner's room, and then entering the room. Thirty minutes elapsed before the officer left the room and coolly walked down the hall to the nurses' station, where he flirted with some of the nurses on duty that morning. This tape cleared Officer Rue of any evil actions on the police force: however, Lieutenant Gorman disciplined him for discussing the active case with Officer Soleman.

"I am afraid that you are going to be one of the people added to Leonard's hit list once Officer Soleman speaks to him," informed Lieutenant Gorman. "I will have to assign you to protect your sister and the Lytle family in order to keep you all together for safety reasons. Will you have any problem with this?"

"No sir," answered Officer Rue. "I will do whatever you order so we can catch this murderer."

Officer Cox suggested, "Dennis, you take Carolyn to the hospital to be with Mrs. Lytle. Officer Rodriguez will fill you in on our duties.

I will take Kay with me to my house to get our clothes and I will have several keys made for Mr. Hughes' home since that is where we will all be staying for the holidays until Leonard is apprehended. We will meet you at the hospital as soon as we finish so we can decide what our next move will be, unless someone else has a better idea."

"Sounds like a good plan to me," smiled Kay looking at Officer Cox.

"If this case keeps going in the direction that it is going, I will have all my officers protecting your family and friends, Kay. There will not be anyone on the force to handle speeders, write tickets, or stop bank robbers," complained Lieutenant Gorman.

"I think this case is coming to an end now that we know that Officer Soleman talked to Leonard. All you have to do is find Officer Soleman and then you can find Leonard," smiled Kay.

"I am assigning two officers to his home and I am going to set up some roadblocks at the city limits," said Lieutenant Gorman.

"I have an idea," alleged Kay.

"Oh, no," whined Lieutenant Gorman. "Go get your keys, clothes, and whatever. I will handle Officer Soleman myself."

Officer Dennis Rue and Carolyn Rue departed the police station in a patrol car headed to the hospital. Officer Cox and Kay proceeded in the opposite direction towards his home to get their clothes. They made one quick stop at a hardware store to have five keys made, one for everyone staying at Mr. Hughes' home. From the hardware store, they traveled west toward Officer Cox's home.

Officer Cox asked, "What were you going to say earlier?"

"You really do not want to know," Kay said.

"Yes, I really want to know," he replied.

"Well, I was thinking, since Officer Soleman knows we are aware of his contact with Leonard, he is not going to go home nor is he going to leave Cortland. I think he is going to hide at one of his girl friends' homes until the coast is clear. When he hurried out of the station he probably did not have time to grab his little black address book from his desk and we both know he is not going to return to the station to retrieve it. He might even try to blackmail Pat into staying at her home, since she did not go with him to Jamaica," Kay supposed.

"I was thinking that you need to return to college to study police administration or forensics. You have some really good ideas when it comes to solving a case," smiled an impressed Officer Cox. "I will telephone Lieutenant Gorman with your ideas about Soleman's girl friends after we get our clothes and return to the hospital."

"Thank you," Kay beamed. "I might re-evaluate college after I take care of Mr. Blackstone's affairs, after handling Pilot Ed's funeral, after purchasing a new plane, after hiring a new pilot, after celebrating the holidays, and after …"

"Ok, one thing at a time, Missy," laughed Officer Cox. "I know you have a busy schedule."

"Speaking of Holidays," Kay reminded him. "Did you really mean it when you said you were going to spend the holidays with my family?"

"I did not think you could hear me over all your crying," said Officer Cox.

"I heard you. Did you mean it?" asked Kay.

"Yes, I meant it. Besides if I am not present, Leonard might show up as Santa," he alleged. "No telling what kind of gifts he would be bringing down the chimney in his bag. Yes, I think I will be there."

Officer Cox drove the car to the garage in the back of the townhouse complex. One of his neighbors watched him as he parked the car, before she hurried over to talk to him. Officer Cox handed Kay the key to his townhouse, opened the garage so she could enter his home, and asked her to get everyone's things ready while he chatted with his neighbor and got his mail. Kay unlocked the door and hurried up-stairs to pack all the clothes that Carolyn, Marie, and she had brought to Officer Cox's home. She thought she could hear Officer Cox down stairs getting his things together.

She yelled, "I am almost finished. Will you help me with some of these bags, please?"

She could hear the creaking of the stairs as if someone was coming. Suddenly, she could smell that special cologne that always indicated trouble was near.

"I need to use the bathroom," she yelled at the person squeaking up the stairway. "The bags are ready. When I finish, I will help you carry them down stairs."

Kay hurried into the bathroom and locked the door. She looked around to find any thing she could use as a weapon. She spotted the toilet bowl plunger just as she heard the person entering the room coming toward the bathroom door. She watched as the door knob wiggled.

"I will be out in just a minute, impatient," yelled Kay.

"Kay," whispered the familiar voice of Mr. Blackstone. "Get into the bathtub, now."

Kay wasted no time to follow her dead friend's orders. She jumped into the bathtub, clinging to her toilet bowl plunger; she pulled the shower curtain across the front of the bathtub to hide herself as she sat near the faucet where she noticed a large family size bottle of tangerine scented shampoo, which she poured over the entire rubber end of the plunger making it slick.

She thought, "If she poured some of this on the floor, whoever came through that door would slip and she could stick the plunger on their face and she could escape."

She opened the shower curtain, pulled the small bathroom area rug away from the door, and poured the scented shampoo in front of the door, emptying the entire bottle all the way back to the bathtub as she climbed back into her white porcelain hiding place, closing the shower curtain.

Officer Cox checked his mail box for any unpaid bills as his nosy neighbor (Mrs. Barbara Hightower) strolled over to talk to him. He had never been very fond of this person due to her constant array of questions about his personal life. She always had something negative to say about the other neighbors in the townhouse complex; however, there was no way for him to avoid having to speak to her today because she was directly between him and his pathway to his home.

"Hello, David," greeted Barbara. "I see you have a new girl friend. She is very cute but I think she might be a little young for you."

"Hello Mrs. Hightower," responded Officer Cox as he tried to get past her. "You have a nice evening."

"It is none of my business to tell the residents living here about some of the things I see, but today I wanted to tell you, I was at the front office paying my rent on time as usual and I saw a police officer come into the office and he asked for your house key. He told Kathy, the new manager who moved here from Oklahoma with her two young sons from her first marriage, that he was your older brother from out of town and he was going to stay with you for a while. Now I know that you do not have a brother because I looked up your life history at the library and I read that you have one sister. Now I am not trying to pry into your personal life but I think it is very strange that this officer would lie to get into your home," tittle-tattled Barbara. "Now I know that policemen can get the best drugs but I am not saying you do drugs or have drugs in your townhouse but I think something is going on illegal in your home because I saw you with three women four nights ago and now this officer is here. Are you listening to me, David? This is a good respectable apartment complex to live in and we want to keep it that way."

Officer Cox was not listening to the scandal seeking busybody. Instead he was reviewing his mail as he walked slowly toward his retreat until she said something about an officer asking for his house key at the front office. He knew that officer had to be Officer Soleman, but did he get into the house and if so, was he still there?

"Did the new manager give that officer my key?" asked Officer Cox.

"Of course she did," answered the gossip spreading Barbara. "It was none of my business to tell her that you did not have a brother. As far as I know, that officer might be an undercover policeman on a surveillance case using your apartment as a stakeout."

"Of course," calmly agreed Officer Cox who was finally interested in what this tattletale had to say. "Do you know if the officer got into my house and if he is still there?"

"Well, I did see him go into your apartment but I did not see him leave. I have better things to do than to keep an eye on your house the entire day," reported Barbara.

"Thank you, Mrs. Hightower," whispered Officer Cox as he put his arm around the scandalmonger. "Will you please do me a favor?"

"Yes, I will, David," answered Barbara thinking Officer Cox was flirting with her.

"Would you call 9-1-1 and ask them to send an ambulance to my home?" asked Officer Cox as he dropped his mail to the ground. "There has been a shooting."

"What? I did not hear any guns fired," buzzed Barbara. "Who was shot?"

"Hopefully, my brother," Officer Cox said as he left the puzzled big mouth busybody standing next to his scattered mail.

Barbara watched as Officer Cox drew his gun from his holster, ran towards his garage to enter his once safe haven of a home through his back door, and disappeared out of her sight. She screamed as she ran back to her townhouse to call the police.

Officer Cox could hear her screaming down the driveway as he quietly sneaked through his kitchen towards his bedroom. He had not heard a word or a scream from Kay which caused him to be concerned about her safety. As he neared the stairway to the second floor, he could hear someone walking around in the guest room and Kay talking to them. He started to yell for Kay but stopped due to smelling a familiar man's cologne that he had smelt two days ago on the airplane before he found pilot Ed dead. He knew Officer Soleman was aware of him being at home and that he would be coming up-stairs to help Kay at any minute. Officer Cox carefully took another step upwards without making a sound. He could see a shadow moving in the room on the door but he did not know who it was. He edged his way quietly up the stairs. The shadow figurine froze on the bedroom door when Officer Cox reached the top of the stairway and the floor creaked under his foot.

Kay sat in the bathtub wondering when Officer Cox was going to discover she was in trouble.

She thought, "Maybe Lover Boy has already killed him and is out there waiting for me to come out of the bathroom. He is going to have to come in here and get me. I am not leaving this spot."

"Officer Soleman, I know you are in there. You are under arrest," yelled Officer Cox. "Drop your gun and no one will get hurt."

"Back off, Officer Cox or I will kill her," returned Officer Soleman as he tried to kick in the bathroom door. "I have nothing to loose so back off."

When Officer Cox heard him trying to kick in the bathroom door, he knew Officer Soleman's attention was not on watching the bedroom door so he made a dive into the room towards the bed to use it for his cover and fired a shot in the direction of the defected officer.

Officer Soleman returned a shot towards Officer Cox but hit the mirror on the dresser causing the glass to shatter to the floor and onto some of the beautiful bedroom furniture. He turned his gun on the bathroom door and shot off the door knob. Officer Cox did not want to fire another shot in the defector's direction because he was afraid he might injure Kay. Once the door was unlocked, Officer Soleman rushed inside, unaware of the shampoo on the floor. He slid across the floor to the bathtub and grabbed the shower curtain to keep from falling. The weight of his body caused the shower curtain to rip at the top and detach from the curtain rod exposing Kay near the faucet area. When he saw Kay, he tried to aim his gun at her with the intent to kill her, but he could not get the leverage he needed to balance himself due to his slipping and sliding in the shampoo. When he fired a shot at her, he missed and shot a hole in the tile above her head.

Kay could hear the distant sound of police sirens coming down the driveway towards Officer Cox's townhouse. Kay knew this was going to be her final opportunity to use the shampoo covered toilet bowl plunger to save her life so she shoved it onto Lover Boy's face causing him to drop his gun and fall into the bathtub. As he slipped, his head struck the wall rendering him unconscious and his body collapsed into the bathtub on top of Kay who was screaming. Kay slowly emerged from beneath the unconscious defector. She could see and feel that he was not breathing so she tried several times to remove the plunger from his face with no success.

Officer Cox hurried to the bathroom to rescue Kay. He had his gun ready to shoot his fellow officer until he looked into the bathroom and saw Officer Soleman in the bathtub with a toilet plunger on his face. As he lowered his gun and started into the bathroom, he slipped on the shampoo covered floor and grabbed the side of the door to balance himself to keep from falling.

"Why is the floor so slippery? What is that smell?" yelled Officer Cox.

"It is the tangerine scented shampoo that Carolyn purchased," she cried as she carefully made her way across the slick floor to Officer Cox. "I think I killed him. I put the shampoo in the plunger and stuck it on his face. I tried to get it off but it is stuck like glue."

Officer Cox carefully slid over to the defector and he tried unsuccessfully to pull the plunger off his face. Once the back up team had arrived, several of the officers ran into the bedroom to secure the area for the paramedics. When they saw how slippery the bathroom floor was, they pulled the comforter off the bed and covered the slippery floor with it so they could rescue the officers. Officer Soleman had no pulse and his fellow comrades could not get the plunger off his face to give him mouth to mouth resuscitation.

Kay could not believe she had killed Lover Boy and felt helpless as she watched the ambulance driver and paramedic carry him (with the plunger still attached to his face) down the stairs to the ambulance. Before the officers could agree on their written report describing how Officer Soleman died (from suffocation), his body would be taken to the morgue for an autopsy to determine what actually killed him and then they can file their accurate report of death with the police department.

Mrs. Barbara Hightower watched from her second story window as they loaded the dead man into the ambulance and drove away. She slithered downstairs and out of her house to the driveway area where Kay and David were informing the officers of what had transpired in the townhouse. She wanted to find out what had happened also, in his apartment, so she would have something to talk about at her next bunko game with the local gossipers. She did not have a chance to say anything to them because they went back into the house to retrieve their luggage. As soon as Kay had finished packing all her luggage, Officer Cox carried them downstairs and loaded them into the trunk of the car. Barbara was still standing in the driveway talking to some of their neighbors when they loaded the last bags into the car.

Barbara hurried over to Kay and she asked," Can you tell me who that man was that was taken away in the ambulance?"

Officer Cox hastily motioned for Kay to get into the car so they could return to the hospital; however, Kay, knowing several people that unfortunately had Barbara's nosy personality (who were her Mother's high school friends) thought of a plan that might keep Barbara quiet and possibly alive.

She told Barbara, "I am a FBI agent and what you saw never happened. It is important for your own safety to keep your mouth shut due to serious consequences. Presently, we have agents everywhere at this point in time watching you. I need to know if I can trust you to keep an important secret."

Barbara leaned her head towards Kay and whispered, "Yes. What is the secret?"

"Good," said Kay as she climbed into the car. "I am counting on you."

"What is the secret?" asked a puzzled Barbara as she watched the car drive down the parking lot and through the townhouse complex gate.

"What did you say to her?" asked Officer Cox.

"If I tell you, I know you are going to be mad, so I am not going to tell you," she answered.

Officers Rue and Rodriguez listened to the events transpiring at Officer Cox's home on the police radio. They waited impatiently for his arrival so they could hear his account of the arrest. When the courageous twosome arrived at the hospital, the first thing that the officers noticed about Officer Cox and Kay was the shampoo covered clothes. As Officer Cox tried to explain what had happened, Kay handed everyone that would be staying at Mr. Hughes' home a key to the house. Carolyn noticed Kay's hands shaking as she handed her the key. Carolyn hugged Kay to reassure her that she had done the right thing.

"You are a hero, Kay," Carolyn said as she moved to the right side of the sofa so there would be more room for Kay to sit besides her.

"I really tried to get the plunger off his face," cried Kay. "The shampoo made it stick to his face like glue."

"It is all right, baby," said Marie as she hugged Kay. "It was either him or you."

"Mother, it was terrible," explained Kay. "I could not find anything in that bathroom that would protect me but that plunger. I was going to hit him with it at first but when I saw that shampoo, I decided to burn his eyes so he could not see me when I tried to escape. When he slid across the room and ripped the shower curtain off the rod, he tried to shoot me. He was looking right at my face, in my eyes, when he started to shoot at me again. I was afraid the next shot would be fatal so I stuck the plunger on his face. He slipped into the tub and fall on top of me. I tried to get that plunger off his face. It was horrible watching the paramedics carry him off with the plunger sticking straight up in the air, still stuck to his face."

Officer Cox asked the other officers to step into the hall so he could discuss the attack. Officer Rue quietly closed the door so they would not disturb Mr. Hughes and the others while they were having their discussion. They walked away from the room so Kay's sensitive ears could not hear their conversation. Once they were far enough from the room, all three officers began to laugh.

"I hate to say it, but the man got far worse than he deserved," laughed Officer Cox. "I walked into the bathroom to see Kay standing over the man pulling on that plunger and there are no words to describe how funny it looked as she pulled on the stick and his head kept going up and down, hitting the porcelain tub. It was a scene out of a comedy movie. Then I slid over to the man and each time I pulled on the stick, Kay would yell, 'try harder, harder'. My bedspread was used to cover the floor so the paramedic could get to him, but the floor was so saturated with shampoo that they slipped even walking on the bedspread. When they finally put him on the stretcher, there was foam and bubbles covering his face and body. He looked like a mad dog," laughed Officer Cox as he wiped the tears from his eyes.

"Did they ever get the plunger off his face?" chuckled Officer Rodriguez.

"No," answered Officer Cox. "It stayed on his face as they carried him down the stairs to the ambulance. I wanted to laugh then, but I could see how upset Kay was, so I turned my back to her to hide my face. She did not notice the other officers on the site, that had arrived to help us, were laughing also."

The officers continued to laugh until Doctor Peterson arrived to bring Mr. Hughes some release papers to sign in order for him to return to his home.

"What is so funny, gentlemen," asked Doctor Peterson. "I love a good joke."

"It is nothing, Sir," Officer Cox snorted. "We should not be laughing at all."

"I heard that an officer was taken into the morgue today. The results from the autopsy report should be available later tonight. I was told that he had a plunger stuck to his face and he was covered with some sort of cleaning liquid. Did he slip in the bathtub?" asked Doctor Peterson, who did not like Officer Soleman due to his constant flirting with the nurses which kept them from their duties.

"Yes, sir," replied Officer Cox. "We are not supposed to discuss a case outside the department."

"I did not realize this was a case," smiled Doctor Peterson. "I have the release papers for Mr. Hughes to sign. Lieutenant Gorman said there would be a van in the back of the hospital to take you to his home. If you need me for anything, I will be available. My home and office numbers are listed on one of the papers I am giving Mr. Hughes. Please feel free to call me at any time."

The men entered the hospital room to find Kay crying about the death of Officer Soleman. Even though Marie and Carolyn tried to comfort her, Kay could not be consoled knowing she had killed Lover Boy. Doctor Peterson asked Mr. Hughes to sign several release papers so he could return to his home. After all the papers were signed, Kay and her team of hideaways were escorted to an unmarked white police van in the parking lot, in back of the hospital. They boarded the van and were driven to Mr. Hughes' plantation style home.

Mr. Hughes was carried upstairs to his fifteen hundred square foot master suite which was decorated in early American furniture. His solid oak bed was given to him by his great grandmother who he was fortunate to meet when he was a child. She was so impressed with the lad that she gave him all her bedroom furniture and a large sum of money to go to college. Back in those days when Mr. Hughes was a child, everyone was suffering from the hardships of the depression and going to college was only a mere dream.

The officers selected a downstairs bedroom so they could hear any intruders trying to invade the house through the front or back doors. They agreed on a weekly work schedule to guard the place until Leonard was apprehended. Officers Cox and Rodriguez would sleep during the night and work during the day, while Officer Rue was given the graveyard shift since it was his fault that the information about the case was leaked.

Marie and Carolyn moved into the bedroom located on the left side of Mr. Hughes' room so Carolyn could hear him call if he needed her. The room was spacious with a huge king size bed and two walk-in closets that had mirrors on the doors.

Kay picked the room to the right of Mr. Hughes's room which was the smallest room in the house but it had the biggest luxury bathroom, complete with a Jacuzzi, separate shower, and two sinks. Mr. Hughes was planning on having a big family and his knowledge of young ladies staying in the bathroom and primping for hours helped him design this bedroom for the daughter he never fathered.

Although life was never going to be normal for Kay or her hideaways until Leonard was apprehended, she managed to create a daily schedule that everyone seemed to be agreeable with. Kay and Officer Cox would pick up the mail at the Post Office and at her mother's home while Carolyn handled all of Mr. Hughes' medical needs and helped Marie prepare the daily meals. Everyone staying at the Hughes' mansion would be in charge of tidying their own rooms and keeping the house from becoming so cluttered.

Mr. Hughes, who was making a healthy recovery, was handling some of his legal cases from his office at his house while his colleagues handled his court cases. He had all the information related to Mr. Blackstone's last will and testament delivered to his home where Kay could finalize the papers so she could take possession of his affairs and properties. Mr. Blackstone left everything he possessed to Kay. His last request was to be cremated and his ashes sprinkled over his wife's grave. Kay had no idea that Mr. Blackstone owned the Hotel in Florida where she had stayed the night before her cruise to the Bahamas. He owned the flight chartering company that had flown her home. He was part owner in a shipping firm in Houston, Texas, and owned some of the property surrounding the Houston Ship Channel. He owned a small ranch in Alpine, Texas that covered twenty-five hundred acres. He had some stocks and bonds in Consolidated Steel where Kay's father, Eager Lytle was president. He owned a chalet in Switzerland and a villa in Austria. The list went on and on as Mr. Hughes continued to read the will to a flabbergasted Kay.

Mr. Hughes explained to Kay that she would have to contact each of her employees and inform them of the change in management and any other changes she might want to impose on them. Kay was overwhelmed by the wealth that Mr. Blackstone was bequeathing her.

"Are you sure there is no one else in his life that he wanted to leave something to other than me?" she asked.

"You were the only one, Kay," said Mr. Hughes. "He thought the world of you. He always talked about how you sang like an angel in

Church. He was proud of you when you selected to attend the college that he had graduated from. Every time you would share a new joke or story with him, he would telephone me and tell the joke or story to me. Kay, you were his world after his wife died and now he is leaving his world to you to show his appreciation. You were good medicine for him."

Kay left Mr. Hughes' office crying uncontrollably as she ran upstairs to her room. Officer Cox thought someone had penetrated the perimeter of the house and alerted Officer Rodriguez as he ran upstairs to assist Kay. Marie was in the kitchen with Carolyn when they heard her crying and they hurried to see what had happened. Marie was hoping that Leonard had been found and killed. Officer Cox entered her room to find her positioned sideways across the bed and crying.

"Kay," Officer Cox asked as he knelt next to her. "What happened?"

"Please, leave me alone. It is terrible," she cried.

"What is terrible, baby?" Marie asked as she and Carolyn entered the room and walked over to the bed.

"Officer Cox," demanded Carolyn. "Get out of the room. This is women's talk. You can go ask Mr. Hughes what happened and we will handle everything up here."

Officer Cox was reluctant to leave her side but he could see that Marie and Carolyn were in control and Carolyn had a tight grip on his arm to persuade him to leave.

Carolyn got a damp cloth from the bathroom while Marie tried to make sense out of Kay's blubbering.

"I should have never left him," she cried and coughed. "I loved him, too. I had no idea that I was all he had left in the world. Oh mother, he left me everything. I should have stayed with him until the end. Mr. Blackstone, if you can hear me, I am so sorry."

"Honey, Mr. Blackstone knew how much you loved him that is why he sent you away," comforted Marie as Carolyn put the wet cloth on Kay's face.

"If you would have been here, Kay, there would have been nothing you could have done to prevent his death," consoled Carolyn. "Look at it this way, you were the one thing that made him happy after his wife died and he wanted you to know it."

"That is right, Honey," agreed Marie. "Be happy that you had the opportunity to make him happy and comfortable during a difficult time. It was hard for him to get over his wife's passing but you were there to help him. Be grateful for your time together as friends. Now stop that crying."

"Thank you Mother, but I would like some time alone," cried Kay. "I will be all right. Thank you Carolyn."

Carolyn and Marie left the room and closed the door to give Kay some privacy. They could hear her crying as they walked down the stairs towards Mr. Hughes' office where they found Officer Cox reading the will.

"What did you say to my daughter, Evan Hughes?" demanded Marie. "She is upstairs bawling her eyes out."

"Now Marie," begged Mr. Hughes. "I was reading over the conditions of Mr. Blackstone's will and last requests. I never got to finish my reading when I noticed Kay was getting disturbed. I knew this was going to be stressful but this is my job, Marie. Kay is going to have to take on some new responsibilities."

"Well, if it was me, I would sell Mr. Blackstone's home and car and use the money to return to college. She said she wanted to go back to college," said Carolyn.

"She is receiving a whole lot more than his home, car, and furnishing, Carolyn," explained Officer Cox. "I can totally understand why she is up there crying. She owns a hotel, a plane company, partnerships and stocks in several other companies. The list goes on and on. That girl has more money than everyone in this town could poll together in one week."

"Let me see that," ordered Marie as she reviewed the will. "How could you do this to my poor baby, Evan?"

"She is anything but poor, Mrs. Lytle," corrected Officer Cox.

"You would think that you would be delighted to hear about her fortune," yelled Mr. Hughes. "She is young and can enjoy her wealth like Mr. Blackstone wanted; however, you are acting as if I sentenced her to death."

"In a way, you have," remarked Officer Cox. "Once Leonard finds out how much Kay is worth, he is going to want to get his hands on some of that money."

"I am not going to put it in the newspaper or broadcast it on the radio," said Mr. Hughes. "This is a matter between me, her, and her family. If the information leaks out, it is because one of you has a loose tongue. I know Kay and she will not say anything or act differently."

"I will not say anything either," agreed Carolyn. "That poor girl. She must feel dreadful. I am going to make her some hot soup."

"I think I will go to that burger place she likes and get some fries and a fish sandwich for her," said Officer Cox. "She should be feeling better in no time."

"What about me?" asked Mr. Hughes in a pitiful voice. "Remember, I am the one that got shot."

"Oh Evan, you will be fine," smiled Marie as she returned the will and patted his hand. "I will take care of you."

While Kay's family and friends were making plans to cheer her up, Kay was upstairs saying a prayer because she knew her life was going to change drastically and she needed all the guidance in the world to help her handle her new responsibilities.

Knelt beside the bed, with her hands together, and looking up towards the sky, Kay prayed, "Dear Holy Father, I am scared and I do not want to disappoint you. Mr. Blackstone thought I was a strong and intelligent person who would be able to walk in his shoes. Please forgive me if I seem ungrateful, but I do not know how to handle all this new responsibility that has come into my life. What am I suppose to do?"

"Kay," softly spoke the familiar voice of Mr. Blackstone. "I will be there to guide and help you when the time comes. You are a strong person that is why I chose you to handle all my affairs. When the time is right, I will need you to use the key I gave you. Go to sleep and get some rest for tomorrow. We will be going on a new adventure."

The next morning, Kay felt refreshed after a good nights sleep. Her first priority was to handle Mr. Blackstone's final request and have him cremated so she could sprinkle his ashes over his wife's grave.

Kay knew attending Pilot Ed Carry's or her stewardess, Miss Sandy Stone's funerals would be impossible; however, she sent flowers and paid the entire funeral expenses, including their caskets. She talked to Pilot Ed's girlfriend for several hours explaining what had actually happened to him. His girlfriend said she would pray that Leonard would be arrested before any more innocent people were hurt.

Kay placed an ad in the local newspapers to take applications to hire a Pilot and stewardess to take her late employees' positions. Then she had a meeting in Mr. Hughes' large formal living room with everyone that was staying at his home.

"I want to apologize for my conduct over the last few days. I have been preoccupied and selfish with my time," explained Kay. "As you know from reading of Mr. Blackstone's will that I will be taking on some new responsibilities and I will need to pay a visit to each of the businesses I have inherited. As for now, I would like to focus on the Thanksgiving Holiday which will be here next week. Once the holidays are over, I would like to complete Mr. Blackstone's requests. I think I will start the New Year off by being more professional and conscientious. I think that is what Mr. Blackstone would want."

"What about Leonard?" asked Officer Rodriguez. "Are you going to stop hiding from him?"

"Leonard, I almost forgot about him," answered Kay. "Right now, I want to focus on the holidays and enjoy my family and friends. I know Leonard is a dangerous man and we all know what he is capable of doing but I do not want him to ruin our holidays."

"Kay," cautioned Officer Cox. "He could care less about the holidays. For the time being, we need to stay alert at all times. We are never going to be safe until he is caught."

"You are right," agreed Kay. "But I am not going to let him ruin my holiday. So we need to go buy a turkey and start making cookies."

Officer Cox was going to say something else but Marie patted his arm to stop him.

"This is her way of dealing with it, son," said Marie. "She knows the danger without you reminding her."

"But I," Officer Cox started to continue his thoughts.

Marie smiled, "Next time I tell you to shoot him, will you please shoot him?"

"Officer Cox," yelled Kay. "We have some heavy grocery shopping to do. Come on, you big baby."

Officer Cox could see he was out numbered so he followed Kay to the car so they could go holiday grocery shopping. Carolyn came alone to select some of her favorite food items to prepare the best thanksgiving feast that they have ever eaten.

The Wednesday before Thanksgiving Day, the ladies spent the entire day making pies, yeast rolls, and iced sugar cookies so the holiday meal would have all the bells and whistles to make it perfect. The smells from the kitchen were driving Officer Cox's stomach crazy. Every time something had finished baking, he appeared from out of nowhere to sample the sweets.

"Not until tomorrow," Marie would yell.

"I am hungry now," Officer Cox pleaded.

Mr. Hughes inspected the kitchen several times during their baking frenzy to sneak a cookie and a kiss from Marie. He was happier than he had ever been in his entire life. Sad, but true, he owed his happiness to Leonard; however, he would never admit this out loud for anyone to hear.

Thanksgiving Day arrived with the televised parades, carnivals, and scheduled football games followed by a wonderful home cooked stuffed turkey dinner complete with hot yeast rolls, turkey gravy, sweet potatoes, yellow corn, and cold jelled cranberry sauce.

Marie did not have to call anyone to the table to eat because Officer Rodriguez had moved the television to the dining room area where they could watch their precious football game from the dining room table. Marie turned the television off so they could have a peaceful and elegant meal without the men yelling at the television because their favorite football team was losing.

"Hey, what do you think you are doing?" yelled all the men in unison.

"We are going to give thanks and eat without that football game interfering with our well deserved meal," demanded Marie. "We all have something to be thankful for and it is time to do just that. I will start."

Everyone around the table held hands as Marie started the Thanksgiving prayer, "Dear Father, thank you for my daughter and keeping her safe from that murderous lowlife of a man. Also, thank you for these new friends, the good food, and the time that we will share together, and Lord, thank you for this home and for helping Evan to get well."

Marie squeezed Evan's hand to indicate that it was his time to pray.

Evan prayed, "Thank you for my friends and for helping me through a tough recovery, but most of all, thank you for Marie and her family for they have been a blessing to me."

Carolyn prayed saying, "Thank you for this job and the joy that I get to share with these people and my brother."

Officer Rodriguez prayed, "Thank you for my family even though I do not get to be with them this year, I know they are thankful, too."

Officer Rue prayed, "Thank you for my sister and for letting us be together again."

Kay prayed, "Thank you for my mother who taught me how to care for others, thank you for my new friends, and for helping me and David Cox through the plane crash, the snow storm, the explosion in Colorado, and thank you for saving us from the late Officer Soleman."

Kay looked at Officer Cox and said," You do not have to pray if you do not want to."

Officer Cox smiled and said, "Thank you for the best home cooked meal I have ever had with the nicest people I have ever met in a free country where we can give thanks to an all mighty God and not worry about persecution or death."

Everyone was surprised at his spiritual prayer as they all said "Amen" and they began to eat.

Mr. Hughes carved the turkey and put a turkey leg on Officer Cox's plate.

As Officer Rodriguez was pouring the gravy on his dressing he mentioned, "My wife's gravy has little pieces of chopped up giblets in it. I have never had such smooth gravy before."

"Our turkey did not come with gizzards, livers, or a neck this year," responded Carolyn. "So I made the gravy from the turkey drippings. I am sorry it is not lumpy. "

"It is good, just different," said Officer Rodriguez.

As Mr. Hughes sliced the huge turkey, he cut into a small bag that was stuffed deep in the back of the turkey.

"I think I found your giblets," laughed Mr. Hughes as he dragged a small hot paper bag full of cooked gizzards, livers, and a turkey neck out of the half eaten turkey carcass. "Would any one like a Thanksgiving surprise?"

"That is not funny," scolded Carolyn.

"I made the same mistake when I cooked my first turkey," laughed Marie as she fondly remembered her first Thanksgiving meal with Eager.

"What should I do with this?" chuckled Mr. Hughes.

"Give it to Officer Cox," giggled Carolyn. "He will eat almost anything."

Officer Cox held up his plate to receive the Thanksgiving surprise while everyone laughed hysterically at him.

After the thanksgiving meal, the guys hurried back to watch the football games and the ladies cleared the table with the help of Mr. Hughes. Marie and Evan washed the dishes while Kay and Carolyn arranged cookies on a platter and plated some slices of pies to add to the dessert cart.

"Would anyone like dessert?" asked Kay as she walked into the dining room pushing the dessert cart sporting the delicious homemade pastries.

"I will explode if I eat another thing," pleaded Officer Rue. "I am going to go rest up for tonight's shift. Thank you."

"How about you, Officer Cox?" asked Kay.

"I never met a dessert I could not eat," he smiled as he took several cookies and a piece of cherry pie.

"Kay," yelled Marie. "Will you play some Christmas music on the piano for us?'

"Oh Mother," said Kay. "Everyone is watching the game and no one wants to hear Christmas music right now."

"I would, Kay," smiled Evan who was wearing a stained white apron to cover his clothes from the dish water. "I remember you wrote a song when you were in grade school. I think you were 10 years old."

"She was 12 years old when she wrote that song," corrected Marie. "Play it for us honey. It will be like old times."

"You wrote a song?" asked Officer Cox who was once again amazed with her talents. "I would like to hear it."

"Oh please, you are embarrassing me," pleaded Kay. "It was silly."

"You won first place at the Christmas pageant at school," bragged Marie. "It was cute. She wrote it for a sick student who was in the hospital during the holidays. Her teacher was so impressed that she made a tape of it and she asked the local disc jockey at the radio station to play it on Christmas Eve for the sick student."

Officer Cox led Kay to the piano and whispered, "If I can pray for you, you can play for me. Please, I would like to hear it."

Kay sat down at the piano to play and sing her song,

> 'Hello Santa, listen to me.
> Put no presents under my tree.
> For all I want is time
> To spend with this family of mine.'

> 'I've been good, just check your list
> But no presents will I miss
> Your sleigh will be lighter in the sky
> For all I want for Christmas is time.'

> 'Don't need candy, toys, or cheer
> We have that all right here
> No winter clothes to fight the <u>weather</u>
> We just want more time <u>to</u> <u>get</u> <u>her</u>'

> 'The snow is falling on the ground
> Everywhere is that Christian sound
> The joy of the season is bright
> With all of the houses in lights'

> 'So Santa Clause please hear my plea
> And put no presents under my tree
> For all I want for Christmas is time
> To spend with this family of mine.'

Marie, Carolyn, and Evan joined Kay in singing the refrain, "

> 'Don't need candy, toys, or cheer
> We have that all right here
> No winter clothes to fight the weather
> We just want more time <u>to</u> <u>get</u> <u>her</u>'

Then they finished the last two stanzas, "

> 'The snow is falling on the ground
> Everywhere is that Christian sound
> The joy of the season is bright
> With all of the houses in lights.'

> 'So Santa Clause please hear my plea
> And put no presents under my tree
> For all I want for Christmas is time
> To spend with this family of mine.'

Officer Cox thought to himself, "This has to be the most strenuous Thanksgiving I have ever experienced; however, look at them singing and laughing as if there were no cares in the world. No, I am wrong – this is a wonderful Thanksgiving. I am glad I am here."

When Kay and the others had finished singing, Officer Cox asked, "Did you ever attempt to make a record out of that song?"

"No, it is just a silly song I wrote. No one would buy this," laughed Kay who was very embarrassed.

"If people will buy records about flying reindeers, singing snowmen, and kissing Santa, they will buy your record. It is cute," complimented Officer Cox.

"I liked it. It is easy to sing. What happened to that student you wrote it for?" asked Carolyn.

"She is married, living in Texas, and has two children," smiled Kay.

"I think you should make a record, too" commented Officer Rodriguez.

"It is not cute enough, but thank you," said Kay. "Not to change the subject, but we need to go pick up the mail tomorrow and get the boxes of Christmas decorations from my mother's home so we can decorate this house. We always do this on the Friday after Thanksgiving. It is tradition."

"I love to decorate at Christmas and drive around to look at the lights," yelled Carolyn. "Can I go and help? "

# THE BIRTHDAY INVITATION

## CHAPTER VI

With Thanksgiving behind her, Kay set out to fulfill all of Mr. Blackstone's expectations and final requests. She contacted a number of airplane manufacturers to have their brochures sent to her so she could purchase several airplanes to replace the two that had been recently destroyed. She notified Peaceful Hills Funeral Home to make an appointment to discuss Mr. Blackstone's cremation request. She called Mr. Blackstone's CPA and asked for a list all the employees' names and addresses so she could interview each one of them to make a decision on whether or not they were hired to handle that position properly at her newly acquired companies. She made a list of the day's activities, complete with telephone numbers, and gave a copy to Officer Rodriguez so he would know where she, Carolyn, and Officer Cox would be in case he needed them.

When Officer Cox was finally awakened by Officer Rue to take his shift, he discovered Kay and Carolyn dressed and waiting impatiently to go get the mail at the post office and Christmas decorations from her mother's house. He hurried through his breakfast without getting choked, grabbed the car keys, and drove the car to the front of the house so the ladies could get in.

On Kay's list, the first stop was the post office to get her mail. She was amazed at the amount of mail that was stuffed in her post office box. There was a large envelope for Officer Cox that was from the Colorado Springs Police Department. She had several thank you cards from Pilot Ed's family and Miss Stone's family and the usual junk mail that everyone who has good credit receives.

Their next stop was to Marie's home to pick up her mail and get the decorations. Marie's mail box was full of letters and advertisements, also. Kay showed Officer Cox where her mother kept all of her Christmas decorations and she helped him load four big boxes into the car. A neighbor across the street, Mr. Mitch Mallard, came over to inform Kay about a package that was delivered to the house that morning and he asked the delivery man to leave it in the back on the patio so no one would steal it. Kay thanked Mitch as she started to go get the box, when Carolyn volunteered to get it for her.

"We should put some decorations on Mother's house so it looks like we are living here since we are still receiving deliveries here," suggested Kay. "I wonder who sent us a present."

"Carolyn," yelled Officer Cox as he waved at her to return, then he whispered to Kay, "We can get the box later. If someone is watching the house, it would be a good idea to make it look like we are here celebrating the holidays. Do you have some more decorations in the house we can use?"

"My mother is the queen of decorations," smiled Kay. "There has to be at least eight more boxes in the house. This is going to be fun. Carolyn, would you telephone Officer Rodriguez and tell him what we are doing? As soon as we finish here, we need to go to the funeral home."

Officer Cox leaned a ladder next to the edge of the house so he could hang some multi colored lights on the eaves of the roof. Kay untangled the strands of lights and handed them to him. Carolyn draped red and green garland on the inside of the windows and over the front door. They hung huge round red, silver, and gold ornaments in the pecan trees across the front yard, and then wrapped the lower part of the boles of the trees with small white blinking lights. Officer Cox plugged the light cords into a timer so it would give the appearance of someone switching the lights on at night and off during the day. The trio stood back and admired their Christmas art work.

"Tomorrow, we can decorate the garage," suggested Kay.

Kay knew the trip to the funeral home was going to be dreadfully stressful for her but she had to do this for Mr. Blackstone. Carolyn and Officer Cox chitchatted as Kay sorted through the mail, selecting the important stuff and tossing the junk advertisement stuff to the floorboard of the car while they traveled to the funeral home.

At the funeral home, Kay felt an eerie peaceful feeling surrounding her as she, Carolyn, and Officer Cox entered the main parlor to speak to the funeral director. Kay listened intensely as the director; Mr. Halcyon showed her several urns so Mr. Blackstone would have an eternal resting place in her home. Kay explained to Mr. Halcyon that his ashes would be taken to Baltimore and sprinkled over his wife's grave so she needed something practical that would travel well on an airplane.

Officer Cox selected an urn that resembled a flower vase on a pedestal.

"After you sprinkle his ashes in Baltimore, you can keep this at the house and put some fresh flowers in it for Mr. Blackstone," he propositioned. "It is small enough for travel, inexpensive, and pretty."

Mr. Halcyon was not impressed. He advised Kay, "These urns are made for the beloved's ashes and not for flowers."

"I like that one, too," smiled Kay. "It is functional, well-designed, and it looks like something he would purchase. I will buy that one. Now, may I see Mr. Blackstone before you cremate him?'

"Yes," answered Mr. Halcyon who did not approve of Kay's choice of urns. "Please follow me."

Officer Cox and Carolyn asked Kay to step aside for a second so they could talk to her before she entered the crematory to view Mr. Blackstone's body.

"Kay, I do not think that is a good idea. I know your emotions are strong for Mr. Blackstone but seeing him in this place might disturb you," said Carolyn.

"This will be the last time I will ever have to speak to Mr. Blackstone face to face," said Kay. "You can come with me or wait for me out here in the parlor but I have to do this."

They decided to follow Kay to comfort her through the entire ordeal.

Mr. Halcyon led them through a short hallway to a large cold room where compartments, like lockers, lined the right wall. He opened one of the compartments which was labeled, "Blackstone's Family" and pulled out a tray containing Mr. Blackstone's naked cadaver covered with a blue sheet.

The room was silent as Kay approached his cold, lifeless body. She calmly placed her hand on his covered forehead, leaned over, and kissed him.

She whispered in his ear, "Thank you, Mr. Blackstone, for saving my life. You are the best friend I ever had. I am sorry if I have disappointed you or hurt you at any time. I am afraid if I cremate you, I will never hear from you again and our friendship will end. I love you, dearly, and I miss seeing your face everyday; although I feel your presents with me wherever I go."

Officer Cox softly placed his hand on Kay's back to get her attention which startled her.

"Kay," he said. "You are going to have to say good bye. It is time for him to rest."

Carolyn wiped the tears from her eyes as she moved closer to her friends and whispered, "Kay, I liked him, too. I am going to go to the front and wait for you. Good bye Mr. Blackstone, it was a pleasure to know you."

Carolyn was crying as she left the others in the crematory area to go wash her face. She had no idea the crematory was going to depress her.

"I think Carolyn needs some assistance," murmured Officer Cox into Kay's ear. "I will stay with him until the end."

"Thank you Officer Cox," Kay said softly. "I would appreciate that."

"Good Bye Daddy Blackstone, DB," Kay kissed Mr. Blackstone's head again. "I will always remember you."

Kay left the room to find Carolyn as Officer Cox watched the undertaker wheel Mr. Blackstone's cadaver into the main cremation area where three huge ovens were located. The mortician prepared his body for the crematory and placed it on the rack that loads the bodies into the fire. Officer Cox stopped the mortician so he could bid his farewells to Mr. Blackstone. The mortician told him to take his time because the crematory oven has to reach a certain temperature before they can load a body into it.

When the mortician walked away, Officer Cox softly spoke to the body, "I was not a religious man until I met this family or I should say, until I met Kay. She has changed my life and I am going to try to save hers. I know you have been there several times to help us – to rescue us. I truly thank you. I promise I will protect Kay to the best of my ability."

"Sir, the fire is ready," informed the mortician. "I will need to take the body."

"Can you see I am trying to talk to the man? Give me a few more minutes," asked Officer Cox.

"Sir, he can not hear you. He is dead," conveyed the mortician.

Officer Cox looked up from the body. His face was full of anger as he showed the mortician his badge and gun and said, "You are going to be dead if you do not let me finish what I started here so step back and wait your turn."

The Mortician moved away from the cold unresponsive corpse to give Officer Cox his space.

Officer Cox whispered in Mr. Blackstone's ear, "I have to go before this spineless insect interrupts me again, but I wanted you to know I appreciate everything you have done for us. Have a safe journey, sir. I hope we get to meet again. I will stay with you until the end."

Officer Cox glared at the mortician as he patted Mr. Blackstone's chest and stepped aside to allow the mortician to take the corpse.

"You can have him now," said the saddened officer.

"You will have to leave during the cremation," advised the mortician.

"I am staying until the end," demanded Officer Cox as he flashed his badge at him again. "He would want it that way."

The mortician was not going to argue with the grief stricken officer. He placed the body of Mr. Blackstone on the loading rack and pushed it into the crematory oven. Officer Cox bowed his head in silent prayer as the flames surrounded and completely engulfed Mr. Blackstone's body.

"Do you smell that?" asked the mortician. "It smells like a

man's cologne. That is strange because the body was washed as a preparation."

"Yes," smiled Officer Cox. "I have smelt that cologne many times. Good bye, DB."

Kay and Carolyn were sitting in the front parlor of the funeral home when they smelt the man's cologne fragrance in the air surrounding them.

"Do you smell that cologne?" asked Carolyn as she wiped her red puffy eyes. "The employees here must use the same cologne as Officer Cox."

Kay knew what that smell was and it was not from the employees at the funeral home. She stood up and gazed out the window as if looking to see an old friend going home. She knew it was over.

Officer Cox joined the two ladies and they had a group hug in the parlor. Kay thanked him for staying with Mr. Blackstone through the cremation. She knew it would have been overwhelming to stay and watch her best friend go up in smoke.

Mr. Halcyon returned to the group and said. "It will be a few more hours before the urn will be ready for transport so it might be a good idea to have lunch and come back later."

"Why is it going to take so long?" asked Kay.

Mr. Halcyon explained that the bones have to cool before they can be sent to the crusher where they are pounded into powder and then placed into the urn.

"I thought the fire destroyed the entire body," said Kay who had never been to a cremation or known anyone that was cremated.

"The fire will only destroy the skin, tissues, organs of the body, and the hair. The residue escapes through the chimney exhaust area; however, it does not destroy the bones. The bones have to be crashed into ashes," explained Mr. Halcyon.

Lunch sounded agreeable to everyone so Officer Cox went to get the car while Kay telephoned Officer Rodriguez to inform him about the delay. Kay suggested that they dine at 'Fish, Fries, and Fast' for lunch. It was the last restaurant that she and Mr. Blackstone had eaten in before the unpleasant bomb shelter incident. Kay brought some of the mail into the restaurant so she could do some work and eat at the same time.

Officer Cox opened his large envelope from the Colorado Springs Police Department. As he read, he discovered that there were four homes in the Colorado Springs and Denver areas that had pools installed where the owners went missing. It also stated that the previous owners were young women, whose names were Katherine, Karen, Katy, and Kate, all were married to a man fitting Leonard's description. Officer Cox excused himself from the table to telephone Lieutenant Gorman and informed him of the discoveries of the missing persons. Then he telephoned the CSPD and asked them to get a search warrant approved to have the swimming pools excavated. He believed that the coroner was going to find the missing owners murdered under their pools.

Kay continued to sort through the bills until she noticed a letter from one of her Mother's oldest high school friends, Susan Hebert.

"I wonder what this is," said Kay as she looked at the envelope.

Carolyn realized that they had left the package that was delivered to Marie's home in the back yard.

"Kay we forgot that package at your Mother's house," reminded Carolyn. "We need to go back to get it so it does not get ruined in the weather. It might be something very valuable."

"When Officer Cox comes back from his calls, I will ask him to return to Mom's home so we can get it," said Kay. "Thank you for remembering it."

When Officer Cox finished his conversations with both police departments, he returned to finish his meal. Kay had taken the liberties to reorder another hot meal for him because his telephone calls were lengthy and his meal had gotten cold. After they had eaten, they return to the funeral home to collect Mr. Blackstone's urn and ashes.

Kay went into the funeral home alone to compensate the bill and claim Mr. Blackstone's urn, while her two best friends waited for her in the car. Mr. Halcyon was very unhappy with Kay's urn choice but he was delighted when she paid him two hundred dollars extra for taking care of Mr. Blackstone's body while she was away.

When Kay returned to the car, she asked Officer Cox to return to her mother's home to get the package that was delivered earlier.

She held the urn in her lap while Officer Cox drove back to Marie's home. When they arrived they were greeted again by, Mitch, the neighbor from across the street. He said that a car had driven up about two hours ago and was parked in front of Marie's home. He thought it was strange so he asked them what they were doing. The man driving asked him if a packaged had been delivered today and he wanted to know where the family was.

"I did not tell them anything, Kay," said Mitch.

"If you saw them again, would you be able to recognize them?" asked Officer Cox.

"Yes," assured Mitch. "One of the men had tattoos all over his arm and lots of pierced earrings in his ears and one in his nose. He would be very easy to spot in a crowd."

"That sounds like the man that I was talking to on the plane trip coming home," alleged Kay. "I thought he said he was going to Las Vegas."

"Both of you stay in the car," ordered Officer Cox. "I am going to call for some back up. That package might have a bomb in it."

Lieutenant Gorman dispatched an unmarked police car to Marie's home with two bomb control officers.

Kay and Carolyn were driven to Mr. Hughes' home and told to stay off the telephone. Officer Cox stayed behind to observe what was in the package and to secure the area from the neighbors while the bomb was being defused. If his hunch was right, the package was from Leonard. According to some of the papers he read during lunch, Leonard liked working with explosives.

When the bomb squad arrived, Officer Cox lead them to the back porch where the package had been delivered that morning. He explained that the person who sent the package had a great deal of knowledge working with explosive and it might have a hair trigger device on it. The bomb squad was very careful in their examination of the box.

Officer Cox returned to the curious neighbor who was standing in the driveway and asked him to stay inside his home until he knew the area was safe. After Mitch and Officer Cox had reached his front door across the street, they noticed a car with the two suspicious men that he had seen two hours earlier cheekily come down the street and started to park in front of Marie's home. The men in the car did not notice Officer Cox and the neighbor standing on the front porch watching them slowly drive past the house because they were more interested in the events that would be transpiring at Marie's house. As they drew near, the Christmas light decorations came on and lit the front of the house giving the appearance that the family was at home. They had no idea that the unmarked cars in the driveway were police vehicles. They were parked in front of the house waiting for something to happen. They were not expecting Officer Cox to come sneaking up on them and point his gun through their open window in their faces.

"Get out of the car and lay on the ground with your hands over your head," demanded Officer Cox.

"What is wrong, Officer," asked the driver. "Is it against the law to go Christmas light looking in this neighborhood?"

"If that is what you are doing, no, it is not against the law," alleged Officer Cox. "However, I understand you were here earlier when the lights were not on, so get out of the car."

The edgy driver looked at his partner in crime and made an indication that he was going to get out of the car; but instead, he sped away down the street. Officer Cox fired two shots at the car, breaking the rear window. He ran into the house to telephone the department to report the license plate number so they could put a trace on the vehicle and a warrant out for their arrest, when suddenly, the bomb squad came running through the kitchen, passing Officer Cox, and dashing through the front door. Officer Cox knew from experience that when you see the bomb squad running, you follow them. He dropped the telephone and made it to the front door just as the bomb ignited and blew the back porch and patio into pieces. The bomb blew out the electricity box shorting out the decorations in the front yard.

"Sorry, we had almost disarmed it," said one of the officers. "Then when we heard the shots fired in the front, the bomb started ticking."

The officers roped off the back yard as a crime scene area while Officer Cox radioed Lieutenant Gorman to inform him about the explosion. He gave him the license plate number of the car that the two suspicious men were driving. Another patrol car was sent to Marie's badly damaged home to take Officer Cox back to Mr. Hughes' home. They made several (off the route) turns to assure they were not being followed.

Officer Cox realized that Leonard did not know where the family was staying because he had sent the bomb to Marie's home instead of Mr. Hughes' house.

When the girls reached Mr. Hughes' home, none of the others were aware of the package or the scene that was taking place at Marie's house.

"Any mail today," Marie asked as she came down the stairs.

"Yes," said Kay. "There were a lot of bills and this looks like an invitation for you, Mother."

Marie took the letter, looked at the return address and sender's name, then tossed it in the garbage.

"You do not want to see what it is?" asked Carolyn.

"I do not care to go," replied Marie. "Where is Officer Cox?"

Kay retrieved the letter from the garbage pail and answered, "He stayed behind due to a package that was delivered to your home this morning. He thinks it is a bomb."

"It was a bomb," interrupted Officer Rodriguez. "Come listen to the police radio."

"Did it explode?" asked Kay.

"Yes," answered Officer Rodriguez. "Luckily, no one was hurt. Officer Cox is on his way here. It looks like we will be staying at this location for awhile longer."

"Good," alleged Evan as he patted Marie's hand. "I enjoy having all this company. You can stay as long as you want."

"Listen to this," demanded Officer Rodriguez as he waved his hand to get everyone's attention. "The car has been found that had the two men in it. One of the men escaped but Officer Cox was able to shoot the driver when they were trying to escape causing him to wreck the car about a mile away from the explosion. He was arrested and they have him in custody for questioning. I bet Officer Cox will be there tomorrow."

"I am glad he was caught," said Carolyn. "He might confess to the authorities where Leonard is hiding and they can arrest him. Then we can have a wonderful Christmas without any more explosions."

"This is a real world, sis," informed Officer Rue. "Nothing is that easy."

"She can dream," scolded Marie who had the same thought as Carolyn except she was hoping Leonard would be killed.

"Mother, what are you going to do with this invitation," asked Kay.

"You can have it," snapped Marie. "If you would like to, you can go in my place."

Officer Cox arrived in time to hear Marie and Kay arguing over the invitation. He closed and locked the door and walked over to Marie to tell her about her home.

"I am sorry about the house, Mrs. Lytle," he apologized. "The back porch is a mess."

"I am glad you were not hurt," said Marie as she gave him a hug. "The house can be replaced. There are some leftovers in the kitchen if you are hungry. I heated them up for you earlier."

"If he is hungry," remarked Kay as she patted him on the back. "I am glad you were not hurt, too."

"There is some good that we can get out of this," said Officer Cox. "Leonard does not know where we are."

"That is right," agreed Kay. "He thinks we are at mother's house. He knows we are on the move searching for a safe place to stay due to the explosion. He is going to start looking for us again."

"Since he is a very intelligent man, he might wait a few months before he starts looking for us since the police know he is alive and they are on the alert. You know how he hates snitches. He will probably focus on killing the man that was arrested tonight and the police will catch him. In view of the facts that will give us time to sprinkle Mr. Blackstone in Baltimore." alleged Officer Cox. "As for the other man that escaped, I do not think he was the man on the plane because he had gray hair indicating an age difference. Plus, we will need to find a better hideaway so he does not destroy this beautiful home."

"You can stay here," begged Mr. Hughes. "I have an unlisted telephone number and the location is perfect. He does not know where I live and my colleagues have been advised not to give out any information concerning my whereabouts if they intend to stay employed."

"It is fine with me if everyone agrees," said Kay. "I like it here."

Mr. Hughes was delighted that everyone wanted to stay with him. His home had never been filled with so much food, laughter, and love. He would hate to see Marie abandon him since their lives were being bonded together for the first time.

"Where is the urn?" asked Officer Cox.

"I placed it on the table in the entrance hall," answered Kay.

"What were you and Marie arguing about before I walked into the house?" asked Officer Cox looking at Kay.

"Mother received a letter from an old school friend. I think it is a birthday invitation but she will not open it," answered Kay handing the letter to him.

Officer Cox opened the letter which contained a red, white, and blue invitation to a 60th birthday party for Susan Hebert. The party was going to be held at her home in Oklahoma City. Attendees needed to respond as soon as possible due to the limitation of rooms at the Cherokee Casino, hotel, and resort where she had a group of rooms blocked for her out of town guest. On November 27th at twelve noon, everyone was to meet at her home for the festivities and meal. No presents were required.

"This looks like fun; however, you only have a few days to respond if you want to attend. I think you should go and have a good time. While you are at the party, Kay and I can fly to Baltimore to take care of business for Mr. Blackstone," suggested Officer Cox.

"You tell him, Kay, because when I start talking about that woman it gives me a headache," alleged Marie.

"You have a headache?" asked Carolyn who was going up-stairs to get Mr. Hughes' medicine. "I have some medicine for that. I will be right back."

"No, Carolyn," laughed Kay. "Mother does not have a headache. By the way, here are two letters for you."

"Are you going to tell me why you do not want to go?" insisted Officer Cox.

"This lady is one of mother's high school friends whose personality is similar to your neighbor's personality," stated Kay. "It is a semi long story, are you sure you want to hear it."

"Yes, go on," eagerly listened Officer Cox. "I have no where to go and all night to get there."

"I want to hear it, too," smiled Carolyn returning with Mr. Hughes' night time remedies and some aspirins for Marie.

"Oh, I will tell the story, Kay, since I was there," frowned Marie. "When I was in high school I had several so-called friends. My mother, Kay's grandmother, would drive me to school every morning. On the way, we would stop, wait several minutes and pick up Susan. Susan pretended to be my best friend in front of my mother (because she was getting a free ride to school). After we had arrived at the school and Mother was out of sight; I became invisible to Susan and was not allowed to be in her circle of friends. Even though, I would be standing right next to her, she would ignore me and talk to everyone standing around her. When it was time to go home, I became visible again and her dearest friend."

"As time moved on so did we. We had to move several miles on the other side of town from my school which meant, I would be attending a new school: however, my parents knew I wanted to graduate with my class mates whom I had known since grade school, so my father paid the out-of-town tuition fee to keep me in that school so I could graduate with my friends. Each morning, he would take me to school on the way to work. My friend, Susan, wanted him to swing by and pick her up so we could ride together. My mother could see through her façade and knew her friendship was superficial. She told her parents that it would be impossible to pick her up for school each morning because my father could not wait on her to get dressed which would cause him to be late for work. I was so glad. I never could understand why Susan's mother or father could not take her to school or why she could not ride the bus; however, I think it had to do with a money issue."

"Are you asking a question, Mrs. Lytle?" asked Officer Cox.

"Shut up, and let Marie finish. That was a statement not a question," scolded Carolyn

"I graduated and went to college," continued Marie. "That is where I met Kay's father and Mr. Hughes. I was a cheerleader in college which is funny, because when I was in high school, I would have never tried out to be on the cheerleading team. I had not seen Susan in 4 years when I received a wedding invitation. Edgar insisted that I make an appearance. He had met some of my true friends from high school but had never met her. We went to the wedding. I was wearing a blue dress and I had left my sun glasses over my eyes when I entered the church because I was so use to wearing them in the summer, outside during cheerleading practice, that I forgot I had them on when I entered the church. Susan and her wedding party were in the Bride's dressing room with some of her family members and a photographer. She greeted me with a hug and introduced me to some of the people in the room as an old high school friend. Her mother insisted that she could not remember me. I thought that was strange because I had known those people since elementary school and I do not have a face that you can forget that easily with or without sun glasses on: however, her mother maintained that she did not know me. So Susan asked me to take off my glasses and show her my face. I thought nothing of it as I took off my glasses until her mother instantly remembered who I was when she saw my eyes. I was so embarrassed. I left the room crying and asked Edgar to take me home."

"There is nothing wrong with your face," complemented Officer Cox. "I think you are a very pretty lady."

"You are too kind, Officer Cox," smiled Marie.

"Mother has always been self conscience of her appearance," consoled Kay. "I think she is pretty, too."

"What happened next?" asked Carolyn.

"Well, Susan moved to Oklahoma City," answered Marie. "She sends me a beautiful Christmas card of her family every year. I wrote her a letter to inform her that my mother had died. I included a short bio of my life with Edgar and how we were told we could not have any children. About five days, after I had sent that letter, she gives me a call. Instead of comforting me through my mother's death, she tells me how healthy and happy her parents are and how happy she was that they were still alive and together. She added that she could not live if she did not have any children because it would make her feel less of a woman. She wanted to know how old I was (even though we went to school together) and asked why I had not adopted any children. She told me that it was a shame that I did not have a family to share the holidays with. I never cared to hear from her again after that hateful conversation until the good Lord blessed Edgar and me with Kay. When I attended my 25th high school reunion, she was there. She was divorced, fat, and had been married several times. My Pastor said that it was wrong to harbor ill feelings against anyone if I was planning on going to heaven when I die. So I greeted her and introduced her to Edgar. Right away, she took out pictures of her only son from the first marriage then she bragged about her children from each additional husband, and showed us pictures of her current husband. Edgar could no longer tolerate her continual bragging so he took out his wallet and showed her pictures of our beautiful daughter, Kay. Susan's mouth dropped wide open revealing her false teeth which fell on the floor, breaking two of the porcelain beauties. While everyone was watching Susan scramble on the floor for her teeth, Edgar asked me to dance. It was the best reunion I ever went to."

"Man, what a witch," commented Officer Cox as he threw the invitation into the garbage pail. "You were right. This is trash."

"Wait a minute," said Carolyn. "If you forgive her, Mrs. Lytle, no disrespect intended, you should go to the party. She must want you there or she would not have sent you this party invitation."

"It is best to stay away from people that try to destroy your happiness," said Marie. "I forgive her, but I do not need to go around her. She causes me to feel uncomfortable and awkward about myself and no one should destroy your confidence. Plus, I do not want her to hurt my baby. I know she has read the newspaper and the only reason she would want me to attend that party would be to say something obnoxious about my daughter and her recent divorce and I will not let that happen."

Kay gave her mother a hug, "Thank you. That is a good story mother. We will have to remember to keep the pruning shears away from you if Susan ever decides to come visit us."

"I wonder why it took her 17 years to invite you to another party?" questioned Officer Cox.

"That is strange," agreed Carolyn.

"I do not care," said Marie. "I am not going."

"Now Marie," argued Carolyn. "What if she has a life threatening disease? She might be calling out to you for some forgiveness."

"I forgive her," spouted Marie. "I am not going."

Officer Cox asked, "Marie, what were the names of the other husbands? It shows on the invitation that her current married name is Walker. How many times was she married?"

"I think she has been married four times, but I do not remember any of her husbands," said Marie. "I only met one of them when Eager and I went to the first wedding."

"You said she bragged about her son at the reunion," reflected Officer Cox. "If my arithmetic is correct, he would have been Leonard's age. Do you at least remember her first husband name?"

Marie's eyes grew twice their size as she suddenly remembered Susan's first husband.

"His name was Morgenstern," answered Marie thinking the name might have been shortened to Morgan.

The room was quiet as everyone stared at Marie. Each person was thinking that her old high school friend might be Kay's mother-in-law.

# THE RING

## CHAPTER VII

Kay put the urn with Mr. Blackstone's ashes on the mantle in Mr. Hughes' home office.

"I think this is a good place for you until I can take you to Baltimore. You will be surrounded by all your friends," quietly whispered Kay so no one in the house would hear her and think she was crazy for talking to a vase.

In the kitchen, everyone except Officer Dennis Rue, was still discussing the birthday celebration and whether or not Marie should attend.

"I have an idea," Kay interrupted the group of party crashers. "I think mother should go to the gala and Mr. Hughes and Officer Rodriguez should attend with her. While she is there, she can search for pictures of Susan's family to see if Leonard is among the honored. If he is, then there is a possibility that she knows his whereabouts and we can go get him."

"What if he is not among her family pictures?" Marie asked.

"Then you can have a wonderful trip to Oklahoma. I heard it is a very large casino, hotel, and resort you will be staying at. Once you discover that she is not his mother, leave the party," smiled Kay. "Simple as that."

"Kay, I do not want to go around that woman. If she is Leonard's mother, she might try to shoot me," argued Marie.

"Mother, what kind of party do you think she is going to have, a lynching party?" laughed Kay. "This is a birthday party, for goodness sakes. She is not going to kill you in front of all her guests. If you discover that she is Leonard's mother, leave the party and get out of that place. Officer Rodriguez will be with you to protect you. Mr. Hughes will be with you, also. I am not sending you into the lions den alone."

"Gee Kay, you have such a way of explaining yourself," chuckled Mr. Hughes. "Marie, the odds of your high school friend and Kay's mother-in-law existing as one human being are a million to one. If, hypothetically speaking, she is related to the eradicator than she may possibly be engaged in his hideous endeavors so we are required to expose this dysfunctional family properly to the media."

"What?" asked Carolyn who was confused after the word 'eradicator'.

"He is a lawyer, Carolyn. He is saying that Leonard's mother might be his partner in crime and we need to arrest them both," translated Officer Cox.

"Evan, you are right," agreed Marie. "I will go to the party to save my daughter's life and clear her reputation."

"My reputation," said a puzzled Kay. "What is wrong with my reputation, mother?"

"Having Susan Hebert as a mother-in-law would ruin anyone's reputation. It would be revolting," complained Marie.

Everyone laughed at Marie as Kay added, "definitely revolting."

Kay decided to depend on public transportation instead of her own private jet chartering company to travel to Baltimore. Each time she used one of Mr. Blackstone's jets; Leonard would kill the crew and destroy the plane, so she and Officer Cox decided to drive to the airport to purchase 4 tickets one for Marie, Carolyn, Mr. Hughes, and Officer Rodriguez to fly to Oklahoma for Susan's surprise party. Then she planned on purchasing 2 tickets one for herself and Officer Cox to fly to Baltimore with Mr. Blackstone's ashes. This was her original plan until the airport ticket agent asked them to wait a few minutes for the tickets because the computer system was down.

Officer Cox watched Kay as she selected a magazine and said,

"One day there will be a computer in every home. We will not have to leave our homes for anything, including shopping or purchasing airline tickets."

"You are a dreamer, OC," smiled Kay. "Have you seen how big those machines are? You would have to build a house to store one in."

Officer Cox signed, "I think it is a good dream."

Frustrated but still pleasant, Kay impatiently waited in the lobby for her tickets. She paged through the bartender magazine she had picked up with hopes she might catch sight of her tattooed friend, Mike, at the Las Vegas Bartending Challenge. She noticed that the air enfolding her became scented with the "PS Design" cologne that she used to purchase for Mr. Blackstone. She thumbed through several more pages of the magazine until she found an article about "the Second Annual Las Vegas Bartending Contest" that Mike Lambie had competed in. There was a picture of a young man, Clifford Barker, holding up the winning trophy next to an article that read, 'He could throw the bottles of liquor higher and catch them better than any of his opponents in the competition. Barker juggled more bottles with one hand than his challengers could juggle with two hands while he poured drinks with his other hand. The Colorado native won every event by impressing the judges and the competitors with his unbelievable bottle handling skills. With his best friend, Mike Lambie by his side, the tattooed bartending expert aced the contest to win $10,000.' There were several pictures of the man posing with his trophy, his best friend, Mike, and four beautiful half dressed female models. In one of the pictures, Kay spotted something that left her breathless. Officer Cox noticed by her expression that something in the magazine had excited her.

"What is wrong Kay?" he asked.

"Look at this picture," Kay pointed at the picture of Mike, the contest winner, the bathing beauties, and the winner's trophy. "What do you see?"

"I see a very lucky man," answered Officer Cox as he took a closer look at the big breasted half dressed beauties. "Did Mike win or the other guy?"

"No," said Kay as she hit Officer Cox on the hand and retrieved the magazine to point at a small object printed on the picture. "Look here. Do you see it?"

"The trophy," Officer Cox replied hoping his second answer would be precisely what she wanted.

"No," growled Kay. "Look at his hand. He has on my Uncle's ring, the one that Leonard was wearing when he fell out of the airplane. Look."

Officer Cox discontinued his jesting and grabbed the magazine from Kay and studied the man's hand.

"Are you sure that is the same ring?" asked Officer Cox.

"Yes, that's my Uncle Billy's ring," said Kay. "I have another one just like it in Mother's safe. I was reading the article which states that the man is from Golden, Colorado. He works at a bar in Blackhawk at one of the casinos there. He likes to go hiking on the weekends up in the mountains near "Oh My God" highway. He must have met Leonard or rescued him in order to have that ring. Mike is his best friend and if he can tell us where Barker is living, we can catch Leonard."

Officer Cox continued to read more about the young bartending winner. He studied other pages that had the man's picture on it to see if he could get a closer and clearer view of the ring, but most of the pictures were close-up facial pictures of the winner and his trophy.

He said, "Kay, I would like to see that other ring before I assume anything."

Once the computers were functioning, Kay purchased only four tickets for Oklahoma City because she decided to cancel the tickets to Baltimore until Officer Cox had an opportunity to examine her father's ring. If the two rings matched, they were traveling to Colorado again.

Kay brought the bartending magazine with her as they left the airport to drive to Marie's damaged house. Mitch, the neighbor across the street was asked to report to the police if any unusual people came near Marie's house or drove through the neighborhood. Officer Cox talked to Mitch while Kay inspected the damaged house. She could not believe all the damage that was done to the back porch and the patio from one small box bomb. The back door was blown off of its hinges. There was crime scene tape draped around the patio area and across the fence to keep nosy people out of Marie's yard. There was broken concrete, burned wood flooring, and destroyed lawn furniture covering the area where her mother's beautiful porch used to be. After examining the damaged area, Kay went to the library to open the safe to get the ring out so Officer Cox could compare it with the ring in the magazine (to see if it matched).

Officer Cox asked Mitch if anyone had been to the house since the explosion. Mitch said a contractor named Allen Green had been by to survey the area to start repairing the house and two officers in a patrol car had stopped by, but nothing unusual. He had been picking up the newspapers and mail each day which he handed to Officer Cox to give to Kay. Officer Cox thanked him for his kindness before entering the house to get Kay and the ring.

Kay handed him the ring that her father had designed and had made for him and his brother. The ring looked the same as the picture in the magazine. He examined both items to see if they matched perfectly. She assured Officer Cox that there were only two of these identical rings made in the world. Her father destroyed the blue print so no more could be duplicated.

"I guess we are flying to Colorado again," said Officer Cox as he handed her the mail, the newspapers, the magazine, and her father's one of a kind ring.

They returned to the airport ticket counter where Kay purchased two tickets to Colorado Springs, Colorado. While she was there, she rented a car to use in Colorado so they could drive to Blackhawk to try to find Clifford Barker, alias Tattooed Man. On the way to Mr. Hughes's home, Officer Cox made a quick stop to speak with Mr. G. R. Morgan, the real estate agent who had sold Kay's house to Teri and Larry Knight. He asked Mr. Morgan if he could list his townhouse in the local newspaper for sale because he had decided to move away from that area. Mr. Morgan was delighted because that was a high income area with good traffic flow and he would not have any problems selling the townhouse. Kay was surprised that Officer Cox wanted to get rid of that beautiful townhouse that faced the lake. She asked Mr. Morgan if he could find her a townhouse or apartment in Golden, Colorado that she could rent on a short term basis instead of having to stay at a hotel. Mr. Morgan was jubilant that Kay wanted to use his services again and told her that he would notify her with any information on available townhouses in that area.

They traveled to Mr. Hughes' home from the real estate office.

"Why are you selling your townhouse, OC?" asked Kay. "I thought it was a great place to live with that lakeside view and the big cedar trees surrounding the property. It was quiet. Well, sort of quiet."

"I am living with you and your family until Leonard is arrested. Once he is behind bars, I am going to take a well deserved vacation to somewhere away from Cortland and Colorado," answered Officer Cox. "Why are you calling me, OC?"

"When I call you Officer Cox, everyone that is in hearing range can hear me and looks around to see who I am talking to and it exposes your cover," replied Kay. "I think OC is cute. If you do not like it, I will stop."

"It will take some getting use to," smiled Officer Cox. "Why do you look so sad? You can call me anything you want to if it will make you happy."

"I am sorry you are not happy working for me," said Kay. "I know I am not the easiest person in the world to get alone with. It is because I have never been an employer nor have I been trained in management so I am going to make some mistakes."

"I have a very bad bed side manner when I try to explain something," OC apologized. "You are the best employer I have ever worked for other than my Army drill sergeant. I am joking. I have to face reality and I know once Leonard is caught, you will no longer need my services, so I will be moving on."

"You can move on when I tell you, 'you can move on', Big Boy. I will need your services for a long time because I am a wealthy lady and there are lots of bad people out there that will try to take my money away from me. Besides, I trust you. That has to mean something," alleged Kay.

Officer Cox was over whelmed by Kay's statement. He had no idea that he would be employed by the Lytle family for life. He did not mention it again as he drove to Mr. Hughes' home.

Carolyn greeted the crime fighters when they drove into the driveway. She informed them that Marie, Mr. Hughes, and she were packed and ready for the trip. Officer Rodriguez was on the telephone trying to get clearance from Lieutenant Gorman so he could travel as their body guard and carry his weapon on the plane. Kay handed the tickets to Marie and told her that a limousine would transport them to the airport tomorrow at 3:00 p.m. She thought it would be a good idea to leave some of the cars in the driveway since Officer Rue would be staying there alone. She showed the picture of the ring in the magazine to her mother and gave her the other ring that belonged to her father. Marie was positive that the two rings matched but she was not happy about Kay returning to Colorado while it was snowing there. Officer Rodriguez finally received the approval to travel as an armed guardian for Mrs. Lytle from Lieutenant Gorman. Now he had to explain where he was going and who he would be traveling with to his wife and family. Kay did not want Officer Rodriguez to have problems with his family, so she telephoned Lieutenant Gorman to see if Officer Rue could take his place. Lieutenant Gorman did not approve of Officer Rue traveling out of the state armed, because he was young and inexperienced. He was afraid the boy might shoot someone at the drop of a hat. Kay explained that Officer Rodriguez was missing valuable time with his family and it was the holiday season.

"Besides," she added, "How can someone get experience if they do not get the experience?"

Lieutenant Gorman was confused with that statement, but finally changed his papers to approve Officer Dennis Rue to travel out of state as an armed guardian for the Lytle family.

"If that boy gets in trouble, Kay, I will hold you responsible," demanded Lieutenant Gorman. "Let me talk to Officer Rue."

Kay handed the telephone to Officer Rue and she told Officer Rodriguez he could take time off with his family. Carolyn was so excited about traveling with her brother.

"Is this a paid vacation?" asked Officer Rodriguez who was relieved to know that he did not have to get on a plane.

"No," answered Kay as she watched Officer Rodriguez lower his head in disappointment. Then she added, "It is paid holiday time; however, I want you to watch both Mr. Hughes' home and my mother's home. Have fun."

Officer Rodriguez smiled until his face hurt. This would be the first time since he had been employed by the police department that he would be able to spend time with his family during the holidays and get paid doing it.

After supper, Kay slipped away into the den to have a private talk with Mr. Blackstone's ashes.

"I have not forgotten you, sir," she explained. "I am going to Colorado again to try to find Leonard. Once I get this behind me, I will fly with you to Baltimore. Please do not be angry, but I think this man may know where Leonard is hiding. The sooner we catch him, the sooner we can live in peace again. I spoke to Allen Green about repairing Mother's home. He seemed excited that I remembered him after all I have been through. He is a nice man and I think he will do a great job on Mother's house."

"Who are you talking to?" asked Marie.

"You probably think I am silly, I know Officer Cox does, but I was explaining to Mr. Blackstone why there was a delay in taking him to Baltimore," she answered. "Most of the time I feel like he is watching over me, Mother."

"I talk to him, too, sweetie," smiled Marie as she hugged Kay. "You go to sleep. We both will have a busy day tomorrow."

Kay left Marie standing next to Mr. Blackstone's ashes as she went upstairs to pack her luggage again and prepare for her trip.

Marie patted his urn and whispered, "Thank you for taking care of our baby. Sleep well good friend."

The next morning was chaos as everyone that was traveling began to stack their luggage at the front door. Officer Rue checked the weather report in Oklahoma City and Colorado, and Carolyn stopped the mail and newspaper delivery at Mr. Hughes' home. Kay had to telephone the airline ticket agent with the name changes on the tickets from Officer Rodriguez to Officer Dennis Rue so he could make the flight as the armed guardian. Then she received a telephone call from Mr. Morgan who gave her the number of a real estate agent located in Golden, Colorado who had a townhouse for rent. Before she and OC left for the airport at noon to catch their flight to Colorado at 3:00 p.m., Kay called the agent to set up an appointment to view the townhouse. The limousine transported the rest of the party crashers to the airport to catch the flight to Oklahoma City. Marie continued to protest about going to Susan's party even after she boarded the airplane. Officer Rodriguez locked the house and went Christmas shopping for his family.

In Golden, Kay rented a car listing David Cox as the main driver. Then she contacted the real estate agent, recommended by Mr. Morgan, to tell her she had landed and asked if she would meet her at the townhouse so she could take a look at the property before she decided to rent it. The totally furnished luxury two story, two bedroom townhouse was lovely and located near the downtown area of Golden, Colorado, close to the police station and a grocery store. It was prefect. The kitchen was large with a wet bar and breakfast area. The living and dining rooms were combined together making it one large flowing living area giving them enough room to work without getting in each others way. Kay said it reminded her of a honeymoon cottage for two people starting a new life together.

Officer Cox thought it was silly to spend money so extravagantly to rent a townhouse when they were not going to be there for a long period of time when they could stay at a local hotel. Kay insisted that the cost of two rooms at a nice hotel would cost the same as renting a two bedroom townhouse. She was not going to rent one room at a hotel because she did not want OC sleeping on the sofa again. She needed him alert at all times if he was going to protect her. She also mentioned how easy it would be for Leonard to trace them to a hotel whereas he would never expect them to rent a townhouse. OC had to agree with that logic and the agent handed Kay the keys.

They unpacked the rented car and carried their luggage to their bedrooms. OC had chosen the bedroom that was the nearest to the stairway so he could hear and respond to anyone other than Kay that was in the house. Kay liked the bedroom she chose because she had a great view of the mountains from a large picture size window. Both bedrooms had a full bath and there was a half bath on the main floor next to the stairs. OC liked the townhouse because there was a telephone in every room. He called Lieutenant Gorman to up-date him on where they were staying and to give him a number where he could be reached. He wanted to know if Officer Rue had reported in and landed in Oklahoma City safely.

Kay unpacked her suitcases in a hurry then stored them in the closet. She did not want to waste any time while the sun was up. The sooner she could get to Blackhawk to search and locate Clifford or Mike, the sooner they could find Leonard.

Kay politely knocked on Officer Cox's bedroom door to see if he was ready for action. He finished his telephone call with Lieutenant Gorman and was unpacking his luggage when she knocked.

"Yes," he answered while stuffing one of the drawers in the dresser with his underwear.

"Are you ready to go?" Kay asked. "We need to go to Blackhawk before the sun sets. I do not want to be out in the snow after dark."

"No, I am not ready. Go and unpack your clothes and rest a few minutes, then we can decide what our next move will be," he said.

"I have already unpacked my clothes, I am rested, and I want to go to Blackhawk," she replied. "You can unpack your clothes when we return. That is my plan."

"You have already unpacked?" whined Officer Cox as he watched Kay leave the bedroom to go down stairs. "I just got started."

He grabbed his gun and an extra clip and followed Kay to the kitchen.

Seeing the kitchen reminded him that they had not eaten and he remembered looking in the empty refrigerator to see if there was any food in there.

He said, "Kay, we need some food in this place incase we get snowed in. My plan is to go to the grocery store and buy a few groceries. When we return, I will fix something to eat and we can rationally decide what our next move will be. I want to find Leonard as bad as you, but right now we are tired, hungry, and you are not thinking sensibly."

Kay wanted to disagree but she knew he was sensibly right. So she changed her plans and they went to the local grocery store that was three miles down the road.

The tattooed man had stopped to purchase some beer when he spotted Kay and Officer Cox in the grocery store. He was quite surprised when he saw them and was wondering why they had returned so soon. He knew they had not seen him, so he left the store to watch from his car in the parking lot to see where they were going to go after they left the store. They were in the store for over thirty minutes carefully selecting their groceries so they would have healthy meals while they were on their manhunt mission. Kay could not believe how expensive the fresh fruits and vegetables were when she was checking out and paying for their provisions. Officer Cox loaded the foodstuff into the rented car while Kay confirmed that she did not get over charged on any of her items.

Office Cox laughed at her because he thought it was amusing that she would shell out an extravagant amount on rent for a townhouse but she would not pay an extra ten cents for a tomato. As they were returning to the townhouse, Officer Cox noticed a car following them in the same lane about three cars behind. When they reached the complex's gated security entrance to enter into the townhouse area, the car continued on the road past them. Officer Cox felt he was letting his over-active imitation get the best of him. He had told Kay hundreds of times not to get scared until she was sure of the situation.

Clifford continued to drive to a subdivision north of Denver on Highway 25 called "Lakewood". In an apartment multiplex one mile away from Highway 25, he parked his car in a covered parking lot. He walked across a manicured courtyard and knocked on apartment door numbered 160. Leonard spied through the peephole before opening the door for the anxious informant.

"She is here, in Golden," squealed Clifford.

Leonard grabbed the mole around the neck, shoved him against the apartment's white undecorated wall, and growled, "Are you sure?"

"Yes," pleaded the fear stricken tattooed man. "I saw her at the grocery store and followed them to an up-town apartment subdivision in Golden. She was with that Officer again. I think they are a couple because they were always laughing."

"So, she is living with a cop," sneered the dirty minded murderer as he released the tattooed king. "Miss goodie two shoes is a slut. I bet her father is turning over in his grave. Ha ha – so I was not good enough for her."

"Do you think they are looking for you?" asked Clifford as he rubbed his aching neck.

"Of course they are looking for me, stupid," Leonard growled again. "She will not stop until she finds me. She is a very determined lady. I have a plan that involves you and Mike. I want you to go find Mike at the bar, then go to the townhouse, and get her."

"How am I supposed to do that when I do not know what townhouse they are living in? That Officer carries a gun and I am not going to risk my life by getting shot for a little whore. You can keep your money. If you want her so badly, go get her yourself," whined the soon to be dead tattooed man.

Leonard punched Clifford in his right eye causing him to fall backwards through a glass coffee table, shattering the glass onto the floor below him.

'YOU WILL DO WHATEVER I TELL YOU TO DO," yelled Leonard. "Or I will turn you into the police."

The bleeding tattooed informant stood up, dusted the broken glass off his butt, grabbed his coat, and started to leave the apartment. His nose was dripping blood onto his shirt so he used his sleeve to wipe his wound.

"Wait," ordered Leonard as he went into the cluttered and filthy back bedroom to retrieve something.

He returned with two small .38 Caliber hand guns (usually known as a 38 special) and said, "Take these and use them if you need to."

Clifford inspected the empty bullet chamber and said, "Where are the bullets?"

"Do you think I would be stupid enough to give you a loaded gun?" bragged Leonard. "Go buy your own ammunition."

Leonard scribbled something in a magazine, tore it out, and handed it to Clifford.

He ordered, "Take her to this location and I will meet you there."

Clifford wrapped the guns in his coat so no one would see them and put the piece of paper in his pocket. He slammed the door to the apartment as he left to return to his car. He drove towards Blackhawk to find Mike to tell him about Leonard's kidnapping plans. Clifford was hoping that Mike would have a better idea that would not get them both killed.

Officer Cox prepared dinner while Kay watched television. The townhouse was filled with the aromas of baked dinner rolls, fresh turnip greens, and steaks being fried in olive oil.

"What are you watching," asked Officer Cox while he stirred his greens and added some fresh lime juice mixed with butter. "You are awfully quiet over there."

"I am watching a documentary on the effects that warm waters are having on the salmon in Alaska. The salmon are getting diseases from the warm waters which make them unsafe for anyone to eat, including animals. Maggots are the only things that get to feed on these fish. The dead salmon pictures are graphic, showing flies and maggots all over them."

"Well, that is a pretty picture to paint before dinner," Officer Cox said sarcastically. "Is there something more pleasant you could watch or could you check on the weather for tomorrow? A good book might be more relaxing."

"That is the problem with the world," Kay alleged. "When an important program is broadcasted (like this one about the warm waters endangering our Native Americans' life style and the fishermen who live in Alaska) people will turn the channel to view something more attractive, like a cooking show or dance contest. This program is as upsetting as the program on those seal hunters clubbing those baby seals to death so they can steal their fur."

"It makes many animal lovers mad, including me, to see any type of animal exploitation," claimed OC. "These men have to make a living to feed their families. This profession has been passed down from one generation to the next and that is all they are trained to do."

"That might be partially true but anyone can learn a new skill," Kay argued. "I believe there should be a government agency that provides a job training department where they could employ these seal killers, paying them good salaries to protect the animals in that area and interact with the public. They could provide them with guns and vehicles to enforce the law which protects these seals and other animals. Most people would pay a reasonable entrance fee to see these live animals interacting together in a natural environment. Why not make a national park or animal reserve so their children could enjoy seeing these creatures. Those beautiful baby seals are totally helpless as their assassins sneak up and club them on the head."

"One problem at a time, young lady," scolded OC. "First, we need to catch Leonard, the people killer. Then we can work on saving the salmon and seals. You live in a dream world wearing pink glasses. I have a question for you. Why does your God allow this exploitation of these animals to continue?"

"You are always blaming God for the evil things that people do," reprimanded Kay. "You have to realize that God has rented this world to us for a short term. We need to solve the problems credited by evil and greedy people. Once we put our humane proposals into motion, then God will assist us (just like any good landlord) with our repairs and improvements. God gives us knowledge and all the materials we need to make our improvements. These baby seal killers could learn to protect those animal in the same way they learned how to kill them. There is more money to earn while sharing and caring than there is in a one time kill. Once the animals are gone, how are they going to make a living?"

"I will say this; you have a good augment and a wonderful solution. You should go into politics," complimented OC. "However, that is another excellent idea that will fall by the way side. Maybe you should send your baby seal saving proposal in writing to Congress. You might be lucky enough to find someone there with brains that will read it and follow through with your ideas. Now can we eat?"

Kay smiled at OC for complimenting her and walked to the kitchen to sample his townhouse cooking.

Suddenly they heard a strange noise coming from inside the garage area. OC knew he had locked the garage when he had finished parking the car so that could only mean intruders were trying to break-in. He hurried to the telephone and dialed 9-1-1 and laid the receiver on the bar. He grabbed his gun that was on the kitchen table and pushed Kay down between the sofa and coffee table to hide her. Just as he started into the garage, they heard the glass from the second story window in Kay's bedroom break. At the same time that the window was broken, the lights in the townhouse went out. OC pulled a cushion off the sofa and covered Kay's body with it. Kay did not make a sound as they listened to the back door being kicked in and someone entering the house. Clifford slithered into the kitchen and maneuvered his way into the dining area. Meanwhile, Mike climbed into the house through the second story bedroom window. Once he had combed the area, he started downstairs to join Clifford. Both men were wearing night vision goggles to help them see in the dark and were carrying loaded guns.

Officer Cox was aware of the danger drawing nigh and he needed to make some dangerous decision and quick maneuvers to help Kay escape. He grabbed another cushion off the sofa and tossed it across the room to get the intruders attention so Kay could make a run for the back door. Both kidnappers fired their guns at the flying cushion, giving OC the opportunity to shoot at the man near the kitchen and draw their attention to him as he ran to the stairs, away from Kay. Mike spotted Officer Cox running towards the stairs so he shot him in the upper shoulder area causing OC to fall against the wall, hitting his head and rendering him unconscious.

Kay could hear someone approaching the sofa. She continued to lay on the floor lifeless not knowing who was standing there. Mike had taken a pillowcase off one of the pillows from Kay's bed and brought it with him as he joined his tattooed friend who was standing in front of Kay. Kay was hoping they could not see her with the cushions on top of her (she was unaware of the night vision glasses) but her fears became reality when Mike grabbed her and Clifford covered her head with the pillow case. Kay was not going to give up without a fight. She screamed for the unconscious Officer Cox in vain. She kicked Mike between the legs and he fell to the floor in agony. When he released her arm, she tried to flee in the darkness but Clifford grabbed her and threw her over his shoulder. Mike followed them to the car that was double parked behind the neighboring townhouse. Suffering from the kick, he tried to help Clifford stow Kay away in the trunk of his car. Kay fought like a wildcat until Clifford hit her on the chin, rendering her unconscious. They tied her hands and feet with a thin rope and locked her in the trunk.

The neighbor watched from the kitchen window as they drove away. He had been a little courageous during the home conquest. For while the kidnappers were invading his neighbor's home, he sneaked over to their car and wrote down the license number; then hurried inside to telephone the police. As the kidnappers were driving out of the security gate, the police were driving in.

The police were met by the heroic neighbor who told them that they had missed the intruders by seconds. He informed the police that he had heard shots fired in the house and watched as they stuffed someone in the trunk of their car. By the sounds of the screams, he believed it was a young lady being kidnapped.

One of the officers entered the house, using a flash light for sight, through the same door the intruders had exited from. He spotted the wounded Officer Cox on the floor near the stairs. While the other officer looked for a breaker box to give life to the house by lighting it up again, his partner checked the vital signs of Officer Cox to see if he was still alive. Once the lights were restored, the officer could see how badly injured Officer Cox was and called for an ambulance.

Officer Cox awoke in the emergency room while he was being

wheeled on a gurney into an operating room. There were several Doctors and Police Officers surrounding him along with some nurses carrying the wire to his heart monitor and intravenous tubes connected to his body. He tried to raise his head but one of the nurses pushed it back down to the gurney. His clothes had been cut off to expose his injury and to see if there were any others. He was covered with a cold white sheet that had a big spot of blood on it where the wound was. Huge lights hung over him as the doctors removed a .38 Caliber bullet fragment from his shoulder. Since the police were able to quickly respond to the emergency call, he did not lose much blood. There were police officers stationed at the entrance of the emergency room and the front of the hospital. Four hours had lapsed when Officer Cox slowly regained consciousness. The Colorado Springs' Police Lieutenant was standing next to his bed waiting for him to recover so he could question him about the shooting at the townhouse. Officer Cox recognized the Lieutenant from his last visit to the Colorado Springs' Police Station.

"What are you doing here?" asked a dizzy Officer Cox. "I thought I was in Golden."

"You are in Golden," replied Lieutenant Blackshear. "The Golden Police Department dispatcher notified me about a disturbance involving a shooting and you. What are you doing here, again?"

"We had a lead on a man that we thought might take us to Leonard," he answered as he studied his body where the operation had taken place. "We were going to ask questions at a casino in Blackhawk about a bartender named Clifford Barker that had won a contest in Las Vegas. He is a friend of Mike Lambie, a bartender that works with the man. Kay spotted a ring…"

Officer Cox stopped talking and looked around the room and realized that Kay was the only person he had not seen since he had arrived and was conscience.

"Where is Kay?" he asked.

"She was taken by the same men that shot you," answered Lieutenant Blackshear.

"How long have I been in here?" he asked franticly.

"A little over five hours," answered Lieutenant Blackshear as he watched Officer Cox pull the IV out of his arm. "What do you think you are doing?"

"I have to get out of here," alleged Officer Cox. "They are five hours ahead of me. Leonard is not going to kill Kay until he can get some money from her to flee the country. The banks do not open until 9:00 a.m. What time is it?"

"It is one in the morning," answered Lieutenant Blackshear.

"That gives me approximately eight hours to find her alive," said a determined Officer Cox.

Leonard in Viet Nam

Kay's baby picture from the safety deposit box

# REUNITED

# CHAPTER VIII

Lieutenant Blackshear watched Officer Cox slowly get out of the hospital bed and asked, "What are you looking for?"

"I am looking for my clothes. Where are my stinking clothes?" he said as he looked around the room and in the closet provided for patients' belongings.

"You have been shot and had surgery. You need to get your rest," ordered the Lieutenant. "You are not going anywhere but back into that bed."

"That is where you are wrong," contradicted Officer Cox. "You can help me or get out of my way. I have had worse injuries in Viet Nam. Kay is in trouble and I need to help her. We were looking for Mike Lambie. If I can locate him, I will be able to find Kay. Where are my clothes?"

"The emergency response crew cut them off of you when they brought you into the hospital," smiled the Lieutenant as he was looking at the back of Officer Cox's open hospital gown. "If you go storming out of this hospital looking like that, I will have to arrest you for indecent exposure."

Before the lieutenant could say another word, Officer Cox grabbed him and spun him around to his hospital bed and said, "You will have to shoot me again to keep me in this place. What size do you wear?"

"Officer Cox, you could get in serious trouble doing this. I read your police service and military files and I know you are a courageous man. I knew you would want to try to find her so I brought you some clothes. Now, will you release me? There are two police officers behind you pointing their guns at your back," demanded the Lieutenant.

Officer Cox knew this lieutenant did not have any jurisdiction in Golden and he knew his authority could only be exercised in certain territories outside of Colorado Springs; however, he needed to get out of the hospital, get a car, and be given access to a computer to help find Kay. He slowly released the Lieutenant.

"I am sorry, but I have to find her, sir," he pleaded. "I need your help. Please, let me make one phone call."

The ruffed-up lieutenant waved at the officers that were pointing their guns at Officer Cox to reassure them that the situation was under control.

"Put down your guns and bring me those clothes I brought," ordered the Lieutenant. "You are the most hard-headed, stubborn man I have ever met. Who were you going to call?"

"A Friend of Mr. Blackstone," answered Officer Cox. "Mr. Blackstone gave Kay the number of General Pickens, of the United States Armed Forces, when we were flying home from the Bahamas. I served with him on my last tour of duty in Viet Nam. I memorized his telephone number in case I needed to use it. I think it is time to give him a call. He has access to any of the government computers in Washington and he might be able to pin point where Kay was taken."

The lieutenant handed the officer the clothes he had brought from the townhouse. He sat on the hospital bed and watched Officer Cox try to get dressed using one arm while the other officers on duty kept the concerned night shift doctor and nurses out of the room.

"As I said earlier, I glanced at your military records while you were in Colorado Springs. You will not need to bother the General," said Lieutenant Blackshear as he jumped off the bed to assist Officer Cox with his pants. "Everyone here is going to help you find Miss Lytle."

Both officers shook hands and Lieutenant Blackshear continued, "I was wondering if you learned that defensive move while you were in the Special Forces with the Army. I would appreciate it if you would teach me that move. After all, you owe me a favor."

Finally, Officer Cox was able to get the pants on his aching body, with the Lieutenant's assistance. Carrying the rest of the clothes in his arms, he started running down the hall to get out of the hospital. The lieutenant was right behind him yelling orders to the pursuing policemen to get his car ready. There was a doctor yelling at both officers to slow down or the stitches would not hold and the wound would break open. Officer Cox had been shot before and this was a piece of cake compared to some of the other injuries he had experienced.

"Officer Cox, put your shoes on," demanded Lieutenant Blackshear. "There is snow out there and you are going to get sick and shot at the same time."

Officer Cox stopped in the hospital lobby to put on his shoes while the squad car was being driven to the front entrance of the hospital to pick them up. Both officers dashed into the warm vehicle and sped away from the hospital. They headed towards the Golden Colorado Police Station so Officer Cox could use the computer to look up anyone named Mike Lambie, Michael Lambie, or Lambie in general. If he could find one of Mike's relatives that knew where he was living, where he likes to hang out, or find one of his friends that Officer Cox could pay an early morning visit to, they might be able to find Kay. He continued to get dressed in the speeding police vehicle, paying no attention to the wound or the intense pain he was experiencing. All he had on his mind was Kay.

He turned towards the window and whispered a quiet prayer, "Lord, please keep her safe."

"What was that you were saying?" asked the lieutenant. "I did not hear you."

"I need a gun," said Officer Cox.

"The police officer that found you at the townhouse, gave me your gun," he said as he handed Officer Cox his gun. "It looks like you got one shot at them. Do you know if you hit him?"

"I missed him," alleged Officer Cox as he reviewed the day's events in his mind. "They had on night vision glasses meaning they were prepared to kidnap Kay. I am wondering how they found our location so quickly when Kay had said it would be harder to track us if we rented a townhouse? We were careful not to use Kay's airline company so we flew in on a commercial airline. We stopped at the grocery store."

Suddenly Officer Cox remembered his over-active imagination.

"There was a small blue compact car that followed us from the grocery store. He must have seen us in the store when we were shopping and waited for us in the parking lot," said Officer Cox.

"That sounds like a good murder mystery, but did you see the guy actually following you?" asked the lieutenant.

Officer Cox could not tell the lieutenant about the man's cologne that indicated danger was near, so he told him it was an uneasy feeling he had when the car passed the townhouse security gate.

"Hypothetically thinking, if those men asked the townhouse secretary at the main office if they had any new occupants, since she did not know Kay and I were trying to stay incognito, she could have given them our townhouse number. That is how they found us!" brainstormed Officer Cox.

"Do you think you can solve the Jimmy Hoffa disappearance?" sarcastically asked the Lieutenant.

Officer Cox was not listening to the Lieutenant; instead, he focused on the ungodly ideas of finding and killing Leonard and the men that kidnapped Kay.

When they finally arrived at the police station, Officer Cox asked to use one of the computers. The Golden Colorado Police Lieutenant and officers on duty were cooperative and helped Officer Cox retrieve the address of Mike Lambie, Sr. who is the parent of Mike Lambie, Jr. The dispatcher printed a hard copy of the directions to the Lambie's home and two squad cars were assigned to assist Officer Cox and Lieutenant Blackshear with their arrest.

It was 2:45 a.m. when Officer Cox arrived and knocked on Mike's senior citizen parents' home. Mr. Lambie opened the door totting a rifle. He aimed it at the policemen with intentions to scare off the unexpected visitors.

He yelled, "My son is not here and get off my property."

Officer Cox, once again, showed off his quick military moves when he grabbed the rifle out of Mr. Lambie's hands to disarm him then handed the weapon to Lieutenant Blackshear.

"We are not here as one of Mike's friends, sir," confessed Officer Cox as he showed his badge to the half conscious man. "I am sorry for the inconvenient timing but I need to know where your son, Mike, or his friends are living. Will you answer a few questions for me?'

Still amazed at Officer Cox ability to disarm him so quickly without either man getting injured, he answered in a timid voice, "Yes, officer."

"Do you recognize this man?" Officer Cox asked as he showed him the picture of Mike and his friend, Clifford Barker, from the article in the bartending magazine.

While Mr. Lambie put on his reading bifocal glasses, Officer Cox peered inside the house and noticed several marksman's trophies and blue ribbons honorably displayed on the fireplace mantle. There were pictures on the wall next to the fireplace of Mike and his proud father holding up trophies together for hitting the bull's eye perfectly ten times in a row. From what Officer Cox gathered by looking at all the trophies and pictures, Mike was an excellent marksman with a rifle and never missed a target.

"Yes, that is Clifford Barker," Mr. Lambie answered as he pointed at Clifford's face. "He is a no good, tattooed convict that convinced Mike to drop out of college and spend his tuition money on tattoos. The man is a loser."

"Do you know where he lives?" asked a victorious Officer Cox.

"He, Mike, and another man live in Lakewood in an apartment. I have the address," answered a concerned Mr. Lambie as he wrote the address on the back of the picture. "Has my son done something illegal?"

"Yes, we have substantiating evidence that he and his constituents have kidnapped a young lady for a large amount of money," bluntly answered the heartless Lieutenant Blackshear.

Officer Cox glared at the lieutenant for being rude to this good man after he had helped them and he asked the lieutenant to send a squad car to the apartment complex and have them wait for their arrival before entering. As the lieutenant was returning to the car, Officer Cox retrieved the rifle and returned it to Mr. Lambie.

When Officer Cox and Mr. Lambie were standing alone on the porch, Officer Cox said, "Your son is a good man, sir. I hope I did not hurt you when I took the rifle away from you. Thank you for your help."

Officer Cox returned to the squad car leaving the puzzled, ashamed and worried father standing alone on the porch. Mr. Lambie went into the house, closed the front door, locked it, and cried into his own hands. His wife, who was standing on the stairway out of sight, hurried to her husband's side and wrapped her arms around him for support. Mr. Lambie told her that their son was in trouble but he had a feeling that the police officer who returned his rifle would take care of him.

The officers quickly drove to Lakewood, following behind a snow plow that was dispatched to clear the highway of snow so they could travel faster.

"Why did you return that rifle?" asked Lieutenant Blackshear. "He could have killed us."

"He was not going to kill us," stated Officer Cox. "He was only trying to scare us. The safety latch was on and the rifle could not fire."

"Well, he got what he deserved," beamed Lieutenant Blackshear. "You showed him good."

"It is three o'clock in the morning and two strangers are standing on his front porch ringing the door bell. He did not know what we wanted or if we were going to kill him. I would have reacted in the same fashion, except I would have killed you. You need to be more sensitive to other people's feelings when you are dealing with the public. That man loves his son and you chastised him."

Lieutenant Blackshear could not believe this sermon was coming out of a man who had assaulted him in the hospital earlier. He was speechless and stayed quiet until they reached the apartment complex.

There was a stampede of angry officers that used a battering device to break down the apartment door. Officer Cox, armed and ready for action, followed the officers into the empty apartment. Inside, he discovered the broken coffee table glass covering the floor spattered with blood, and there was a dent in the wall next to the front door that was caused by someone being shoved against it. Two of the bedrooms were filthy but livable. The back bedroom door was locked so Officer Cox kicked the door down, completely off its hinges. There were pictures of Kay posted on all four walls in the bedroom. There were several newspaper clippings of both plane crashes and a newspaper article on Mr. Blackstone's death among some of the wall hangings. There were other articles with pictures about Kay on the floor in one of the corners of the bedroom that had been saturated with human urine and manure. Flies and maggots crawled all over their filthy apartment haven. The odor was horrendous. While the Crime Scene Investigators took samples of the blood spackled broken glass, one of the officers in the filthy back bedroom mentioned that the air around the desk smelled like an expensive man's cologne.

"Where did you say you smelled a man's cologne?" asked Officer Cox as he hurried in that direction.

"It smells nice in this area," repeated the officer pointing towards the desk. "He must have poured some of the cologne over here to cover that terrible odor in the corner."

Officer Cox studied the pictures and newspaper articles on the desk, hoping to get a clue of where Kay might have been taken. He noticed a beautiful picture of a country road that was leading into some snow covered mountains and trees which seemed very familiar to him. In the picture, the road was partially snow covered and there was one tiny black spot on the white snow next to the road. He borrowed one of the officers' eye glasses to magnify the object to get a better look at the spot.

"What are you looking at?" asked Lieutenant Blackshear.

"This black spot seems out of place on the snow. What do you see?" questioned Officer Cox.

"It looks like a dead bird," said the Lieutenant as he examined the picture. "No, it is a black glove. What would a glove be doing way out there?"

Officer Cox's eyes widen as he said, "I know where they have taken her. We have to hurry. We will need an ambulance equipped for hypothermia."

"How do you know where she is?" asked the Lieutenant as both men hurried to the car.

"That is my glove," confessed Officer Cox as he put the picture in his pocket.

The confused Lieutenant radioed for an ambulance, while Officer Cox explained to the driver where he wanted to be taken. The driver sped towards Highway 25, traveling away from the city. Officer Cox showed him the picture of the country road.

The time was fifteen after four in the morning. The sun would be rising in two and a half hours. Officer Cox was sure that was the place that Leonard had taken Kay. He had a religious feeling that someone from above was leading him to her. He said a silent prayer as the squad car slid on the icy highway; however, the driver never lost control and continued to speed towards the country road.

"Use the siren," whispered a soft, comforting voice in Officer Cox's ear.

"Turn on the siren. Tell all the officers to use their sirens," yelled Officer Cox. "She needs to know we are on our way."

Mike telephoned Leonard from a service station, letting the phone ring twice as their signal, to let him know that Kay was with them. He ran back to the car and Clifford drove to the desolated area located on a country road off of Highway 25 that Leonard had described on the paper.

Kay was able to take the pillowcase off of her head. Since there was no lighting in the trunk, she felt around to find something she could use as a weapon. She noticed the car was built for snow skiing because there was an opening in the back seat constructed for skis to fit through and be stored. She lightly pushed the covering forward to open it so she could hear what the kidnappers were saying. She had no idea that one of the kidnappers was Mike.

"When we get our money, we are going to open our bar," said Clifford.

"I think we should take this girl to the police and give ourselves up," pleaded Mike. "I shot a man and I do not want to spend the rest of my life in prison. We have ten thousand dollars from that contest we can use to start our bar. We don't need that man's blood money."

"SHUT UP, MIKE," yelled Clifford. "You are confusing me. If we turn ourselves in to the police, that man will find us and kill us. As long as I wear this ring, he will remember that it was me that saved his life. I did not turn him into the police when I could have. He is going to give us twenty thousand dollars for this whore and we are going to get out of Dodge."

Kay could not believe that she was reunited with Mike and he had shot OC.

She thought and silently prayed, "Is OC dead or did Mike miss him when he shot at him? From the conversation it sounded like Mike was being forced to kidnap me. Please, Lord, let Officer Cox be safe."

Kay could smell her favorite cologne covering her body.

"Kay, do not move or panic. I am with you," whispered her invisible friend, Mr. Blackstone. "Help is on the way."

The car slowed down as Clifford made a sharp right turn onto the snow covered country road, drove a short distance, and parked near the edge of the cliff. They opened the trunk to view their valuable but illegal cargo.

"She smells nice," said Clifford as he shined the flashlight in Kay's face.

When Mike saw Kay's bruised face, he said, "This is the wrong girl. You made a mistake. I met this girl on the airplane during my flight to Las Vegas for the contest. Her Name is Katy, not Kay."

"Are you sure?" asked the terrified tattooed man as he moved closer to view Kay's face. "I saw her with an Officer at the store."

"Yes, I am sure," Mike said as he wiped some of the blood from her nose on the pillowcase. "I would recognize that pretty face with or without bruises anywhere. I asked her to attend the contest with me but she was visiting some friends in Cortland. She told me that I had potential. She likes to watch old western movies. We can not kill this girl because you kidnapped the wrong one!"

Kay was alert but pretended to be unconscious (following Mr. Blackstone's orders) and she listened to Mike as he tried to save her life. She could smell the bouquet of "PS Design" cologne as it perfumed the air around the opened trunk and she knew Mr. Blackstone was with her.

"Smear some of this oil on her face and cover her head with the pillowcase again so Leonard can not recognize her. In this light, he will think it is Kay and we will get our money and leave," planned Clifford. "He will never know the difference."

"No, I am not going to do that. We need to get out of here before Leonard arrives and we need to drop Katy somewhere so she can be found unharmed," argued Mike. "I am in trouble enough for shooting that man, probably her boy friend. We need to leave now while we can."

"I have a better plan, boys," snarled Leonard as he shot Clifford in the back. "You imbecile, so you kidnapped the wrong girl and thought you would get paid. This is your third and final mistake."

As Clifford fell to the ground, he cried, "It is her. Look at her face. Please don't shoot me again."

Mike watched in terror as Leonard shot Clifford two more times then turned his gun toward him.

"Do not move," Leonard ordered as he walked toward the trunk to glare at Kay to see if he could identify her.

Leonard examined the oil and blood covered face of the lady lying in the dark trunk with the flashlight. It did not look like his beautiful ex-wife Kay.

Mike was scared for his life and for Kay (alias Katy) so he said,"Sir, she is still unconscious. She does not know you are here and she can not identify me. I could take her into town and drop her somewhere so she could be found unharmed. I could take her to the police station and say I found her in an abandon car. You could escape into the mountains while the police questioned me."

"KID," screamed Leonard uncontrollably. "I needed Kay to get money to leave this stinking city. Since this is not Kay, this woman is a liability just like you."

Mike's eye widen in horror as he watched Leonard shoot him. He fell lifeless to the snow covered ground. Leonard picked up his body, stuffed it into the trunk of Clifford's car on top of Kay's body, and slammed the trunk to close it. He knelt next to Clifford dead tattooed body to search for the keys to the mobile coffin so he could drive it over the cliff. When he could not find the keys on Clifford, he decided to look in the car to see if the keys were still in the ignition but all the doors were locked. That meant that Mike must have the keys in his pocket and Mike was locked in the trunk. Leonard was so furious that he kicked the car in frustration making a dent in the side. He knelt next to Clifford's body again and pulled Kay's ring off his finger. Then he covered Clifford's bloody body with snow and left the area to go get his car. He returned driving a small compact foreign truck which he was going to use to push Clifford's car over the cliff. He lined-up his bumper with Clifford's and began to push the car toward the cliff.

Kay knew she had to make some quick decisions because Mike was starting to softly wail from the pain of being shot. Kay gently covered his mouth with her hand so Leonard could not hear him.

"Mike, do not move," whispered Kay. "He might hear us and come back to shoot you again."

The car inched closer and closer to its final resting place as Leonard slowly pushed it toward the edge. Suddenly, he smelled the scent of that man's cologne which filled the air on his last airplane flight over Colorado. He remembered that fragrance accompanied Kay wherever she went. The car started tipping over the edge of the cliff, as Leonard jumped out of his truck and ran to the back of the car, hoping it had not reached the end so he could rescue her in order to get the money he needed to leave the country. He heard some sirens coming in his direction so he decided it would be better to leave the car as it was and get out of that place before the police arrived. He returned to his truck to leave but his truck was stuck to Clifford's bumper. As the car began to fall over the cliff, his truck was pulled with it. He adjusted the gear shift into reverse and floored the gas pedal to get the two vehicles unstuck but the front two tires had already slipped over the edge and it was too late. He jumped to safety and watched as both vehicles fell over the cliff. He did not have time to see if the vehicles had hit the bottom of the ravine because the police were arriving in numbers and he did not want to be captured. He fled the crime scene to be free to kill another day.

Kay could feel the car falling over the cliff so she moved closer to Mike and recited a Psalm of David from the Bible, "The Lord is my shepherd, I shall not want. He maketh me to lie down in green pastures; he leadeth me beside the still waters. He restores my soul. He leadeth me in the path of righteousness for his name's sake. Yea, thou I walk through the valley of the shadow of death."

As the car fell, Kay closed her eyes to prepare herself for the explosive impact and prayed, "I will fear no evil."

There was a thick forest of snow and ice covered trees growing on the side of the cliff which caught and lodged the car in their trunks and branches. The truck was not as lucky and fell past the car to the bottom of the canyon and bust into flames upon impact.

The car was secured between two large white aspen trees with several smaller snow covered aspen trees against the side. Kay was cold, covered with blood, and afraid to move. She did not know if she was on solid ground, safe enough to escape or if she did climb out of the car, would Leonard be there waiting for her.

Mike was alert enough to untie Kay's hands. Kay used the pillowcase to apply pressure to Mike's wound to try to stop the bleeding.

"It is not bad," whispered Mike. "He was a poor shooter."

"How do you know this?" asked Kay in a soft voice so no one would hear her.

"I was pre-med in college before I dropped out to become a kidnapper," smiled Mike. "I am sorry Katy. I would never hurt you, honest."

"My name is Kay," She confessed. "I lied to you because my friend, Carolyn, said not to trust anyone you meet that you will only know for a short period of time. I am sorry. I had no idea that we would be reunited."

"I do that myself when I go bar hopping," laughed Mike as he turned to position his feet on the back seat and tried to kick it out. After several kicks, he was successful and the back seat fell forward. He said, "You are small enough to climb through there. What is that perfume you are wearing?"

Kay could smell the fragrance, too, and she knew help was on its way. She climbed through the trunk onto the back seat to look out the windows so she could see where they were. Below, she could see flames from the truck burning which lighted the area. All around the car were white leafless aspen tree trunks covered with ice and snow. Looking up, she could see the edge of the cliff and she realized that the car had fallen a few feet from the top of the cliff. She carefully pulled Mike, who was bleeding and needed a doctor, out of the trunk into the back seat.

Mr. Blackstone's voice softy ordered, "Climb into the front seat and turn on the lights."

Kay started climbing over the seat when she heard Mike yelling, "Don't do it Kay. It might be that crazy man again."

Kay knew it was not Leonard and continued over the seat to the front and turned on the head lights. With every move she made, she could hear the cracking of the ice on the white aspen trees or it might have been the tree's branches. She lowered the window, causing a small amount of snow to fall into the car, and she listened for any sounds that might be someone coming to help them. The fresh air felt good on Kay's face but it was cold and she did not want Mike to get hypothermia so she closed the window.

"Are you scared," asked Mike.

"Yes," said Kay. "Anyone would be scared if they were in our shoes. When that fire goes out, no one will be able to see us. I do not think anyone will look over the cliff to find us."

"Who were you talking to," asked Mike. "It sounded like a man's voice was talking to you."

"It was my best friend," answered Kay as she climbed over the front seat to the back seat to check on Mike's condition.

Kay felt Mike to see if he was warm. She could tell by holding his hand that his temperature was dropping. She wrapped her arms around him to give him some of her heat.

"You were reciting the Bible earlier," alleged Mike. "It sounded pretty."

"I try to read it every morning," said Kay while rubbing Mike's arms. "I am sorry I did not finish it. My favorite line is, 'and I will dwell in the House of the Lord forever.' I have been told that it is one wonderful place."

"When I was a child, my parents would take me to Church every Sunday. I had to learn the Ten Commandments," he said softy. "Do you know the Ten Commandments?"

"Yes," answered Kay. "I try to live my life by them."

"Would you recite them for me," requested Mike.

"Sure," agreed Kay. "The first four commandments are God's major rules concerning him because he is a jealous God. Number one is, Thou shalt have no other gods before me for I am the Lord your God. Number two is, thou shalt not make any graven images. Number three is, thou shalt not take the Lord thy God's name in vain. Number four is, keep the Sabbath holy. Those are the most important commandments because they pertain to God. The rest of the commandments pertain to our lives so we can live healthy and happy. Number five is, honor thy mother and father. Number six is, thou shalt not kill."

"Stop, Kay. I think I have broken the first four commandments on a day to day basis," admitted Mike. "And I probably broke the remaining four but I am not proud of it."

"Sometimes, I fall short of my religious convictions," acknowledged Kay. "I wanted to kill you earlier for shooting OC, but instead, I prayed."

"I did not kill your boy friend, Kay," confessed Mike. "I shot him through the shoulder to avoid hitting any vital organs. He will be sore and the area will be sensitive for days, but I did not kill him."

"Thank you," cried Kay, holding Mike closer to her heart. "He is not my boy friend. He is my."

Kay had to think for a minute before saying what Officer Cox was to her. He was a friend, a protector, a recent proclaimed cook, a war and police hero, and an employee.

She finally said, "He is my every thing, but do not tell him that because he will get the big head and will be impossible to be with."

"Your secret is safe with me. If I would have known he was an Officer, I would have gotten out there in a hurry," said Mike. "Why does that man want to kill you?"

"Money is the root to all evil," answered Kay then she lowered her voice. "I think I hear something. It sounds like police sirens."

"Honk the horn," whispered Mr. Blackstone. "They will hear you."

Kay climbed back into the front seat to honk the horn. The first honk broke the silence and startled both of them, but she continued honking the horn with hopes that someone would hear her.

A small Police brigade drove into the area where Officer Cox believed they would find Kay. They could see the light from the burning truck in the distance when they turned onto the snow covered country road. Officer Cox recognized the area from when Kay and he had stayed at the invisible but warm hotel. He hurried to the edge of the cliff to see if anyone had survived the burning truck at the bottom of the gully. Another officer yelled when he tripped over Clifford's cold bloody body under the snow. Officer Cox was about to leave the cliff side to look at the body when he saw the headlights of Clifford's car shining from the side of the cliff. He could see that the car was stuck in a group of trees growing on the side of the mountain. He could smell Mr. Blackstone's cologne filling the air around him. Then, like an angel's trumpet, he and the other officers could hear the car's horn honking.

"SHE IS ALIVE," yelled Officer Cox as he wiped a tear from his eye.

# THE ICY RESCUE

## CHAPTER IX

"We are going to need some lighting out here, a strong rope, some chains, and winch to pull that car up and out of there," ordered Officer Cox. "Have the ambulance ready to transport her immediately to the nearest hospital and notify them that we are bringing in a lady suffering from hypothermia. I need bandages, blankets, and some warm water. Now, move it."

Officer Cox knew Kay was not warmly dressed nor did she have on a coat or shoes when they kidnapped her. He also knew that hypothermia was deadly. The sooner they could reach her, the sooner they could start treating her for hypothermia.

He did not know if she was cut, shot, or if she was seriously injured from the fall and he did not know that Mike was with her, shot, and nearing death. He was assuming the worst so they would be prepared to help her.

All the policemen, paramedics, and recovery crew were working together like a finely tuned machine. Generators were brought in to supply more lights so everyone could see what they were dealing with. Officer Cox flashed a light towards the car to let Kay know she had been spotted. Kay returned the signal by turning the car's lights on and off and honking the horn a few more times. One of the officers reported that a snow storm was headed in that direction and they needed to speed up the rescue process or they would not be able to see her in the storm and the wind would blow the car off the mountain. A large wrecker was driven to the location which backed up towards the cliff and using the winch, lowered the cable to the car to secure the vehicle for hauling up. Three Officers, wearing lighted head gear, were lowered by ropes down the side of the icy mountain to the lodged vehicle. The first officer, to reach the car, knocked on the window to get Kay to lower it.

"Do not worry," he said. "We are going to try to get you out. Are you injured?"

"No," answered Kay. "But Mike is. He was shot, cold, and is bleeding. He needs a doctor."

The officer handed Kay a blanket and told her to try to start the car to use the heater to warm the vehicle. Kay tried several times, but the engine would not turn over. The officer told her that he would bring another blanket and some warm water. Kay climbed back into the back seat and wrapped the blanket around Mike to keep him warm.

The other two officers began painlessly working to attach the hook at the end of the cable to the car's bumper. The white snow covered ghost like trees, embracing the car, cracked and quavered under the weight of the men. This caused some huge ice sickles and clumps of snow to fall out of the trees on to the car, breaking out the front windshield with the impact. The shattering noise scared Kay and Mike and they trembled because they were thinking the car was going to fall forward.

Once the officers had the cable securely fastened around the car's bumper, they made plans to pull the quivering victims to the top of the mountain. The first officer returned to get a gurney flat board to haul Mike up on. Officer Cox was surprised but relieved to hear that Mike was in the car with Kay. He was glad she was not down there alone.

The lieutenant asked an officer to radio the hospital to alert the emergency room staff that a man with a gun shot injury was coming in. The officer ran to his squad car that was parked behind the ambulance, slightly out of sight from the rescue activities. As he opened his door to radio the hospital, Leonard jumped him from behind and knocked him to the ground. He grabbed the car keys, started the police vehicle, and fled the area to escape without anyone (other than the assaulted officer) knowing he was there. Everyone was focused on the rescue attempt.

A metal cutting device (called the jaws of steel) was lowered so the police officers could cut the door off of the car to gain access to Kay and Mike. They gave them two more blankets to cover their bodies from the sparks and the flying metal splinters. After they had separated the door from the car, they tied a rope to it and hauled it to the top of the mountain, instead of letting it fall into the ravine. Everyone watched as the board was lowered to the two officers holding on to the car for support. One officer tried to carefully and slowly enter the back area of the compact car but it was crowded so he asked Kay to slide the board under Mike's blood soaked body. Mike was able to help her as he rolled to one side and Kay placed the board under him. Then Kay was asked to securely tie Mike onto the board so the officer could pull him out of the car. With every vibration the car made, the small aspen trees would break under the weight. Kay could not feel her fingers and her hands were trembling as she tried tying all the security lines around Mike. When she was finished, she gave the awaiting officers the thumbs up sign and they pulled Mike out of the car. Slowly the crew on the top of the mountain pulled Mike to safety with one of the officers following him up the mountain to make sure he did not fall or get tangled in the trees. When he reached the top, everyone cheered and the paramedic carried him to the ambulance.

"Is Kay hurt?" yelled Officer Cox as he followed Mike to the ambulance.

"No, sir," said the cold and quivering kidnapper. "She is very brave."

Mike was loaded into the ambulance, escorted by two officers, and it sped down the snow covered country road to the Golden hospital. Officer Cox ran back to the cliff. He was anxious to see what kind of condition Kay was in.

Below, the remaining officer tied a rope securely around Kay's tiny waist. He could tell, by shining the flashlight in her pale face that she was beginning to exhibit traits for hypothermia. He wrapped her in a blanket then wrapped his arms around her as he yelled for the rescue crew to hoist them up to safety. The wind had increased in velocity and the snow started to fall heavily. Kay and the officer were pounded against the side of the mountain as the rescue crew struggled to haul them to the top. When they finally reached the top, once again there was a cheer of relief.

Officer Cox rushed to Kay's side. As the paramedics untied the officer from her, she walked over to her hero and collapsed into Officer Cox's arms.

She looked into his eyes and said, "I was waiting for you."

Officer Cox smiled, "I got here as fast as I could."

As He carried her to the ambulance, he whispered a silent prayer, "Thank you."

A paramedic caught sight of the assaulted officer lying next to the ambulance and yelled for some help. The paramedic observed an injury to the back of the officer's head. The unconscious officer was given a whiff of ammonia to bring him back to conciseness. The officer was taken to the same ambulance Kay was in. He kept babbling about someone sneaking up behind him and hitting him on the head to steal the police car.

"I bet it was Leonard," said Kay. "He could not get his bumper unstuck from the car's bumper and it went over the side. I could hear him yelling and cursing inches away from the trunk as the car was falling. He is still alive."

Officer Cox asked Lieutenant Blackshear to assign a guard to Mike and alert the hospital that a man (Leonard) might try to assault him. They knew he was armed and driving a police vehicle.

"I will follow you to the hospital to cover your back," said Lieutenant Blackshear as he watched Kay and Officer Cox climb into the ambulance. "I am glad we were able to find you, Miss. Officer Cox was determined to find you before nine o'clock. It is 8:30 a.m. Officer Cox, good job. I will see you at the hospital."

The ambulance driver closed the door and they sped down the country road.

Lieutenant Blackshear returned to the cliff area to thank all the officers and rescue team that had helped save Kay. He watched as the wrecker driver slowly drove forward to tow Clifford's car up the cliff. The car's bumper ripped away from the car as the winch began to haul it to the top. The car fell through the trees and dropped to the bottom of the canyon. Kay's rescuing officer said he was surprised that the car had not fallen sooner because there was nothing holding it to the side of the mountain except air.

"She must have a troop of angels watching over her," said the officer.

It had stopped snowing and the sun was bright enough for the Lieutenant to look over the side of the cliff to see a shear drop and the residue of two burned vehicles at the bottom of the gulch. He thanked the officer for helping and ambled to his car. Still puzzled about the location and how Officer Cox knew how to find Kay, he radioed the dispatcher to send some officers to the hospital to guard Mike.

The lieutenant thought, "Since Officer Cox was right about Mike's father and the kidnapping location, he probably was right about Leonard and his plan to kill Mike."

He gave strict orders to the dispatcher that no one was to be allowed to see Mike but his doctor and him. The driver hurried down the isolated country road towards the hospital where the lieutenant was hoping that Officer Cox and Kay could enlighten him on some very puzzling questions.

One paramedic wrapped several blanket around Kay's half frozen body while another paramedic vigorously rubbed her feet. Kay did not realize that she was freezing to death until she saw her blue lips in a reflection on one of the silver drawers in the ambulance.

"OC, are my lips blue or am I seeing things?" Kay asked in a weak voice.

"Your lips are blue," answered OC who was rubbing her arms and hands. "Next time you are kidnapped you will need to wear the appropriate clothing. Did you over hear anything that they were saying while you were with them?"

"Yes, the tattooed man got my Uncle's ring as a reward when he saved Leonard," alleged Kay. "That is why he did not inform the police about Leonard when he found him. Were you able to get my ring from him?"

"No," apologized OC. "I was about to take a look at his body when I heard you honking the horn. When we arrive at the hospital, I will check with the coroner to see if he still has it on his finger. Did you get a look at Leonard?'

"Yes, I peeked at him when he shot Mike," smiled Kay. "He never saw me move. Mike tried to save my life by saying I was the wrong girl. He smeared oil on my face so Leonard could not recognize me.

He said he was sorry for shooting you, but he was not going to kill you. He was pre-med in college and knew you would live."

"He is a champion marksman with a rifle," said OC. "I saw trophies of him and his father at his parent's home. I know he could have killed me but instead he chose to shoot me below my shoulder bone and away from my main organs. If he can give us any insight of where Leonard might be hiding, I might be able to get him off with a light sentence."

"He said it would be sensitive for days. Does it hurt?" asked a concerned Kay.

"Only when I try to carry my frozen boss to an ambulance," smiled OC as he rubbed his arm. "Ouch."

"You big baby," grinned Kay.

The ambulance screamed into the hospital emergency driveway and stopped at the entrance where a group of nurses and doctors were waiting with a gurney to take Kay into the hospital. OC followed the group as they hurried into an emergency room to examine Kay for any serious injuries. OC was not allowed in the room so he stood outside the door waiting in the hall. Lieutenant Blackshear arrived at the hospital a few minutes after the ambulance. He asked the front desk nurse where he could find Officer Cox and the lady that was recently admitted. Following her direction, he was able to find Officer Cox at his post. Both officers asked about Mike who was taken into surgery when he arrived, to remove the bullet. Officer Cox telephoned the Golden Police Lieutenant and asked him if he would drive out to Mr. Mike Lambie's home and bring him and his wife to the hospital to be with their son.

"I will telephone them and they can drive up there," said the Golden Police Lieutenant.

"No, I want you or one of your officers to bring them to the hospital," ordered Officer Cox as if he had jurisdiction in Colorado. "There is a dangerous man linked to their son that might try to hurt them. Please bring them here so they can be with their son."

The Lieutenant decided that Officer Cox was right in his analysis and sent a patrol car after Mike's parents. While the two policemen were waiting to hear Kay's and Mike's prognosis on their condition, the lieutenant decided this was a prime time to talk to Officer Cox about Leonard.

"Last time you were here you asked me to investigate any disappearances of any rich ladies who had purchased a swimming pool," reminded Lieutenant Blackshear. "Do you remember this?"

"Yes, I do remember asking you to do this and I received a large envelope from the Colorado Springs Police Department after Thanksgiving," claimed Officer Cox.

"Yes, we found all four of the ladies that had been missing for years," alleged the Lieutenant. "Each woman had been buried under their swimming pool and there was a bomb attached to their lower extremities like the one you found on Kaylyn Cross' body. As I informed you, each woman had married a man that fit Leonard's description. All four women had money embezzled from their checking accounts and jewelry stolen from them. All four women were college students with similar names. It looks like the man you are chasing is a homicidal serial killer who enjoys murdering young ladies whose names are Katherine, Kaylyn, Kate, and Katy; but they all are labeled by their nick name 'Kay'. "

Officer Cox was impressed that Lieutenant Blackshear not only sent him information about the missing ladies but had done his case home work. He was about to say something when a mature gray headed doctor approached them with news about Kay condition. He told them that she had a bruised chin bone (not serious) from a blow to the face. There were multiple small cuts and abrasions on her feet and arms but over all she was in fine condition. He requested that she stay over night for observation but she wanted to leave.

"She must be as hard headed as you are when it comes to staying in the hospital," grinned Lieutenant Blackshear.

"I will talk to her," smiled Officer Cox as he and the Lieutenant followed the Doctor to Kay's room.

"Have the parents of Mike Lambie arrived," asked Officer Cox.

"No," said the Doctor.

"When they arrive, I would like to talk to them before they see Mike," requested Officer Cox.

"I will have them brought to my office to wait for you," said the Doctor.

Kay was sitting up in the hospital bed in a blue and white hospital gown. There was a guard stationed at the foot of her bed and one at the door of the room.

"We need to get out of here," said Kay. "Leonard can find me and Mike here. This is not a safe place."

"We can not go back to the townhouse," said Officer Cox. "We thought it would be safer than a hotel and they found us there."

"He probably knows where Mike's parents live and they will not be safe either," said Lieutenant Blackshear.

"Leonard does not know where the townhouse is located," alleged Kay. "We can return there with Mike and his parents. They can stay with us until we have a better plan."

"Kay, the second story window is broken, allowing snow to blow in and there is blood on the walls down stairs," informed Officer Cox. "The townhouse will be freezing inside. I do not think that is a good idea."

"I can rent another townhouse with three or four bedrooms," said Kay. "Leonard will not know where any of us are staying."

"I think that is a good idea," agreed Lieutenant Blackshear. "We can talk to the front desk secretary and tell her not to give out any information on you. This way Leonard will not be able to find you again. In fact, I will call them right now and see if there is a four bedroom townhouse available."

"Wait one minute," yelled Officer Cox. "I did not agree to this arrangement."

"OC, you need to chill out," replied Kay. "Plus, the doctor said you need to rest. This would be the prefect place. Mike probably will need to get some rest after his surgery to recover which will give him time to get reacquainted with his parents. If you are worried about me spending too much money, well, stop."

A policeman interrupted their conversation to notify Lieutenant Blackshear that Mr. and Mrs. Lambie had arrived. He asked the policeman to have them wait in the doctor's office so they could talk to them.

"This argument is not over. When I return, try to have a better plan," ordered Officer Cox.

Both officers left the room to speak to the Lambies, while Kay made a telephone call to the townhouse complex to see if there were any available four bedroom units. Officer Cox asked the Lieutenant if he could speak to the Lambies alone. The Lieutenant was offended but agreed to wait outside the door until he was needed.

Officer Cox greeted Mike's parents with a smile and asked them to have a seat. Before he could get started, Mr. Lambie apologized for being rude to him and the other officer when they came to his home.

"I would have reacted in the same manner," said Officer Cox as he shook Mr. Lambie's hand. "I asked to speak to you alone before we take you to Mike."

"Is my son dead, officer?" asked Mike's Mother.

"No, however he was shot trying to save my friend," answered Officer Cox.

"Thank God," cried Mrs. Lambie as she leaned on her husband. "Can we see him?"

"Let the officer talk, mama," said Mr. Lambie as he hugged his wife. "Is he going to jail?"

"No sir," responded Officer Cox. "Neither I or my friend are going to press charges. He could have killed me and my friend, but choose not to. However, he is in trouble with the man that set him up to do the kidnapping. This man is very dangerous. He will try to get to Mike through you."

"We will not say anything," replied Mr. Lambie.

"He will kill you if he does not get what he wants from you," informed Officer Cox. "We are going to have to move you to a safe house until this man is captured."

"Move us," said Mrs. Lambie. "Where? What will we do for clothes, or food, or how will we get our mail? We can not move. We have lived in our home for forty-one years. "

"I know I am asking you to give up a lot," alleged Officer Cox. "It will only be for a short time until we can apprehend this man. Mike might be able to tell us where he is staying or going and this information will keep him out of jail but will put him in danger with this murderer. I know you love your son and want to keep him alive. Will you help me?"

"We will help you, sir," responded Mr. Lambie.

Mrs. Lambie nodded her head to agree with her husband and said, "Thank you officer. Can we see our son now?"

Officer Cox opened the door for the concerned parents and led them to the recovery room where Mike was being treated. To his surprise, Kay was sitting next to Mike's bed telling him about their moving arrangements. Mrs. Lambie hurried to her son's bedside. Mike's father followed behind her and grabbed Mike's hand and kissed it. Kay moved towards Officer Cox to give the family more room to talk.

She, Lieutenant Blackshear and Officer Cox started to leave the room when they heard Mike say, "I am sorry I shot you, sir."

Officer Cox smiled at Mike and he departed the room with Kay. Lieutenant Blackshear followed, taking a quick look at Kay's firm butt as they left the room. Officer Cox noticed the Lieutenant's sudden interest in Kay's back side then remembered his own experience wearing the hospital gowns. He dashed behind Kay thinking she was exposing her behind and he noticed that she was wearing two gowns, one backwards, to cover her butt.

"She is not as intrepid as you are," whispered the Lieutenant. "Even in a hospital gown she looks nice."

Officer Cox replied, "We are here to protect her. Remember that."

Kay was not paying attention to either officer as they continued down the hall to her room. She was thinking about helping Mike start a new life. They were half way down the hall towards Kay's hospital room when they heard someone hurrying behind them. They all jerked around to see Mr. Lambie coming towards them.

He walked straight up to Officer Cox; he hugged him and said,"Thank you for my son." Then he turned around and departed to the recovery area to be with his family.

"You were right again, Officer Cox," said Lieutenant Blackshear. "I need work on my social skills."

Officer Cox was speechless and thought to himself, "It takes a big man to do something like that in a crowd. If Lieutenant Blackshear says another sarcastic word I am going to punch him out."

They continued to Kay's room.

Once in the room, Officer Cox asked Kay if she had an alterative arrangement.

Kay responded, "I do not think you are going to like my plan but I was thinking we could take a flight home and take the Lambies with us. Mike told me that he knows how to fly a plane and has been to aviation classes in college. Along with being a pre-med student, he can handle a gun. I told him that when he recovers I would like him to come and work for us."

"You are right," said Officer Cox. "I do not like it. You can not hire every hard luck case in town. You do not even know how well this man can fly a plane or what kind of planes he can fly. We need more information on this man before he becomes one of your employees. We need another plan."

"It is either that or we have to move into a bigger townhouse," replied Kay. "I know the safe house will not be safe, no offence Lieutenant Blackshear."

"None taken," smiled the Lieutenant.

"We have to take action now or Leonard is going to be on top of us, OC," said Kay.

"Our police force can handle Leonard, Miss," bragged Lieutenant Blackshear. "He will not get past any of the officers here."

Officer Cox and Kay looked at each other as if they were thinking the same thoughts.

"I will ask the doctor to see if Mike is able to travel while you get dressed," said Officer Cox. "You can call the real estate agent to see if there is another townhouse that we can rent."

"I have already done that," Kay said farsightedly. "It will be ready to move into at one o'clock today. I explained that we did not want anyone to know our whereabouts. She said she would inform her staff to take extra precautions not to give out any information regarding us and to discreetly move our clothes to the new location."

"When did you call her?" asked Officer Cox.

"Right after you left me the first time to speak to Mike's parents," said Kay. "As for the repairs to the damaged apartment, she is going to make it look like they are modernizing the entire complex so it will not draw attention to that one unit. Leonard will think they are refurbishing the place. He will not realize that is where we were staying."

Officer Cox handed Kay her clothes and stepped out of the room with Lieutenant Blackshear who was amazed with Kay's ability to plan ahead.

"How old is she?" he asked Officer Cox.

"Why?" replied Officer Cox.

"She is amazing," said the Lieutenant. "I need to give her a job working in our department."

"She does not need a job," responded Officer Cox. "She is a one woman, powerhouse cooperation that amazes me every day."

Both Officers spoke with the Doctor to see if Mike could be transported to a different location. He was asked to keep any information, regarding Mike, restricted to police personnel only. Lieutenant Blackshear notified the Golden Police Department, he explained the situation, and requested an unmarked police car for transporting Mike to the townhouse.

Officer Cox remembered how they had fled the hospital in Cortland in the same manner. He thought, "If Leonard is watching the hospital, he will be watching from the rear entrance. Why not leave the hospital from the front?"

"I have a plan," said Officer Cox. "I will need two nurses' uniforms. Tell the lieutenant that we will need a car to pick up some people from the back of the hospital and drive them around the block. If Leonard is watching, he will follow them while we leave from the front entrance of the building. If we are lucky, he might be spotted and arrested; however, he is very cleaver and hard to capture."

Officer Cox went to the nurses' station and asked if he could borrow two nurse uniforms. Officer Cox took one of the nurse's uniforms to Kay and asked her to change into it. Once Kay had changed into the nurse's uniform, Officer Cox asked her for her clothes. The lieutenant thought Officer Cox had a good plan and it was going to work until he handed him Kay's clothes.

"Officer Cox, these clothes are not going to fit me," complained Lieutenant Blackshear.

"I know it is going to be a tight fit, but you have to wear those clothes in order to make this plan work," smiled Officer Cox who knew this was going to be humiliating. "Wrap his head in some bandages so Leonard will think it is Kay."

"You owe me big time, Officer Cox," whined Lieutenant Blackshear.

He gave the other uniform to Mrs. Lambie. He telephoned a rental car company and asked them to meet him in front of the hospital. Kay, Mrs. Lambie, Mike, and Officer Cox took the rented car to the townhouse complex. Mr. Lambie tailed their car at a sensible distance so he could make sure they were not being followed by Leonard. The unmarked police car picked up the Lieutenant, who was dressed in Kay's clothes, and another officer who was pretending to be Officer Cox. They sped out of the back parking lot adjacent to the hospital. Lieutenant Blackshear did not notice any cars following them until they had driven several blocks away from the hospital when he spotted a police squad car pulling in behind them. He knew Leonard had stolen one of the police cars at the rescue site so he did not use the radio to contact the station for back up assistance. Instead, he asked the driver to lead him to the police station where he would be surrounded by other officers. The police car followed them straight to the station. When they reached the station and had parked the car, Lieutenant Blackshear jumped out of the car, pointed his gun at the pursuing squad car, and yelled at the driver to get out of the car. The pursuing policeman stopped the car and got out. What a surprise for the Lieutenant when he discovered that it was a Golden Policeman returning the stolen car to the station. He and his partner had found the car parked two blocks from the hospital and he was returning it to the station for figure printing. His partner drove up and said that a vehicle was stolen in the hospital parking lot as they were driving to the station. Several other officers, who were laughing, gathered around the Lieutenant to see what was happening in the parking lot. This was when the Lieutenant remembered he was dressed in Kay's attire. He never noticed Leonard watching him from a stolen parked car across the street from the station. Leonard realized he had been following the wrong car and sped away.

Kay and her band of hideaways arrived at the townhouse without any problems. Just as she had informed Officer Cox earlier, their clothes had been delivered to the new townhouse. The real estate agent was waiting for them in the living area so she could give Kay the keys to the unit. The townhouse was spacious, with a roomy living area fully decorated in contemporary furniture. The bedrooms were all fashionably furnished with comfortable beds. Kay was satisfied with everything. Officer Cox studied the alarm system which was located near the front and back doors. Mike and his parents thought it was a beautiful place and, like

Kay, were satisfied with everything. Mr. Lambie was especially excited to discover that there was a television in all the bathrooms. After Officer Cox spoke to the real estate agent, he asked everyone to have a seat in the living room for some safety briefing. He wrote down the sizes of all the Lambie family so he could have someone from the police department go purchase them some clothes. They would need some groceries and personal items, also. He explained to the Lambies that their house would be under twenty-four hour surveillance until it was safe for them to return home. He knew they were tired so he said he would finish his talk with them after they had some rest. When they had left the living area, he told Kay he needed to talk her.

"I see no need for us to stay in Colorado since Leonard has escaped us again," he said. "The Lambies will be protected when we leave and after we are gone. Leonard is not going to try to hurt them because he is after you. Mike does not know where he is hiding now since the apartment complex where they were staying was raided. Leonard could be on his way back to Cortland as for as we know."

"I know you are right this time," agreed Kay. "But I would like to stay a few more days to make sure the Lambies are comfortable with their new environment."

"One more day would be fine; however, the sooner we leave this area, the safer they will be," argued Officer Cox. "Besides, we need to finish Mr. Blackstone's request and you own some companies that you need to research."

"I have not forgotten my responsibility to Mr. Blackstone or his companies," disputed Kay as she stood up to walk to her room. "I just fell over a cliff. All I want to do now is take a nap."

"Kay, I am tired, too," quarreled Officer Cox. "But we need to talk."

"No, OC, we can talk later," said Kay. "I want to get out of this nurse's costume and into a bath."

"Kay," he yelled as she closed her door to end their conversation.

Officer Cox was mad. He could not understand why she was as hard headed as he was. He left the townhouse to get something to eat and clear his mind. He remembered seeing a fast food hamburger restaurant a few blocks away as they were traveling to the townhouse. He had not eaten anything since the kidnapping and his stomach was doing some flip flops. He decided to buy several hamburgers for everyone because it would be late before Lieutenant Blackshear arrived with the groceries and clothes. While he was waiting, he noticed a shivering lady with two children standing outside next to the restaurant. As he was leaving he asked her if she needed a ride to some place.

"No, I do not need anything," she yelled at him and grabbed her children. "Get away from me."

Officer Cox could tell that the frightened lady had been hit in the face due to the big black and blue eye she was sporting and the bruise on the left side of her face. He identified himself as an officer to calm her down and asked again if he could help her.

She began to cry as she told him that her husband had thrown her and the children out of the house after he had beaten her. She claimed that she reported it to the police but the dispatcher said that there was not an officer available to send to her location at that time due to a rescue mission off of Highway 25.

She said she had no where to go and had been walking all morning to find a safe place to stay.

"I was praying someone would be kind enough to help me when you walked up," she cried.

Officer Cox asked them to come inside the restaurant and have something to eat. He ordered some more hamburgers and watched the hungry homeless family eat.

He thought to himself, "If Kay can help a hard luck case, so can I. I will give them my room and sleep on the sofa."

He said, "I am staying at a townhouse a few blocks from here. You are welcome to come with me and stay the night until we can find you a better place."

"I do not want to inconvenience you," replied the lady.

"There is a family staying there already," he said. "One more family to feed will be fine."

He grabbed the second order of hamburgers and led the family to his car. As he drove to the townhouse, the lady said her name is Debbie Beaufort. Her son's name is David and her daughter's name is Kelly Ann.

Officer Cox smiled, "My name is David Cox. I am an officer from the Cortland Police Department here on a special assignment. It is very important that you do not say anything about me to strangers. It would jeopardize my cover. Once we have arrived at my townhouse, I will explain everything to you."

While Officer Cox talked to the children, Debbie carefully slid her hand into her purse to grab a container of pepper spray. She wanted to be prepared in case he was an axe murderer taking her to his crib. He parked the car in the garage and held the door open to the townhouse to invite the battered family in. Debbie was impressed with this officer's expensive living life style. Her children were well mannered and stayed close to her side as Officer Cox led them to his bedroom to get warm, refreshed, and rested. He told Debbie he would be in the kitchen if she needed him for anything.

Kay soaked in a warm bath thinking how wonderful she felt when she saw Officer Cox at the top of the mountain waiting for her. She decided that she would tell him that they would take the next flight home like he recommended. She could hear him in the room next to her as she was getting dressed. She knocked on his bedroom door to tell him what she had decided when a woman, wearing one of his shirts, opened the door to greet her.

"You must be one of the members from the other family that is here," greeted Debbie. "It is nice to meet you." Debbie turned her head to tell her children, which Kay could not see, to get off the bed.

Kay could not believe her eyes. She thought, "How could he go out and bring a hired woman into her townhouse?"

Kay politely smiled and slowly returned to her bedroom thinking, "We go to church on Sunday to praise God. How could he do this? He knows how I feel about things like that."

She could hear some voices coming from the kitchen area so she decided to join the Lambie family to see what they were doing. In the large kitchen breakfast area she saw Mr. and Mrs. Lambie talking to Officer Cox.

"If OC is down here," thought Kay. "Who was up stairs in his bed?'

"Have a seat, Kay," smiled OC. "Have a hamburger. I know you must be hurry."

"OC, who is that person in your bedroom?" asked Kay.

"So you met Debbie," answered OC. "She and her children are

homeless. Her husband beat her then threw her and her two children out of the house to stay on the cold streets."

"She should have called the police," said Kay.

"She did," alleged Officer Cox hoping Kay would understand. "But most of the police force was out on Highway 25 trying to rescue you. She did not have any where to go so I brought her here to get warm and rested. When Lieutenant Blackshear arrives with groceries and clothes, I will ask him if he can help her."

Kay smiled, patted him on the back, and said, "That was very nice of you. She is welcome to join us. The more the merrier. Does she know about Leonard?"

OC knew Kay would understand because she was that type of person.

"I have not told her about him," he answered as he handed her a hot hamburger. "I thought I would let you explain our circumstances since you can relate to her situation.

"Did you buy some fried apple pies," smiled Kay. "I am hungry."

"No apple pies today," laughed OC.

"I forgot to tell you that a Lieutenant Gorman called earlier while you were out," informed Mr. Lambie. "I told him you would return his call when you returned."

"Thank you," said OC. "I will call him now. I wonder if he has any news from Officer Rue and Mrs. Lytle. I would like to know how the party is going. "

"I hope she is having a good time at Susan's party," said Kay. "I bet Susan got a big surprise when she saw mother there."

# THE BIRTHDAY SURPRISE

## CHAPTER X

The flight to Oklahoma City, Oklahoma landed on schedule. Officer Rue and Carolyn went to get the rented car while Marie and Mr. Hughes waited for their bags on the luggage carrousel. Carolyn asked for a map of the city and for directions to the hotel where they would be staying. Mr. Hughes paid a porter to carry the luggage to the car. All four of the party goers were eager to get to the hotel, unpack, and go site seeing. Marie continued to complain about going to Susan's birthday party. She had a dreadful feeling that Susan was going to say something hurtful or do something that would embarrass her.

The drive to the hotel was slow due to a traffic jam on the road connecting Interstate 35 to Interstate 40. Cars were backed up in bumper to bumper traffic for ten miles. This gave the four adventurers an opportunity to read some of the advertisements on the side of the road. Carolyn wanted to ride the trolley for 25 cents and take the boat tour on the water taxi. Dennis read an advertisement about the botanical gardens' crystal bridge tropical conservatory which captured his interest. Mr. Hughes wanted to go to the ancient history center and American museum to learn about the Cherokee Legends and to see their beautiful hand made art exhibits. Then he wanted to play some golf on the Choctaw Creek Golf course. Marie wanted to go shopping on the

Bricktown Canal to purchase a birthday gift for Susan. Even though she did not like Susan, she was not going to any party without a gift. Then she wanted to dine at one of the romantic sidewalk cafés locate on the canal facing the water so she could watch the dinner cruises and boat tours floating down the river.

"I could stay a week here and still not see everything this city has to offer," said Carolyn. "I want to ride on Route 66, too. Do you think we could stay a few days longer once we get this party out of the way?"

"I do not think it would hurt if we changed our itinerary and stayed a few days longer," said Marie. "We can inform Kay that we are having a nice visit and we want to stay two days longer."

"Business before pleasure, dear," remarked Mr. Hughes. "I would like to stay and play a few rounds of golf but our primary and foremost objective is to see whether or not Susan is the treacherous creature that we imagined her to be. Once this question has been resolved, then we can vacation."

"Mr. Hughes, you are going to have to learn to relax," smiled Carolyn.

Officer Rue turned off Interstate 35 on to Interstate 40 and drove on it until he reached the Robinson exit. He went left on Robinson to Sheraton and turned right. He stayed on Sheraton Street until he reached Broadway Boulevard and he turned right again. From Broadway he drove to One Park Avenue to the beautiful historic Skirvin hotel which was located in the center of Oklahoma City's recent exciting revitalizations.

Marie looked at the beautiful hotel and said, "This is not the casino where the party guests are supposed to stay."

"I know, Mrs. Lytle," said Officer Rue. "Officer Cox thought it would be a good idea to stay in a location away from the party in case Susan is Leonard's mother. This way she will not know where you are staying and will be surprised when you arrive at the party. Kay picked this hotel because it is in the center of the city, near everything that you are interested in."

"My daughter is wonderful," smiled Marie.

"Since the party is tomorrow, we can get our rooms and tour the city today," said Carolyn who was eager to start on their excursions.

Kay had made registrations for adjoining suites with a view of the city. Marie and Carolyn roomed together while Mr. Hughes and Dennis were in the room next to them. Carolyn unlocked and opened the door between the rooms which made the suite even larger. Each room had two double beds, a desk with a chair for a work station, a light blue couch in front of a huge television, and a refreshment center equipped with a small refrigerator, wet bar, and coffee maker. There were several bags of coffee, tea, and a variety of sugars and creams. There were two terry cloth robes in the closet and two large complimentary bottled waters on the bar. There was an iron, an ironing board, small safe and extra pillows in the closet.

While Marie stored her clothes in the closet, Carolyn read the information booklets on the desk.

She read to Marie, "The hotel is 80 years old. It is walking distance to the Mayrid Botanical Gardens, Bricktown Canal, the Art Museums, and five minutes from the State Capitol. There is 24-hour room service and several restaurants we can eat at without leaving the hotel. There is a piano bar here and a heated indoor swimming pool. I never want to leave this place. There is even a fitness center that is complimentary to all the hotel guests. I can swim, work out, and then call for room service."

Marie asked, "Carolyn, are you going to unpack? There is plenty of space in this closet for your clothes."

"I would rather go site seeing. Besides, there is an ironing board so I can iron my clothes in the morning before the party," she answered.

Officer Rue telephoned Lieutenant Gorman to inform him of their location and to give him a telephone number where they could be reached. Mr. Hughes knocked on the open door before he and Officer Rue entered the room and sat on the couch.

"Well ladies," said Mr. Hughes. "The day is still young. I am ready to take a trolley ride and visit a museum, if you are."

"Before we do anything," advised Officer Rue. "Officer Cox gave me some ground rules that we need to follow."

Carolyn and Marie sat on the sofa next to Mr. Hughes as Officer Rue began to read, "First he said we need to stay together at all times. If we find out any information on Susan, he wants us to report it immediately to the local authorities. He wants us to..."

"Dennis," said Carolyn interrupting her brother. "We can follow Officer Cox's rules tomorrow."

"I agree with Carolyn," said Marie. "I would like to get started before everything closes and the sun goes down. There is so much to do here; I do not know where to start."

"We can go down to the lobby area and explore our hotel," replied Mr. Hughes. "The concierge can give us information and directions on places to see."

"What is a concierge?" asked Officer Rue.

"That is a lawyer's fancy word for doorman or caretaker," answered Carolyn. "I told you he needs to loosen up."

All four of them laughed as they left the room to have a visit with the concierge, who was located in the hotel hobby, to inquire about the popular site seeing places and to get some information on the hotel. Officer Rue asked the concierge if he could have a taxi waiting for them in the morning. The concierge said he would have the taxi ready to take them anywhere they wanted to go. He gave them a map of Oklahoma City's downtown area and highlighted several places of interest plus a few fashionable stores to do some serious shopping in. He showed them where to catch a ride on the Oklahoma's trendy trolley car and gave them some free coupons for food and admittance to the Museum and Botanical Garden.

"That was a good idea, Mr. Hughes," smiled Officer Rue. "That man knows his town."

The four adventuress tourists rode the trolley to the state capital building and took a thirty minute guided tour. Then they walked two blocks towards the hotel to the History Museum, which was adjacent to the Convention Center and near the entertainment district. They used their free admittance coupons to enter the beautiful and informative museum. They went on a two hour self guided tour reading, studying, and admiring all the American Indian's art work and artifacts. Mr. Hughes would have stayed at the museum the entire day to learn more about the Chickasha and Shawnee heritages but Officer Rue wanted to go to the Botanical Gardens before it closed for the day and the ladies had some serious shopping to do.

They used their free admittance coupons to enter the breathtaking Botanical Gardens. Carolyn thought it was like walking into paradise.

They walked past water and rock formations, huge tropical plants, and walked across a crystal bridge. There were hundreds of species of birds flying over their heads and in the atrium areas; they spotted large colorful parrots eating fruit in the top of the palm trees. The sounds of the water fountains and bird's singing were so calming that they stayed at the gardens until it closed.

Carolyn purchased several souvenir T-shirts for herself, Kay, and Officer Cox.

From the gardens, they walked to the Bricktown Canal to dine at one of the water front cafés. Carolyn ordered a salad because she spotted a dessert cart that had a selection of alluring desserts that she could not resist. Mr. Hughes and Marie ordered the catch of the day, seasoned fish served with rice and mixed vegetables. Officer Rue ordered the Oklahoma steak and potatoes. Mr. Hughes and Marie drank a glass of wine while Carolyn and Dennis drank tea. After the meal, they all ordered a different dessert. The waiter told them to take a ride on the canal at night. It was romantic and beautiful for couples in love. They decided to take the ride after they had finished their shopping. All though Dennis did not want to get separated, Carolyn and Marie went into some feminine shops while the guys waited outside. Mr. Hughes asked Dennis to wait for him while he stepped into a jewelry store. He returned with a small box while the ladies finished their shopping. They never knew he left. Once the ladies were finished with their shopping, they all went on the boat ride down the canal. Marie showed the guys what she had bought for Susan's birthday present which was a lovely floral mid-waist bed jacket with some matching house slippers. She apologized for taking so long but she wanted a bag with tissues to wrap it in instead of a box. She purchased a card and wanted everyone to sign it when they returned to the hotel. Mr. Hughes admitted that he had been shopping, too.

"What did you buy, Evan?" asked Marie with Dennis and Carolyn quietly and intensely watching.

Mr. Hughes reached into his pocket and pulled out a small black box. He got down on one knee and looked into Marie's very surprised face as he opened the box to reveal a two caret diamond engagement ring.

With the boat slowly floating down the canal and the music softly playing in the distance, Mr. Hughes asked Marie to marry him.

"You have always been my first and only love but Eager beat me to you," he said. "I can not take his place but I would love to make a place of my own. Will you please be my wife and marry me?"

The unplanned moment was like a scene out of a romantic movie when Marie said "yes" and kissed Evan. He could not stop smiling as he put the ring on her left ring finger. Carolyn was crying and clapping with the rest of the cheering tourists on the boat as they floated back to the dock to end the romantic fairytale cruise. Officer Rue shook Mr. Hughes hand and said congratulations along with all the other passengers that were leaving the boat.

Marie was crying tears of joy as she hugged Carolyn and some of the well wishers leaving the boat.

"When we get to the hotel we can celebrate at the piano bar," said Carolyn. "This is the best vacation I have ever been on."

They returned to the hotel toting their precious merchandise and went straight to the piano bar where they listened and danced to some very entertaining live jazz music until mid-night. It was announced at the bar that Mr. Hughes and Marie had just gotten engaged. Mr. Hughes bought expensive Champagne for everyone at the bar. Officer Rue toasted the happy couple saying, "May you live a long and happy life together."

The night ended with a kiss at the separating door and the two lovers went to their own rooms.

"If you would like Mr. Hughes to stay with you in here tonight, I can change rooms with him," said Carolyn. "My brother will not mind."

"No dear," said Marie as she kissed Carolyn on the head. "I am a little old fashion and I want to wait until we get married even though I have been married before. Thank you anyway."

The next morning brought more surprises for Marie. Mr. Hughes had ordered breakfast in bed for her and Carolyn. There were roses and a romantic card on Marie's breakfast tray. He knocked on the separating door and asked to speak to Marie for a minute.

"I know this is sort of sudden; but I do not know how much time I have remaining in this world," stated Mr. Hughes. "I asked the concierge if there was a Wedding Chapel nearby so we could get married. I know you would like to have Kay present but we can redo our vows, when we return home, for her."

"I had a big wedding the first time I got married to Eager, complete with all the bells and whistles and it lasted thirty years," replied Marie. "A small wedding would be wonderful and you are right, I would like Kay present; however, I do not know how much time I have left, if any, once we attend this party. I would love to get married to you today. It will give me something to brag about at the party and we can redo our vows for Kay when we return home."

Marie and Evan kissed in the doorway between the rooms.

After everyone had eaten and gotten dressed, Mr. Hughes handed the taxi driver a slip of paper with two addresses on it. The first stop was to a chapel on Sheraton Street and the second address was the location of Susan's birthday party.

"Why did you want to take a taxi?" asked Carolyn looking out the window at downtown Oklahoma City as they rode to the chapel.

"A taxi driver knows the city and will not get lost going to the party," said Officer Rue. "If someone is following us, he will know how to drive defensively and he will know which streets to take to get out of harms way to get us to safety."

"I thought Lieutenant Gorman said you were inexperienced," commented Mr. Hughes. "That was a great idea, son."

Sheraton Street was east of Broadway Boulevard. The taxi driver had to drive three streets down Sheraton to the chapel which was located on the left side of the street. Officer Rue asked the driver to join them in the chapel as an extra witness for the couple. Carolyn was the bride's maid and Dennis Rue was the best man. Marie was so excited that her hands were shaking like a young bride.

The pastor started the sermon as usual with "Dearly beloved we are gathered here today to join this man and this woman in holy matrimony in accordance to the laws of the great state of Oklahoma."

Before they knew it, the pastor was asking if this man takes this woman and saying, "You may kiss the bride."

Mr. Hughes stared at Marie. He could not believe that his life was finally fulfilled.

"I love you," he cried as he kissed his bride.

"I love you, more," said Marie with tears of joy filling her eyes.

Mr. Hughes paid and thanked the pastor for the short but modest sermon while the others hurried to the taxi to go to the birthday party. Once the newlyweds and the two party crashers were in the cab, the driver started the taxi and drove in the direction of Susan's home. Marie never replied to Susan's invitation.

"This is going to be a birthday Susan will never forget," smiled Carolyn.

"Here is the plan," informed Officer Rue. "I will pretend to be Carolyn's husband and she will masquerade as Kay. Officer Cox said we are not to get separated at any time, however, I will look for any pictures that might have Leonard in them."

"You do not know what Leonard looks like," said Marie. "I will look for his pictures while you keep Susan enchanted with your charms. If I find anything, I will put it in my purse and bring it to you."

"I think we need to use a key word or phrase incase there is trouble," alleged Carolyn. "Like the 'weather is looking bad' or 'I feel sick'."

"We are not international spies," replied Mr. Hughes holding Marie's hands.

"No wait, I think Carolyn is on to something," agreed Officer Rue. "If something is amiss we can use 'I feel sick' as the cue to get out of there. Whatever you do, please do not call me Officer Rue."

Mr. Hughes paid the driver a full day's wages to park near the house so he could rush to their rescue to take them either back to the hotel or to the police station. The driver handed Officer Rue a hand held radio device to keep in his pocket. He showed him how to operate it so he could call him if he needed him. With the signal and plan all set, they were ready to attend the party.

The taxi driver dropped them off at the front gate entrance. He parked the cab several houses down from Susan's but close enough for Officer Rue to see it. They walked through the gated yard and up a brick sidewalk to the front door. They could hear people laughing and music on the inside. Marie was about to ring the door bell, when Evan gave her a reassuring kiss.

"Are you ready, Mrs. Hughes?" he asked.

"Yes, Evan, I am ready," she smiled. "I hope we are wrong about her."

Marie rang the door bell and they waited for someone to come to the door to let them in. A tall man in a black turtle neck sweater answered the door and opened it to let them enter the birthday party of the century. Marie did not see Susan anywhere but was greeted by some of her party guests. Marie introduced herself and Mr. Hughes, then she introduced her masquerading family. She asked a lady, who was wearing a big black hat and smoking a long cigarette, where Susan was hiding herself.

"Susan loves to make a grand entrance, sweetie," the snob said. "She wants everyone's eyes on her."

"She has not changed one little bit over the years," whispered Marie to Evan.

"Neither have you, dear," smiled Evan as he kissed Marie.

While Evan, Marie, and Carolyn mingled with the birthday guests, Dennis walked around looking at the family's pictures. Finally people started singing 'Happy Birthday to Sue' and Dennis rejoined his imaginary wife. Susan made a magnificent entrance riding on the back on a half naked muscular man that looked and acted like a slave from an Egyptian movie. Everyone was singing and applauding as he slowly and carefully lowered her frail body to the floor so she could greet her admirers. She was wearing a tight formfitting blue sequined and beaded dress with a black feathered boa around her neck. She had rings on all of her fingers except her thumbs and her shoes matched the blue sequined dress perfectly. She greeted her guests as she promenaded across the room and acted as if she was the queen of Egypt. She was half way across the room when she spotted Marie. The expression on her face conveyed that she was surprised.

"Everyone, let me introduce you to my old high school friend, Marie," she announced as she strolled over to where Marie and her imaginary family were standing.

"Hello Marie," said Susan as she kissed Marie on both of her cheeks like the French people do when they greet a familiar friend. "I am surprised to see you. Did you come alone?"

"No," replied Marie. "I brought my family. This is my husband Evan, my daughter, Kay, and her husband, Dennis."

"Oh," said Susan. "I read about Eager being killed in an automobile accident. It was dreadful."

Marie knew what Susan was leading to so she changed the subject.

"I brought you a gift," she smiled. "I did not know where to put it."

Evan gently squeezed Marie's hand because he knew exactly what she was referring to and he wanted to stick it there, too.

"It is a pleasure to meet you, Susan," he lied. "You sent Marie a beautiful Christmas card each year. I feel as if I have known you for years."

Susan smiled, then turned her attention to Carolyn (alias Kay) and said, "I read about your terrible marriage in the newspaper, dear. You were lucky to escape that animal."

"You have such a lovely home and so many friends," replied Carolyn. "I bet you are having a wonderful birthday."

When Susan put her hand out to greet Dennis, Marie noticed Kay's blue topaz and diamond ring on Susan's right index finger.

"Susan, I can not stay long so is there some place where we can go and have a girl talk?" said Marie.

"Yes, dear," smiled the aging snake. "Follow me. We will be back in a few minutes."

She smiled at her guests as she and Marie went up stairs to her private sitting room.

"What did you want to talk to me about, Marie?" asked Susan.

"I wanted to thank you for inviting me and my family to your birthday party," responded Marie. "It was a refreshing opportunity for me to get out and be with someone I had not seen in a long time and celebrate a happy moment instead of going to another funeral. Since I have been through so much sadness with my daughter, I knew this social event would brighten my day. You have not even opened the present I bought you."

"I will open it now," said Susan. "You know, your daughter does not look any thing like her pictures in the newspapers."

"Those pictures always make you look fatter than you are," said Marie who was beginning to feel uneasy. "I noticed that beautiful blue topaz ring on your index finger. May I see it?"

"Certainly, dear," toyed Susan. "It was a gift from my oldest son. It is one of my favorite rings."

Susan removed the ring from her finger and handed it to Marie. Marie held the ring up to the light to look at the inside of the band. It read, "To Kay from Pa Pa."

So Susan would not know what she was doing, she said, "The color is so bright and vibrant in this light. It matches your dress perfectly."

Marie lowered the ring from the light and saw a small hand gun pointed at her heart. Susan was through playing cat games. She knew why Marie was there but she was not sure who she brought with her.

Evan began to get worried and told Dennis that he was going up stairs to see what the delay was. Carolyn had left the men to go to the bathroom. Since the guest bathroom was occupied, she was told to use the bathroom in the maid's quarters. On her way back, she spotted a small picture, on the dresser in the bedroom. She recognized Leonard's face immediately. She put the picture in her purse and hurried back to Mr. Hughes and Dennis.

"I do not feel well," said Carolyn

"Would you like something to drink," replied Dennis who did not pick up on the clue.

"What did you say, Carolyn?" asked Mr. Hughes.

"I thought her name was Kay," said a guest who was introduced to them earlier.

Dennis looked into Carolyn's eye as if an alarm went off in his head.

"Marie is in trouble," whispered Dennis to Evan. "Go call the police while I go up stairs to help her."

"Carolyn," Evan ordered. "Go call the police. I am going with Dennis. Marie needs me."

"I thought her name was Kay," repeated the drunken lady.

Carolyn hurried to the nearest telephone to call the police. Dennis and Evan ran to the top of the stairs to try to find Marie.

After looking into three bedrooms, they found Marie with Susan, who was pointing a gun at Marie's heart.

"Please do not shoot her," cried Evan.

"DROP THE GUN, LADY," yelled Dennis. "The police are on their way. We know who you are. Where is your son?"

"Evan, stay where you are," ordered Marie. "I am fine. Susan is not going to shoot me."

"How do you know what I am going to do," growled Susan. "Your daughter ruined my son's life. We had it all until your precious Kay stepped into our life."

"Why did you want to kill Kay?" asked Marie. "She never did anything to hurt you."

"I always wanted a daughter but instead I had three dirty boys," confessed Susan. "You had the perfect child that was pretty and smart. My late husband divorced me and he left me with nothing but bills and these dirty boys. I did not know how we were going to survive. When my oldest son returned from Viet Nam, he married a young beautiful woman named Rosie, who had a brilliant plan to make money fast. Leonard would pose as a student in college when in reality he was stalking rich young ladies. The first girl he married was very rich. She disappeared after they were married three months, so we used her bank account to payoff all of our debts. It became a game with him and Rosie until he married Kay. I told him to kill her like the others before burying her under the pool, but he wanted her to suffer."

"You said your late husband divorced you, how can that be," asked a terrified Marie who never realized how evil Susan was until now.

"Leonard fixed his brakes," laughed Susan. "He went down that hill so fast."

"I am very sorry," cried Marie.

"Sorry, why are you sorry?" bellowed Susan. "You had everything. The perfect husband, nice friends, and then you had Kay. I hated you when you came to the reunion and Eager showed me those pictures of your perfect family. You embarrassed me in front of our senior classmates. I vowed that I would get my revenge."

Marie began to laugh at Susan.

"Why are you laughing?" yelled Susan. "STOP IT."

"I thought you had everything, Susan," laughed Marie. "You were pretty and popular in school and your boys were all handsome and popular like you. That is what you used to write me in my Christmas cards. I always thought you were the lucky one. Susan, please put the gun down. Help us end this madness before someone else gets hurt."

When the police officers arrived, Carolyn pointed to the room at the top of the stairs where the trouble was happening. The birthday guests were asked to step outside so they would not get hurt. Susan saw the policemen coming up the stairway. She knew she did not have any escape from the horror she had inflicted on those innocent girls.

"Why did you come to my party?" Susan asked. "Everything was going fine until I saw you standing in the corner with that man. WHY ARE YOU HERE?"

"Because you invited me," softly and calmly answered Marie.

"You will have to find Leonard for yourself. I will never help you," she said as she watched as two more policemen pointed guns at her.

"I guess the birthday surprise is on you," smiled Susan as she aimed the gun at her own head and fired one shot.

"NO," yelled Marie, but it was too late.

Susan killed herself in front of her oldest friend. Marie ran to her lifeless body and cried, "Please forgive her, Lord."

Evan hurried to Marie's side and wrapped his arms around his sobbing wife.

"Thank you for keeping her safe," he prayed as he helped her stand up and walk away from her dead high school friend.

"I never knew she was in so much pain," cried Marie. "Please forgive me Lord. I am so sorry."

"Honey, you did not do anything," assured Evan. "She was mentally ill and she needed professional help. You did nothing wrong. Her death is not your fault."

Dennis joined them as they walked down the stairs to the birthday party area where Carolyn was waiting. Carolyn used a birthday party napkin to wipe some of Susan's blood off Marie's hands.

A maid from the kitchen brought Marie a glass of water and a wet towel to help remove the blood. Marie thanked her and wiped the rest of the blood from her hands on the towel.

"I want to go home, Evan," begged Marie. "I hate it here. Please get me out of this house."

"The taxi is waiting for us outside, Mrs. Hughes," said Dennis.

"I did not even get to brag about my beautiful ring," Marie said as she looked at her wedding band.

Then she remembered she was still holding Kay's blue topaz ring that Eager bought her when she graduated from high school. She dropped it in her purse and planned on giving it to Kay when they returned home.

Carolyn pulled the picture of Leonard and his two brothers, that she had taken off the dresser, out of her purse and showed it to Marie. The three handsome boys looked happy and content standing side by side in front of the house.

"I found this when I went to the bathroom," confessed Carolyn. "You had already gone up stairs with the lady so I tried to get Dennis's attention by using the cue phrase but it did not work."

"It worked, sis," Dennis told her as they walked towards the taxi. "I will never make a good spy because I am too slow with my interpretation."

"Leave that picture here, Carolyn," demanded Marie. "I do not want anything belonging to that woman near me.

Carolyn put the picture on the dinning room table next to Susan's elaborate three layer chocolate birthday cake.

All four party crashers sat quietly as they rode in the taxi back to the hotel. Dennis telephoned Lieutenant Gorman to inform him of the tragedy. Marie took a bath to wash any blood and residue from the party off her body. When she was finished, she wrapped her clean nude body in the terry cloth robe provided by the hotel.

She looked at her face in the mirror and softly prayed, "Thank you for my life and my daughter, Lord."

She was about to end her prayer when she remembered she had a new husband and imaginary family that has been with her through the entire ordeal.

She continued, "Thank you for Evan, Dennis, and Carolyn and for blessing me with this new family. I love my family. Amen."

She stepped out of the bathroom into the sleeping area to discover red roses on the desk and red rose petals on the bed.

"What is this?" she asked while studying the rose petals that were scattered on the bed and floor.

"I know you probably do not want your first night with me filled with intense romance and love so I brought you some roses to cheer you up," confessed Evan.

"Where is Carolyn?" asked Marie.

"I moved her to the suite across the hall," answered Evan. "Do you need her? I will ask her to come back."

"No, I do not need her, Evan," said Marie as she dropped her robe to the floor. "I can do this on my own."

Evan turned out the lights as the two newlyweds climbed into the rose petal covered bed.

"Good night sweet heart," said Evan.

"It will be," smiled Marie. "Good night to you, too."


Crime scene tape was draped across Susan's fence and taped across her front door.

"I came for Susan's birthday party," said Leonard. "It must have been some wild party."

"We have not lived here long and she invited us to the party," said the neighbor. "My name is Bill Chick."

He and Leonard shook hands and he invited him into his home to finish his story. His wife, Ellie, fixed some coffee for him and brought out a plate of fresh baked cookies.

"Susan made a grand entrance," informed Bill. "She looked beautiful."

"Thank you for the coffee," said Leonard. "Where is she?"

"I think she is dead," supposed Bill. "They said her son, (Leon, Leo, Lee or something like that) was a murderer and she was helping him kill innocent ladies."

"Really," glared Leonard. "How did she die?"

"I am not sure," answered the unsuspecting man. "Everything seemed to be going great until some people arrived."

"She said her name was Kay but the man kept calling her Carolyn," added Ellie.

"Susan and a guest went up stairs and we were asked to leave," completed Bill. "The party was over, the police came, and we went home. The out of town guests are staying at the Casino. Susan reserved rooms for them."

"I think her son murdered her," alleged Ellie. "He probably needed money to get out of the country."

"I do not think that is what happened, Mrs. Chick," smiled Leonard as he stood up to leave her home.

"Why is that?" asked Bill.

"Because I am Leonard, Susan's murdering son," he confessed then shot both of the new neighbors in the head as he left their home. "Thank you for the information."

Leonard climbed over the fence to enter his mother's home through the back entrance. The back door was locked but he had a key. He walked through the kitchen and dinning room, passing the birthday cake, and went up stairs to the crime scene area. There was blood on the floor and splattered on one of the walls. He looked through Susan's desk to see if he could find any money or valuables that he could take to use to finance his trip out of the country. It was his lucky day; he found some jewelry and his mother's check book. He stuffed that into his pocket then continued with his scavenger hunt. He found a small suitcase in her bedroom and began filling it with anything that was of any value. As he was going down stairs, he heard a police siren coming in that direction. He figured someone must have heard the shots and telephoned the police. He was leaving the same way he came in when the picture next to the birthday cake caught his eye. He looked at the picture with tears in his eyes as he remembered the happy days with his brothers. He cut himself a piece of the chocolate cake and took a huge bite of it.

He took one last long look at his mother's home and said, "Happy Birthday, Mom. I will give you your present later."

He walked through the kitchen door just as the police drove up to the neighbor's home, next to the Chick's house. He could hear the lady telling the officers that she had heard two gun shots at her friend's home. They never noticed Leonard walking down the street and escaping the crime scene area.

# THE ROAD TRIP TO OKLAHOMA

## CHAPTER XI

Officer Cox returned to the kitchen, after speaking to Lieutenant Gorman on the telephone, to tell Kay the tragic news about Susan's deadly birthday party.

"According to the police report," informed Officer Cox. "Susan killed herself in front of your mother. No one else was hurt."

"That is horrible," cried Kay. "Is mother all right?"

"Officer Rue reported that he witnessed the suicide and your mother was doing fine," said Officer Cox. "I also received some bad news from Lieutenant Gorman."

"That was not bad enough?" Kay said sarcastically. "What else happened?"

"The two neighbors, Mr. and Mrs. Chick, who lived across the street and were new to the neighborhood, were murdered and Susan's house was broken into," answered Officer Cox. "Some finger prints were lifted off of the back door window, that were identified as Leonard's. He is in Oklahoma City, Kay."

"He is going to be looking for Mother," cried Kay. "We need to leave."

"Officer Rue is taking every precaution to protect your mother and the others," said Officer Cox. "I do agree with you that we need to go there. We might get lucky and stumble onto Leonard. If he is watching the airport for our arrival or flight departure, he might hurt other passengers. I think we should drive to Oklahoma."

"You want to drive?" repeated Kay. "It is going to take us all day to get there."

"He drove," remarked Officer Cox. "I asked Lieutenant Gorman to tell Officer Rue and your family to stay at that hotel and wait for us."

"What about the Lambies?" Kay asked.

"They can stay here until we return to Cortland," planned Officer Cox. "Lieutenant Blackshear will assign an officer to watch over them. Leonard is not coming back to kill them. He is looking for you. We will stay here tonight then leave early in the morning for Oklahoma City."

"We will need a bigger car," said Kay.

"Take my car," said Mr. Lambie. "It has four new tires and the engine purrs like a kitten."

"That is a great idea," agreed Kay. "Although I think you are going to need your car to take Mike to the doctor. Thank you."

"I will telephone Lieutenant Blackshear and ask him to rent us a car," said Officer Cox. "He can bring us the car and we can drop him off at the police station as we are leaving."

"What about me?" asked Debbie who had been standing there listening to their brainstorming session. "Could I ride with you to Oklahoma? I have some relatives that live there who will let me stay with them. My children will be no trouble at all to travel with."

Kay and Officer Cox had forgotten about Debbie and her children. They did not want to leave her here for her abusive husband to beat her again and they did not want her to go to a shelter where her children might be subjected to pedophilia and be molested.

Debbie could see she had put them in a compromising position and said, "We will be fine. I will find a place in the morning where we can stay."

"You can go with us," insisted Kay. "I would rather have you with us than have you go back to that abusive husband. Please join us on our road trip to Oklahoma."

Debbie looked at Officer Cox to see if he agreed with Kay. When he smiled, she knew she was going with them.

"Thank you. Thank you so much," she cried with excitement. "I have to go tell the children. They will be trilled."

"It is very nice of you to do that for that girl," complimented Mrs. Lambie. "I am going to check on Mike and take him one of these hamburgers. Thank you, Officer."

Mrs. Lambie left OC and Kay to take care of Mike giving them some time to talk in private.

"So, you found a hard luck case to help," said Kay.

"I could not leave her and her children standing there, in front of the restaurant," responded the helpless Officer Cox. "I thought you would understand since you had been married to Leonard. What was I suppose to do? Leave her there for some wacko to hurt and abuse again. Say something."

"I think you did the most unselfish and kind act by bringing her and her family here," smiled Kay as she kissed him on the forehead. "I think you are wonderful, even with your short comings."

"What short comings?" asked an embarrassed Officer Cox. "Where are you going?"

"I am going up-stairs to pack my clothes again," answered Kay. "We are going to have a long trip ahead of us tomorrow. You better get some rest, big boy, because you are doing all the driving."

Officer Cox smiled and rubbed his forehead as he watched Kay leave to get ready for their long road trip.

Lieutenant Blackshear, accompanied with a Deputy from the Golden Colorado Police Station, arrived with some clothes for the Lambies and eight bags of groceries. Officer Cox assisted in unloading the trunk and carrying the groceries to the kitchen. While the three men were working, Officer Cox explained the situation with Debbie and her children. Lieutenant Blackshear had no idea that he was becoming Officer Cox's personal errand boy. Now he had to return to the stores to purchase some warm clothing for Debbie and her children.

"I promise you will be reimbursed for everything you have done," said Officer Cox. "I will need you to rent me a comfortable car, big enough for five adults, to drive to Oklahoma."

"Is there anything else I can get for you?" asked Lieutenant Blackshear.

"Yes, I would like the address of Mr. Edward Calley," requested Officer Cox.

"Is Mr. Calley kin to Debbie? Is he the abusive husband?" asked Lieutenant Blackshear.

"Yes, he is the husband," answered Officer Cox. "I would like to introduce him to the Battered Women's Rehabilitation and Counseling Agency where he can get some anger management therapy."

"Let me think about that request before I give you that information because you have only heard Debbie's side of the story," smiled Lieutenant Blackshear. "I will do my home work and get back to you. As for the car, I will bring it to you in the morning."

"What about the clothes for Debbie and her family?" he asked.

"Before you take her to Oklahoma, I am going to do a background check on her," informed the Lieutenant. "Then I will see about buying the clothes."

Officer Cox liked Lieutenant Blackshear and how he was handling Debbie's situation. All Kay and Officer Cox wanted to do was help the homeless lady. She could be a fugitive running away from the law or a kidnapper. If there was something Debbie was not telling them, Lieutenant Blackshear would have that information for them in the morning.

Lieutenant Blackshear asked the deputy to drive him to the station so he could investigate the dysfunctional Calley family.

Officer Cox distributed the clothes to the Lambies and he stored the cold groceries in the refrigerator while Mrs. Lambie and Kay assembled the dry foodstuff in the cabinets. The Lieutenant bought some bandages and medicines for Mike, which Mrs. Lambie took up stair to her room.

Kay was so excited about driving across Colorado to Oklahoma that she could not sleep. She tossed and turned in the bed but could not get comfortable. Then she read her Bible, but nothing could help her sleep. By three in the morning she was dressed and ready for the road trip. She sat in the chair next the window to watch the snow slowly falling on top of the fence as she wondered when Lieutenant Blackshear was going to bring the car. The slowly floating snow covered the roof tops, bare tree limbs, and the fence post. It was relaxing and hypnotizing to watch and soon Kay was sound asleep sitting in the chair.

Kay was awakened the next morning by the sounds of people moving around in the room next to hers and voices in the hallway. She looked at her watch to see what time it was and discovered that she had slept for two hours in the chair. She grabbed her luggage and carried it down the stairs to the living area. Mrs. Lambie was making breakfast for Officer Cox, Debbie, and her children.

"Good morning, Kay," greeted Debbie. "Come over here and have some breakfast. Mrs. Lambie is a wonderful cook."

"Is there any milk left?" asked Kay.

"Yes, dear," answered Mrs. Lambie.

Kay sat at the dining room table next to David Calley who was sporting a white milk mustache.

Mrs. Lambie handed Kay a tall glass of milk and asked if she could get her anything else.

"Yes, please," said Kay. "I would like a small glass of ice."

"Ice?" replied Debbie. "Whatever for?"

"I like ice with my milk," said Kay. "It keeps it cold."

"Yuk," laughed David and his sister, Kelly Ann.

"You have to try it to like it," said Kay as she passed her glass in their direction. "Here, have some."

"Not me," David refused.

"Not me," Kelly Ann refused, too. "It sounds terrible."

"Well, it is delicious," Kay said as she took a big drink.

The children started laughing at her because she had a big milk mustache under her nose. Officer Cox and Debbie joined the children laughing at Kay's mustache. Mrs. Lambie handed Kay a napkin to clean her face.

"Thank you," laughed Kay. "Where is Mr. Lambie?"

"He is in the bathroom," answered Mrs. Lambie. "There is a television in there and he is watching the early morning news and weather reports. Last night he fell asleep in there while watching the Night Show. He would eat his meals in there if he could."

"Yuk," they all said simultaneously and they laughed.

"I am going to go feed Mike," said Mrs. Lambie.

There was a knock on the front door that ended the laughter. Officer Cox put his hand on his gun as he looked through the peephole in the door. Lieutenant Blackshear and the deputy were standing on the porch waiting to get out of the cold. The Lieutenant was carrying a black brief case and a road map.

"Good Morning," greeted Officer Cox and the others in the kitchen. "Did you have any problems renting the vehicle?"

"No," said the Lieutenant who was dropping snow on the floor.

Kay took a broom and dust pan over to the door and swept the snow into the dust pan and threw it outside. Lieutenant Blackshear smiled at Kay and held the door open for her.

"Good morning, Miss Lytle," he greeted. "Are you ready for your road trip?"

"Yes, I am," she answered shyly. "I could not sleep a wink last night thinking about this adventure."

"I would not have known it because you look beautiful this morning," smiled the Lieutenant.

"Hello, there are other people here," growled Officer Cox. "Do you have some information that you want to share with me?"

Kay returned to the kitchen to replace the broom and dust pan in the pantry. The Lieutenant followed her with his desirous eyes until she was out of sight. He asked Officer Cox if there was somewhere they could talk in private. Officer Cox led him to the garage and closed the door so no one could hear them.

"What did you find out about Debbie?" asked Officer Cox. "I noticed that you did not bring any clothes in for them. That brief case would not hold much."

"There was a file on her husband for being abusive and causing a public disturbance at a local restaurant. Mr. Calley has been arrested and been in jail several times for drunken and disorderly conduct at his wife's place of employment which got her fired. He does not have a job and sits at home waiting for Debbie to bring him the pay check. I paid a visit to Mr. Calley's home last night to find him watching a football game and drinking beer. I could tell he was drunk by the way he yelled at me when he answered the front door. He thought I was bringing Debbie and the children home for another beating. I arrested him for probable cause (cause I did not like what I saw). He will be locked up at the Golden Police Station long enough for you to reach the state line. I left their clothes in the trunk and there are three coats in the back seat for them. Debbie is a good hard working mother with no criminal record on file," informed the Lieutenant.

"Thank you," smiled Officer Cox. "I was dreading having to tell her that she had to stay. What is in the brief case?"

"Are you getting soft hearted, Officer Cox," asked the Lieutenant. "I read your files and you are one bad dude. Why are you concerned about this woman, who you do not know, and her children? Most police officers would have taken her to a shelter or batter woman's facility."

"I did not put the lady's husband in jail so she could get out of the state safely," replied Officer Cox. "You put the man in jail. I think we are both getting soft."

"You are right," smiled Lieutenant Blackshear. "I guess I am getting soft but don't tell anyone. I brought you a portable telephone. It is a new device that plugs into the lighter socket to be charged. Once it is charged, you can make a telephone call anywhere without having to stop the car to use a phone booth."

"Really. Show me how it works," asked Officer Cox. "I told Kay that there were going to be devices like this some day. American Modern Technology is incredible."

While Lieutenant Blackshear was teaching Officer Cox how to use the portable telephone, Kay was helping Mrs. Lambie wash the dishes and clean the kitchen. Debbie and her children were watching television and Mr. Lambie was in the second story bathroom watching television. Mike was slowly getting dressed to come down stairs to tell Kay and her cross country crusaders to have a safe trip. After he was dressed he dragged himself to the stairway and was about to start his mission down the stairs when Debbie and the deputy spotted him. They hurried up the stairs to help him down to the main floor.

"You should not be walking around by yourself," scolded Debbie. "There are plenty of people here that can help you."

"Yes, mother," groaned Mike. "I wanted to talk to Kay before she leaves for Oklahoma and I knew I did not have a lot of time to do it."

Debbie asked her children to move off the sofa so Mike could lay there. She went into the kitchen to convey to Kay that Mike wanted to talk to her while the deputy guarded the front door.

"I will be right up as soon as I finish drying these dishes," said Kay.

"He is on the sofa waiting for you," informed Debbie.

"WHAT?" yelled his mother. "I will spank that boy's behind for getting out of that bed. I am still his mother and he in not to big for me to spank."

Kay hung up her dish towel and rushed to the sofa to see if Mike was all right.

"What are you doing down stairs, Mike?" scolded Kay. "I would have gone to your room if you needed me."

"I sure have a lot of mothers here," smiled Mike. "I am fine. Besides, any doctor will tell you 'the sooner a patient can get up and move around, the sooner he will get well'. I wanted you to know how much I appreciate all you are doing for me and my parents. You could have sent me to jail."

"I could not do that to a fellow who loves old westerns like you," smiled Kay as she covered his legs with the blue afghan that Officer Cox had used for his covers last night. "You are a handsome man that would have been used as some prison cell mate's joy toy. I could not let that happen to a friend."

"Joy toy," laughed Mike. "Ok, you saved me twice. Thank you. I wanted to know if you were serious about hiring me as your pilot."

"Are you a certified licensed pilot that can fly small commercial jets?" asked Kay.

"Yes I am and I can fly any type of plane you have," bragged Mike. "Will you allow me to prove it?"

"My son is a good pilot, Kay," interrupted Mrs. Lambie. "He made the highest grades in his flight class at Aviation School."

"I need to make you aware that if you work for me, you will have to wear a company uniform that will cover all your tattoos," said Kay. "Plus, all those rings in your ear will have to go. I want my entire flight crew to look professional and qualified for their jobs; however, what you do on your own time is your business. Will you have a problem with that?"

"No, Miss Lytle," agreed Mike. "I will do whatever the job demands and follow your requirements. I need to clean up my life. I have been walking down the wrong path long enough. I need to be a responsible person. So, do I get the job?"

"Not so fast," smiled Kay. "I still have to see you fly."

"Yes ma'am," said Mike. "I hate to brag but I am really good in the air."

"When you recover, I will have you flown to Cortland to demonstrate your aviation skills for me," said Kay. "You can bring your parents with you when you come. I might have a job for your father, too."

"Thank you, Kay," smiled Mike as he looked at his proud mother. "I promise I will not disappoint you."

Officer Cox was carrying the small black briefcase when he and Lieutenant Blackshear re-entered the house from the garage. The deputy was asked to load Kay's luggage and Officer Cox's briefcase into the car. Officer Cox went to his room to gather his things and pack for the trip. He was surprised to see everything, including his tooth brush, packed and waiting for him at the bedroom door. He carried his bags down the stairs to the car and thanked Debbie for packing his things.

"I did not do it," she said. "My children packed your bags for you."

"Thank you David and Kelly Ann," smiled Officer Cox. "That was a very nice thing to do."

Mr. Lambie finally came out of the bathroom to see what all the noise was about. Kay hugged Mrs. Lambie and told her to call if she needed anything. She wrote her home telephone number on a piece of paper then remembered she was not going home.

"I will call you each day to see how things are going," she said. "I do not know what my telephone number will be since I will be staying at hotels for the next few days."

"You have a safe trip Kay and thank you for helping my son," replied Mrs. Lambie as she hugged Kay again.

"If I see Leonard, I will call the police and tell them to notify you," said Mike. "I will see you soon."

"I think we might move into this place permanently," said Mr. Lambie. "I am comfortable here and I can get use to climbing those stairs."

"When Mike is well, I will change the lease over to your name," agreed Kay. "Then you can start paying the rent."

"How much is the rent," asked Mr. Lambie.

Kay softly whispered the monthly cost of rent into his ear.

He coughed and his face turned red as he said, "I guess I will have to enjoy that bathroom while I can."

Everyone laughed at him and continued packing the car. Debbie and her children rode in the back seat and Officer Cox was the designated driver. Kay was the map reader and navigator for the trip. When she opened the door to sit in the front passenger seat, there was a black briefcase filling her spot.

"What is this?" she asked as she lifted it off her seat.

"We will need this in case of an emergency," answered Officer Cox.

"Does it have to ride in the front with me?" she inquired.

"Yes," said Officer Cox. "It has to be plugged into the cigarette lighter socket to charge while we are driving. Put the case on the floorboard in front of you so you will have more room."

Kay set the briefcase on the floor in front of her and climbed into the car.

Looking at the Lieutenant, she asked, "Will the Lambies have someone protecting them while we are gone. Leonard is a sneaky man. He can get in and out of a place without anyone ever knowing he was there."

"This deputy is assigned to stay with them during the day and another man is coming at night," assured Lieutenant Blackshear. "Will you be coming back to Colorado again?"

"It all depends on whether or not we arrest Leonard," said Kay. "Why?"

"I would like to show you some of the hot spots in Colorado that some people never get to see," he shyly smiled. "Would you be interested in going out with me?"

Kay never got a chance to answer because Officer Cox interrupted their conversation saying, "Hello we have to get on the road before it gets too late in the day."

"Give this envelope to Officer Cox," ordered Lieutenant Blackshear as he handed it to Kay. "I hope you have a safe trip."

Officer Cox drove the vehicle towards Denver to merge onto Interstate 70 East, traveling towards Kansas; however, he missed his exit and turned onto Interstate 25 traveling towards Pueblo, Colorado.

When they reached Pueblo, he stopped at a gas station to study the map the lieutenant had given him. He decided to travel towards Albuquerque, New Mexico to Interstate 40 which would take them straight into Oklahoma City. Kay told him to make a U-turn in Denver to get back on the highway that the Lieutenant wanted them to take but Officer Cox was stubborn and wanted to take his own route.

After everyone had used the restroom, bought something to snack on, and Officer Cox had refueled the tank, they were back on the highway to Albuquerque. Kay bought each of the children a coloring book with colors so they would not be bored to death on the road trip.

The day was beautiful with traces of snow covering the roofs of houses, trees, and mountains along the way. In Trinidad, Colorado, Officer Cox stopped to ask if he was going in the right direction. The Children got out of the car to stretch their legs. Debbie folded her coat to make it into a pillow for her head so she could take a nap. When Officer Cox returned, he reassured everyone that he was going in the right direction to Albuquerque, New Mexico and they were back on the highway to Oklahoma. There had been very little talking during the road trip because they thought they were lost and did not want to disturb Officer Cox while he was concentrating on his driving. Debbie and her children were taking a 'car' nap in the back seat when Kay finally decided to talk to Officer Cox.

"It is beautiful here," said Kay. "I would like to come back. We could come back here for a family vacation during the summer time so we could go rafting, hiking, or mountain climbing. Would you be interested in doing that?"

"I think any time in Colorado is a good time," replied Officer Cox. "No matter what we do it would be a great vacation here."

"What is in this briefcase?" Kay asked. "Is it some kind of secret weapon?"

"No, it is a portable telephone," laughed Officer Cox. "Lieutenant Blackshear showed me how to operate it so we would not have to stop on the road to make an emergency call. He has it programmed to call the nearest police station in case we need some help or something."

"Can we order a pizza with it?" asked Kay.

"Pizza, no we can not do that. Are you hungry?" inquired Officer Cox.

"Yes, we have been traveling for hours and all I had for breakfast was a glass of ice milk," whined Kay. "Could we stop in the next town and get something to eat?"

"We will do that," agreed Officer Cox who was always hungry.

"Can I have a chocolate shake?" asked David.

"Hey, I thought you were asleep back there," alleged Kay.

"I was but I heard you talking and I am hungry, too," confessed David.

"You can have a chocolate shake if you promise to eat something healthy," said Kay.

"I will," agreed David. "Can I sit with you in the front?"

"Sure," answered Kay. "Climb over and bring that coloring book with you."

David grabbed his coloring book and carefully climbed over the front seat to sit with Kay. His sister and mother never moved a muscle while they were sleeping in the back.

"This is a great coloring book," said David as he showed it to Kay. "It has games and lots of cool pictures to color. It even has stickers."

"It does?" said Kay. "Show me what you have colored."

David showed Kay several pictures of super heroes that he had colored and stuck stickers on. He turned to one picture of a villain that had been entirely colored in black.

"What happened here?" asked Kay.

"I do not like this crook," confessed David. "He is one bad dude. I colored him all in black because I dropped a bomb on him."

"A bomb," remarked Kay.

"Yes, and it burned him up," explained David. "Sometimes superheroes need some help from outsiders so I help them."

"I think he should of used some red for blood," said Kelly Ann who was looking over the seat. "Can I come up there with you, too?"

"Sure," answered Kay. "The more the merrier."

The seat was large and Kay was small enough that David sat besides her and Kelly Ann sat on her lap. She pulled the seat belt across all of their bodies and attached it for safety.

"I hate wearing this thing," Kay whined.

"One day there will be a law passed that everyone will have to wear one in the front and back seat," informed Officer Cox.

"That law will never pass," said Kay as she tried to make the seat comfortable for the children.

Officer Cox smiled at Kay being surrounded and tied in the seat with children. He kept on driving to Albuquerque and looking for a restaurant.

"Do you know any stories?" asked Kelly Ann.

"I know Bible stories," answered Kay.

"I like stories about superheroes," said David. "Do you know any stories like that?"

"Sure," admitted Kay. "I can tell you the story of David (a young boy like you) and Goliath."

"Is Goliath the superhero?" asked Kelly Ann.

"No," answered Kay. "Goliath is a giant of a man that is not afraid of anything. Not even God because he thinks he is a God. All the people, including King Saul, are afraid of him because he is strong and has never lost a battle."

"How can David be a superhero if he is just a boy like me?" asked David.

"David is a good boy who believes in God," answered Kay.

"How can God help him?" inquired Kelly Ann.

"Let her tell the story," scolded David. "I want to know what happened to Goliath."

"How tall was Goliath?" asked Kelly Ann. "My mother said to always get the facts. Facts are important. Knowledge is power."

"Goliath was a giant," said David. "She said he was a giant and giants are taller than trees. Was David afraid of Goliath?"

"David was a young boy who believed that God could and would help him through anything," answered Kay. "Jesse, David's father, asked him to take some food to his brothers, who were hungry from fighting all day with Goliath. When he arrived at the camp, he heard that Goliath had challenged anyone brave enough to fight him. He said, if they won, his people would be their slaves, but if he won they would have to give up their God and serve his people as slaves forever."

"What do slaves do?" asked Kelly Ann.

"A slave is like a maid but they do yard work," answered David.

"A slave is a person that is held in servitude as property to their masters," explained Kay. "You have to do whatever your master tells you to do."

"You would have to clean the toilet?" asked Kelly Ann. "I would hate to clean the toilet because of all that stuff in there."

"Yes, you would have to clean the toilet, mop the floor, and take care of any live stock on the property," explained Kay. "It is a hard job to be a slave but no one was going to fight Goliath to stay free. They were all afraid. All were afraid except for David. He told King Saul that he would fight Goliath and win."

"I bet that king laughed at him because he was a little boy," remarked Kelly Ann.

"The king did not laugh at him. Instead he gave David his royal armor to wear and his shield to carry," continued Kay. "The king's servants dressed David in the King's breastplate and put the King's spear in his hand."

"What is a breastplate?" asked Kelly Ann.

"It is like a bulletproof vest," answered Officer Cox who had become interest in the story.

"That is right. Thank you OC," smiled Kay as she continued. "David was a small boy and the breastplate was too heavy for him to wear. The shield and spear were too heavy for him to carry. He thanked the king for all the nice battle gear but he wanted to fight Goliath with his sling shot and his flat rocks."

"Oh no," cried Kelly Ann. "He is going to be killed."

"Quiet Kelly Ann, I want to hear what happened," scolded David. "Will you please continue?"

"So David marched over to the hill where Goliath was waiting with his large army of men. As he marched, he prayed to God and asked him to help him slay this giant so the war would stop and his people would remain free from slavery. When he reached the top of the hill, Goliath laughed and asked 'what kind of dog is this you send to defend your country? He is not even full grown, but a puppy'."

"David took one of his flat stones out of his pocket and put it in his sling shot. Goliath yelled, 'come child, let's get this over with.' David moved closer towards Goliath to get a better shot at his face. Goliath threw a spear (the size of a weaver's beam) at David and it missed him. Now it was David's turn. David took his sling shot and spun it around his head faster and faster. Then he prayed, 'God please help my people,' and he released the stone from the sling shot. The stone flew through the air and hit Goliath right between the eyes. At first, everyone was laughing at what David had done; however, when Goliath started swaying back and forth, the laughter stopped. Goliath fell to the ground and David ran as fast as he could and took Goliath's sword and cut off his head. When the lawbreaking invaders saw this, they ran back to their country and God saved David's people from slavery and he became a great and mighty King," Kay finished the story.

Kelly Ann and David cheered and clapped at Kay's wonderful superhero story so loud that it woke Debbie from her "car" nap. Officer Cox even gave Kay the thumbs up on her story.

"Are we here?" asked a sleepy eyed Debbie. "What are you doing in the front seat?"

"They are fine," said Kay.

"I see a restaurant ahead and I think they serve chocolate shakes there," said Officer Cox as he exited the Interstate to go to a restaurant called Emily's. "That name seems familiar to me."

"As long as they serve good food, I do not care what the name is," confessed Kay. "I am hungry."

Kay kept her promise and bought David a large chocolate shake for eating all his vegetables. The food was good, fresh, and inexpensive. Everyone was satisfied with their choices. Kay ordered an extra burger and five shakes to go for the road. Kay told Officer Cox that she would drive awhile, until it got dark, so he could get some rest. When they reached Albuquerque, New Mexico, she merged onto Interstate 40 to go to Amarillo, Texas. While she was driving, Debbie told her sad life story of abuse and hardships.

"My first husband died in an automobile accident on Highway 25 about five years ago. I swore I was never going to get married again until I met this man. I thought he was a great man, but looks can be deceiving," she said. "I guess that is why I was afraid of you, Officer Cox. I am sorry. This man was good with the children and fun to be with. After we got married a year ago, everything changed. He lost his job because of his drinking and his bad attitude. Then he had fits of pique, mood swings, and started beating me. When he hit David, I knew I had to get out of there. That is when I was praying for someone kind to find us. The rest of the story you already know."

"When he started hitting you the first time, why did you stay?" asked Kay.

"I thought it was my fault," said Debbie. "However, I knew my son had not done one thing to him when he began to beat him. I will not allow anyone to hit my babies. They are my life, so we left."

"You are a brave woman," Kay replied. "I am glad you are with us on this trip."

"Will you tell us another story?" asked David.

"You tell good stories, Miss Kay," added Kelly Ann.

"I have to focus on the road but when we get to the hotel if we are not too tired, I will tell you another story," smiled Kay. "OC probably has a lot of stories stored in that brain of his. Maybe he will tell you a story."

"Will you tell us a story, OC?" asked the children.

Officer Cox frowned at Kay for volunteering him as the road story teller. Debbie could see that it was time for the children to color so she handed them their colors and coloring books.

Kay reached Amarillo, Texas at five o'clock in the evening. She drove the car to a convenience store to refuel the tank and so everyone could stretch their legs again. Officer Cox resumed the driving and Kay returned to the front passenger seat. Debbie picked up all the trash in the car and the children threw it in a garbage can near the gas pumps. David asked the cashier if they had any sling shots for sell. He was disappointed when the cashier told him 'no'. Officer Cox told him that he would make a sling shot for him when they reached Oklahoma City.

There were two more hours to drive before they reached Oklahoma City. Kay could see that the children were starting to get antsy from being on the road for ten hours so she asked them to make a list of all the things they wanted for Christmas.

"We do not celebrate Christmas at our home," said Debbie. "It is our religious belief."

"What?" said Kay. "Why don't you celebrate?"

"Now Kay, some people do not believe the way you do," commented Officer Cox. "All religions are different."

"Oh, I do not mind telling you," said Debbie. "It is a pagan holiday where everyone tries to out do the next person. There are lots of lights and fake emotions that are followed by stupid Christmas songs and programs. I am not going to be a part of it. I can buy my children toys whenever I please without having to put them under a sacrilegious tree."

"You are so wrong," scolded Kay.

"Now Kay, that is her opinion and she has a right to it," alleged Officer Cox.

"Yes, she does have an opinion and I listened to her opinion for over two hours and now it is my time," claimed Kay. "Celebrating Christmas is in the Bible. If you read St. Luke, it reads, "A multitude of Angels filled the sky in celebration while the shepherds were watching their sheep. Where in the world did you get sacrilegious tree? It is a symbol for everlasting life which represents our Lord who will always be with us. The lights, candles, and stars are for the glory of God which shown over the Christ when he was born. Some religions believe that the star was over Bethlehem for three years; but if that was so, the star would not be special. Instead it would be like one of those lights in a mall parking lot that announces a new store is opened or there is a carnival in town. The first time that it appears, people rush to see what it is announcing; however, after a week or a month of seeing it, it becomes old news and no one is interested anymore. If the star hovered over Bethlehem for three years, the king would have known where the baby was abiding and would have killed him. I was taught that the star hovered over the baby for three days, long enough for the Wise Men to find the baby and long enough for Mary to recover from his birth, so they could escape into Egypt. The presents from the three wise men are represented by the gifts that we shower on our children. Sure we can buy them something each day, but this day; Christmas day is special and they deserve something special in memory of our Lord. Let me tell you my story, Debbie. My father came from a poor family. My Grandfather left when my father was in high school. My Grandmother would sew, to put food on the table. When they could not afford food, they would stand in soup lines for hours, just to get something to eat. They lived in a rented garage that did not have any inside dividing walls. The rooms were divided by sheets and there was one light in the middle of the garage that was used for studying, cooking, and sewing. My father worked at a grocery store after school and he would bring home the damaged items, that no one would buy, and the bones from the butcher shop so grandma could make soup that would last for two or three meals. My father received a football scholarship to a good college where he met Mr. Hughes who was studying law and he met my mother who was a cheerleader. There was a war back then and my father and Mr. Hughes were shipped over seas to fight the enemy. This is where they met Mr. Blackstone. "

"That is fine and dandy, Kay. What does this have to do with Christmas," smarted off Debbie.

"I listened to you tell your life's story so I would appreciate it if you would listen to mine," scolded Kay.

"I like her stories, mommy," David commented.

"Thank you David. I will try to make it short and condensed," Kay continued, "Mr. Blackstone use to tell me the story of their Christmas that was over seas during the fighting. He said that all the fighting would stop on Christmas day. Not one bomb was dropped or shot was fired during that time. He said they could hear the other troops singing Christmas songs from the dug outs. When Christmas was over the following day, the fighting resumed. When the war was over, Daddy, Mr. Hughes, and Mr. Blackstone became forever friends. My father worked for Mr. Blackstone until he was able to purchase his own company. My Grandmother bought war bonds when she could afford them, then later, she invested her money buying stocks in my father's company. Her foresight made her a wealthy woman. They worked hard to accomplish their wealth; but, even when they were poor, they never forgot God and always celebrated Christmas. When we were able to move to a better neighborhood, my father taught me to always remember our humble beginnings, back when we were struggling to stay afloat. Christmas is a time for sharing with others that are less fortunate than we are and are struggling with their finances or personal problems. You said you were afraid to leave your abusive husband but you had the choice to stay or leave. I was not given a choice. My husband married me for his love of money. He buried me alive in a bomb shelter in my own back yard and then tried to cover it up with a swimming pool. I never stopped believing in God and I was able to escape a horrible fate."

"That is horrible," agreed Debbie.

"When I think of that precious baby's humble beginnings, lying in a manger, and I remember the pain and torment that he suffered to save us, nothing will ever stop me from celebrating Christmas. I know I have so much to be grateful for," cried Kay.

"I know you are a religious lady, but I think Christmas is over advertised," remarked Debbie.

"Over advertised," Kay repeated in a low tone.

"Ladies, we have one hour and thirty minutes before we reach Oklahoma City," said Officer Cox. "I think we need to change the subject before this gets out of hand."

"No, since I had to listen to her for four hours while riding to Albuquerque, New Mexico, without interruptions, she is going to listen to me for a few minutes," argued Kay. "I understand where you are coming from when you see all of the Christmas sale signs, the store decorations, and parades; but if it was not for Jesus' birth over two thousand years ago, there would be no Christmas or a reason to celebrate the season. There would be no forgiveness of sins or resurrection day. God wants us to remember his son in joyful celebration so we can celebrate with the angels when we die."

"How can you say there is a God after being buried alive?" cried Debbie. "Where is he? Why has he forgotten me?"

"God has not forgotten you, Debbie. Look where you are now," said Kay. "Just because you do not see God does not mean he is not near. God is…."

"Let me explain it, Kay," interrupted Officer Cox. "God is like the sun in the sky. When a cloud covers the sun that does not mean that the sun is gone forever. It is hidden behind the clouds. When the clouds move, the sun is right where it always was. That is God. He is here and will make his appearance when he is ready."

Kay could not believe her ears.

She whispered, "You were listening."

"Did I explain it right?" asked Officer Cox.

"Wonderfully," replied Kay. "I could not have explained it any better than that."

Debbie looked at her children and thought to herself, "How strange it was when she met Officer Cox right after she had prayed for help.

Now, she is in a better place with nicer people. Maybe she was wrong about God and they were right."

The sun set behind them was beautiful as it covered the sky with orange and purple colors. Kay remembered her stay at the Florida hotel and how she watched the sun disappear into the ocean.

"Can you hear it sizzle," she thought quietly. "Yes, daddy, I hear it."

They arrived at The Skirvin Hotel at10:15 p.m. Kay went to check in while Officer Cox, Debbie, and the children waited for her in the car. She returned with a bellman and luggage cart to take their baggage to a suite on the tenth floor. The children could not believe how beautiful the hotel was and they were excited to see their room.

"This is better than the circus," remarked David.

Kay gave the money for the tip to Kelly Ann so she could give it to the bellman. Kay did not want to disturb her mother until the morning so she asked Officer Cox not to call. Once the door was closed and locked, Kay asked Debbie to select a room for her and her children to sleep in.

"Any room is fine with me, Kay," said Debbie. "May I borrow something to sleep in?"

"No," said Officer Cox. "I have some clothes for you and your children in these bags. There should be something for you to sleep in without borrowing from Kay or using my shirt."

Debbie was overwhelmed by all the nice things that were purchased for her and her children. She hugged Kay and Officer Cox with appreciation. Her children were yelling, "Look at this mommy".

Officer Cox never had seen children so happy before over tooth brushes and underwear. Kay helped them carry their new clothes to their room and closed the door so they could have some privacy. As she was walking away, Kelly Ann came running out of the room, hugged Kay around the waist and said, "This is the best road trip ever. Good night."

Kay and Officer Cox went to their separate rooms.

"See you in the morning, Kay," Officer Cox yawned. "That was one long drive."

"You did good, big boy," smiled Kay. "I bet mother is going to be so surprise to see us in the morning."

# THE CHRISTMAS LIST

## CHAPTER XII

Kay woke up early as usual and she read her Bible. After she dressed, she went to the lobby to inquire which room her mother was staying in. She explained that she was her daughter and wanted to surprise her. At first, she was going to hurry to her mother's room, burst in, and yell surprise but since they were hiding from Leonard she decide that might scare her and Officer Rue might shoot her. She decided she would knock on the door and bring her mother and Carolyn some breakfast. Kay knocked several times before her mother opened the door.

"Good morning," smiled Kay as she walked into the room unexpected. "I brought you and Carolyn some breakfast."

"Kay," whispered Marie. "I thought you were going to call us when you arrived."

"We traveled all day, for twelve hours to get here, because Officer Cox missed his turn in Denver. You know how stubborn he can be and he would not make a U-turn to get on the right interstate." explained Kay as she glared at another body in the bed thinking it was Carolyn. "We were so tired when we arrived that we decided to see you in the morning."

Kay walked over to the other bed and sat next to the person she thought was Carolyn and said, "Wake up sleepy head. We have a lot of work to do today."

"Kay," said Marie. "I have something I need to tell you. It may come as a shock, dear, but I..."

Kay noticed a man's hairy foot hanging out of the covers on the bed. She looked at her mother and quickly jumped off the bed.

She suddenly realized that her mother did not hug her when she entered the room which alerted her that something was wrong.

"Run mother," Kay yelled as she grabbed the lamp off the table to use as a weapon to bash the head of whoever it was in her mother's bed. "I will protect you."

"No, Kay," yelled Marie to stop her from hurting Evan. "That is Evan. We got married."

Kay replaced the lamp on the night stand and uncovered Mr. Hughes' face. Marie waved her hand at Kay to show her the beautiful wedding ring. Kay was embarrassed. She walked over to her mother, hugged, and kissed her.

"I am so happy for you, Mother," she cried. "I will come back when you are ready for visitors. Where is Carolyn's room?"

"It is across the hall," answered Marie. "You are not up-set or mad at me?"

"I wish I could have been present," replied Kay. "After all, I am your only daughter."

Kay returned to her room and sat on the sofa to read the hotel tourist magazine. Debbie saw the light on from under her door so she slid carefully out of the bed, not to wake the children, to join Kay in the sitting area.

"Good Morning, Kay," greeted Debbie. "How did you sleep?"

"I was so tired that I think I fell asleep before my head reached the pillows," replied Kay. "How are the children?"

"They are sleeping like babies in their new pajamas," answered Debbie. "I wanted to thank you for all you and Officer Cox have done for us. I never dreamed that I would be sleeping in a luxury hotel like this one."

"You are welcome. I am glad we could help you," smiled Kay. "Where do those relatives live that we are supposed to take you to stay with?"

"It is my mother and father. They live on North Luther Road next to a big guest ranch," she said. "I can telephone them to come get me so you will not have to drive out there. I have not seen my parents since I got married. They will be delighted to know that I am going to get divorced because they never liked my husband."

"I do not mind driving you out there," said Kay.

"You have done enough for us," thanked Debbie. "I will never be able to repay you."

"You just did," smiled Kay as she hugged Debbie. "What would you like for breakfast?'

"Anything is fine with me but the children will want to eat pancakes," alleged Debbie. "I will call my parents while you order breakfast."

Kay was wondering why Officer Cox had not joined her and Debbie in the sitting area. She knocked on his bedroom door but there was no reply. She opened the door to find the bed untouched and no one was in the room.

"He must be down stairs talking to Officer Rue," thought Kay. "I will call Carolyn and ask her to join us for breakfast.

Kay picked up the room phone to contact Carolyn and over heard Debbie talking to her parents. She was surprised by the tone of her mother's voice and her tense attitude.

Debbie's mother asked, "Do you have those snotty nose children with you? I am surprised you would call me for help."

"I am sorry mother, but I did not have any where else to go," replied Debbie. "I could not let him hurt my children. They are your grandchildren. Most grandparents want to be with their grandchildren."

"I am not like most grandparents," the wicked mother said. "Your father and I are going on a cruise to Jamaica, leaving on Tuesday; where are you going to stay?"

"I can watch the house for you mother," cried Debbie. "I promise the children will not break anything. When I find a job, I will move out. I need your help."

"What kind of job?" remarked her mother. "All you know how to do is wash dishes and clean houses. You can not make enough money doing that to support you and those children."

"Mother, I am sorry I bothered you," cried Debbie. "I will find someone else to help me. I hope you have a safe cruise."

Debbie ended the conversation, went into her bathroom so her children could not hear her cry, and she prayed, "Lord what am I going to do? Where am I going to go? Please help me and my children."

Kay could not believe Debbie's mother was so mean. Those children were very disciplined and polite. Any grandparent would be happy to see those children. Kay ordered breakfast for ten people because she knew when Officer Cox returned he was going to be hungry. Debbie returned to sit with Kay and tell her about her parents' plans to come and take her home with them. Kay could see how painful it was for Debbie to perjure herself.

"My parents are going on a cruise and they want me to take care of things while they are away," fibbed Debbie. "After the children get dressed and eat, we are going to take a taxi to their home. My parents love being around my children."

Kay could not stand it. She knew Officer Cox was going to tell her to stop hiring hard luck cases but this lady (like Carolyn) deserved a chance at a better life and not to be beaten because the beer was warm. Debbie finally ended her fabricated story and decided it was time to go back to her room to get dressed to take her children on a taxi ride to nowhere.

Kay lightly grabbed Debbie's arm to stop her and she asked, "Debbie, how would you like to work for me? I will have to start you at a trainee level and you will make minimum wage but your salary will be steady. That will mean you and your children would have to transfer to Cortland and rearrange your lives. Plus, you will see me on a regular basis. I know you want to help your mother but I need someone now that I can depend on. Would you be interested in the job?"

Debbie's eyes filled with tears as she realized that once again her prayers had been answered. She hugged Kay around the neck and wept.

"Thank you, Kay," she cried. "You are a life saver."

"Now, Debbie, life savers can only be found on cruises. Does this mean you will take the job?" asked Kay as she wiped tears from her eyes.

"Yes, yes, I want the job," answered Debbie. "Now I need to get me a good lawyer so I can get a divorce from that mad man."

"Lawyer," remembered Kay. "I was supposed to call my mother. You get dressed and I will introduce you to my new family."

"Your new family," Debbie said puzzled.

"Yes," replied Kay. "I can not tell you anything about them until they tell me what is going on."

There was a knock on the door and Debbie said she would answer it. Kay stopped her because she did not have a description of Leonard and it might be him. Kay looked through the peephole to spy her mother and Mr. Hughes.

"Good morning again, mother," greeted Kay. "I would like to introduce you to Debbie Beaufort. Debbie, this is my mother and my step father, Mr. Hughes."

"Hello," said Debbie. "If you will excuse me I am going to get dressed."

Debbie returned to her bedroom to wake the children so they could all eat together. Kay invited her mother and new husband in to join them for breakfast.

"Where is Officer Cox?" asked Marie. "I am surprised that he is not at the table eating."

"He must be in Officer Rue's room discussing police matters," assumed Kay. "He never slept in his room and he was gone when I woke up. Now, will you tell me what has been happening since I have been in Colorado?"

Before Marie could start talking, there was another knock on the door. Kay, once again, looked through the peephole to see Carolyn and Officer Rue at the door. She invited them in to join them for breakfast and to listen to her mother's fabulous romantic wedding story. While Marie was gearing up to discuss her wedding day, there was another knock on the door.

"This is becoming Grand Central Station," remarked Kay as she peered through the peephole for the third time to see room service with the breakfast.

The waiter arranged the food on the dining table that could seat six people for a meal. The rest of the drinks and the pastries were on the cart to be served when requested. Kay asked Carolyn and Officer

Rue to eat with her on the sofa so there would be room at the table for Debbie and her children.

"What children?" asked Marie.

"I will tell you about them after I hear about you and Mr. Hughes getting married. Was it romantic?" asked Kay.

"It was like a moment out of a fairy tale," smiled Marie as she kissed Evan. "He proposed on a boat going down the canal at sun set. I was totally caught off guard."

"I wish I could have been there," whined Kay.

"We are going to have another ceremony for you, dear, when we get home," said Marie. "I would never leave my baby out of anything."

"Where is Officer Cox?" asked Carolyn. "I figured he would be the first one at the table."

"I do not know," confessed Kay. "I thought he was with you, Officer Rue."

"I have not seen him," alleged Officer Rue stuffing his mouth with a hot butter crescent roll. "Maybe he is still asleep. Have you checked his room?"

"Yes," admitted Kay. "His bed has not been slept in. Do you think he is in trouble?"

"No, he is probably handling some police business down stairs so we would not interrupt him," replied Officer Rue.

"He is missing a great breakfast," commented Carolyn. "Now tell us about the children."

"While we were in Colorado, we met a battered wife and her children," explained Kay. "We could not leave her in Colorado to get beaten again so we brought her and her children with us. Wait until you meet these kids; they are so well mannered and polite. You are going to love them."

"Where is she going from here?" asked Carolyn.

"Well, it is a long story and I will share it with you when we are alone," said Kay. "She is coming home with us."

"With us?" whined Carolyn. "She does not have any where else to go?"

"No she does not," glared Kay at Carolyn. "You of all people should understand what it is like to have no where to run or no place to stay after being used. She is just like you and me; a lady scorned, abused, and unloved. Since the Lord has blessed me, I wanted to help her."

"I am sorry Kay," apologized Carolyn. "You are right. If I had been there, I would have done the same thing."

"Why are you a lady scorned, Carolyn?" asked Dennis.

Kay remembered that she and Carolyn had never told anyone about Lover Boy so she told Officer Rue, who was ready to kill anyone that hurt his sister; that her boy friend had left town after going on their first date and she never heard from him again. It was a little lie that had a lot of truth to it.

"He probably was not able to find you to ask you on a second date, sis," he said optimistically. "You have lived in so many different places since you have been hiding from Leonard."

"I never thought of that," agreed Kay as she winked at Carolyn to secure her secret. "That is probably what happened to him."

A contented Debbie and her children entered the room to have breakfast with the others. David and Kelly Ann hurried over to Kay and gave her a wonderful morning hug.

"Good morning, Miss Kay," said Kelly Ann. "Mommy said we are going to live with you in Tartland. Did they name that place Tartland because there is a lot of candy there?"

"No sweetie," smiled Kay as she hugged both of the children. "You are going to Cortland."

"I told you it was too good to be true," scolded David.

Everyone laughed at David's remark. Kay stood up to introduced Debbie and her children to everyone in the room. She led the children to the table to enjoy their breakfast. The waiter, who laughed at David's remark, too; served the children hot pancakes covered with hot maple syrup.

"I am glad we are going to be with you, Miss Kay because our grandmother hates us," said David.

"David, do not talk with your mouth full," reprimanded Debbie. "Eat your breakfast."

"I am sure your grandmother loves you," smiled Marie.

"No she doesn't," said Kelly Ann. "She…"

"Would you like some pastries," Kay interrupted Kelly Ann so

Debbie's secret would not be public. "When you get through eating I will tell you about a plane trip we are going to take."

"I have never been on a plane," confessed David. "Where is OC?"

"Who is OC?" asked Marie.

"This is what I call Officer Cox so no one around us will know he is an officer," answered Kay. "I am getting worried about him. This is not like him to miss a meal."

"Maybe he is out there fighting the bad guys," remarked David. "He looks like a superhero to me."

Officer Rue told Kay that he would check in the lobby to see if anyone fitting his description had left the hotel. Kay suggested that he ask to see the security tape from last night which would show Officer Cox leaving if he left the hotel. Officer Rue said that was a good idea and left the suite to track down their missing friend. As he was waiting in front of one of the four elevators, the elevator to the left of him opened and Officer Cox accompanied by an Oklahoma City sheriff, stepped out of the elevator, carrying bags and boxes of pictures and papers from Susan's home. He was dirty and exhausted from being up all night looking for evidence at Susan's house that might guide him in Leonard's direction. He handed Officer Rue the portable telephone briefcase to carry for him.

"I was looking for you, Officer Cox. Everyone has been worried since you did not show up for breakfast," welcomed Officer Rue.

"Is everyone in the suite?" asked Officer Cox.

"Yes, we are having breakfast," answered Officer Rue.

"Good. I am starving," said Officer Cox. "By the way, this is Sheriff Owens from the Oklahoma City Police Department. I have a key to the room in my coat pocket so you can open the door for us."

Kay was telling everyone about the beautiful sights they passed as they traveled to Oklahoma from New Mexico. She said that there is a place called "Taos, New Mexico" that is the residence of the oldest established Indian population in the United States.

"I want to return there because the gas station cashier in Albuquerque, New Mexico said it was a good place to sight see, shop, and study history. He said the hotels are built like an Indian village but have all the modern conveniences," informed Kay. "He said that Taos is the best place to purchase authentic hand made Indian art works and jewelry made out of Spanish silver and American turquoise mined from that area."

Mr. Hughes was going to ask Kay if there was an airport located there so they could fly there on their next vacation but his question was interrupted when Officer Rue opened the door to allow Officer Cox and Sheriff Owens to enter the suite. Kelly Ann ran from the breakfast table and hugged Officer Cox around the legs.

She said, "We thought you were fighting some bad guys."

Officer Cox was surprised and taken by the affection shown from this child he had only known for two days. He placed the box on the coffee table, knelt down next to Kelly Ann, and he gave her an affectionate fatherly hug. She returned to the table to finish her breakfast with her brother. Kay was not so affectionate but was mad because he did not leave a note or tell her where he was going.

"Where have you been," she scolded him. "You told me to leave a note or tell someone when I left the premises. I have been worried sick about you."

Kay suddenly noticed some blood on his shirt as he removed his coat.

"Carolyn, I need your medical bag," ordered Kay.

"I am on it," replied Carolyn as she ran out of the suite to get her medicines and bandages.

"How bad are you hurt?" asked Kay as she led him over to the sofa.

"I think that is blood from that gun shot wound I received in Colorado," replied Officer Cox as he sat on the sofa. "I might have pulled a stitch or two."

"I told you he was a superhero," shouted David as he ran to see Officer Cox's wound.

Kelly Ann began to cry, "I don't want him to die Mommy. I love him."

Once more, Officer Cox was moved by that little girl's remarks.

He said, "They can not kill a superhero, Kelly Ann. I will be all right. Please stop crying."

"I think we need to take him in the bedroom so Carolyn can have more privacy," suggested Officer Rue. "I will help you with him Kay."

Officer Rue and Kay assisted Officer Cox to his bedroom and David followed as his guard.

He said, "Don't worry OC, I have your back covered."

"David," yelled Debbie. "Get back over here and eat your breakfast."

"I will later, mother," said the brave little man. "OC needs me to protect him."

Carolyn arrived with her medical bag and hurried into Officer Cox's room. Everyone in the room was asked to leave so she could evaluate the seriousness of the injury. David started to cry when Carolyn asked him to leave.

"I will be all right, little buddy," smiled OC. "You can stand outside my door and guard my room."

"Yes, sir," agreed David as he wiped his nose on his sleeve.

While Carolyn doctored Officer Cox, Kay was getting bombarded with questions about the shooting in Colorado. The waiter asked Sheriff Owens if he would like to have something to drink.

"Some coffee would be nice," answered the Sheriff as he placed the second box next to the one on the table.

"I am sorry, sir," apologized Kay. "I forgot my manners for a moment when I spotted that blood on OC's shirt. My name is Kay Lytle and this is my family. Would you please join us for breakfast and tell us what happened last night."

"Yes, by all means," said Mr. Hughes as he stood up to give the sheriff his seat. "My name is Evan Hughes and this is my wife, Mrs. Hughes."

Marie looked around to see who Evan was talking about because this was the first time she had ever been referred to as Mrs. Hughes. She smiled at Evan and shook the Sheriff's hand.

"I am pleased to meet you sir," she said. "You are welcome to call me Marie."

The maître d', who was attentive to all their dining requests, poured the sheriff a cup of coffee and served him some hot pancakes and eggs. Kay consoled Kelly Ann and told her that OC would be a brand new man when Carolyn got through with him.

"I like the old man," she cried. "Miss Kay, may I sit with you."

"Sure," smiled Kay. "First, let me get one of those pastries and a glass of milk."

"Don't forget the ice," reminded the sweet five year old child.

"You can ask the waiter to fix that for me," Kay said.

The waiter fixed a glass of ice milk for Kelly Ann while the others waited impatiently for the sheriff to finish his breakfast and tell them where he and Officer Cox were last night and what secret information was harbored in those boxes. The waiter asked everyone if they were finished so he could clear the table.

Everyone was satisfied with their breakfast but Kay asked him not to remove anything from the room because Office Cox had not eaten and she was not sure if Carolyn was finished. The waiter said he had to report to the kitchen but would return later to clean the room. Officer Rue suggested that the waiter stay until he was informed about the situation and told not to repeat anything that he had seen. The waiter telephoned the kitchen and told them he would be down as soon as he was finished serving his guests.

Carolyn asked Officer Cox to remove his shirt so she could see how bad the wound was. Officer Cox slowly and painfully removed his shirt to reveal a blood soaked bandage on his shoulder. She carefully removed the nasty blood stained bandages to find a small gun shot wound that had been stitched up on his shoulder. One stitch was missing that caused it to bleed. She poured some hydrogen peroxide on the wound to kill any bacteria that might be growing on it and she cleaned the injured area with a soft white cotton ball. Next she applied an antibiotic and pain relieving ointment with a cotton tip swab and covered the wound with butterfly tapes. She wrapped his entire shoulder with a light bandage and secured it with surgical tape.

"I hope I did not hurt you, Officer Cox. How in the world did you get shot?" she asked as she cleaned the bed area of all the blood covered bandages and repacked her medical supplies in her bag.

Officer Cox had fallen asleep during Carolyn's professional medical repairs to his body. She covered him with the comforter on the bed and turned out the light as she left the room so he could sleep in peace. David asked if he could sit by his bed so no one would disturb him. Carolyn suggested that it would be better to guard his door so no one could enter his room while he was sleeping.

"How is he doing?" asked Kay who was very concerned about her hero.

"He is a big boy and he will be fine," assured Carolyn. "It is a miracle the bullet did not hit any of his major organs."

"The man that shot him was the man I met on the flight home from Colorado. Do you remember I told you he had tattoos of snakes all over his left arm?"

"I hate snakes," added Kelly Ann who was sitting on Kay's lap.

"Yes, I remember you mentioning him," answered Carolyn. "Why did he shoot Officer Cox?"

"He and another man kidnapped me because Leonard promised them lots of money," explained Kay.

"Kidnapped," exclaimed Marie. "You did not tell me you were kidnapped."

"I have not had time, with you getting married and Officer Cox missing, so much going on around us; I just have not had time to tell you anything," said Kay.

Sheriff Owens burped very loud surprising everyone. They all looked in his direction and the children laughed.

"Excuse me," he said. "The food is delicious. May I have another cup of coffee?"

The waiter poured him another cup of hot coffee and Sheriff Owens thanked him.

"This has to be the best breakfast I have had in a long time," complimented Sheriff Owens. "I need to come here more often. Did they arrest the men that kidnapped you and the man that shot Officer Cox, young lady?"

"No, sir," answered Kay. "Leonard killed the tattooed man named Clifford Barker and I hired the other man named Mike Lambie to be my body guard and pilot to assist Officer Cox."

The conversation was becoming extremely scary for Debbie's children to be listening to, so she asked them to go to the bedroom with her to watch their favorite cartoon program.

"I have to stay here and guard my friend," argued the stubborn but brave eight year old superhero. "I am not leaving."

"Can I guard him for you while you take a short break?" asked

Officer Rue who was using reverse psychology on the child. "I promise I will not let anyone past this door unless I talk to you first."

David thought that was a good idea because he needed to use the bathroom in the worst way. He and his sister followed their mother into their bedroom.

The conversation continued with the sheriff asking Kay, "Why would you hire a known criminal to protect you?"

"I know it sounds crazy; but Mike is an expert with a gun, mainly rifles, and he could have killed OC by shooting him in the head but he did not do that," answered Kay.

"That answers my question about the gun shot wound," interrupted Carolyn. "I am sorry, Kay, please continue."

"Leonard shot Mike then threw his body in the trunk with me to die," said Kay. "If it had not been for Mike, I might be dead now. We shared body heat to keep warm and we talked about the Ten Commandments to keep from falling asleep and freezing to death. When they pulled us up the side of the cliff, Mike gave me his blanket to stay warm."

"I thought you were in the trunk of a car?" inquired Mr. Hughes. "I am so confused."

"I was in the trunk until Mike kicked the back seat out," said Kay. "Leonard pushed the car over a cliff. It lodged in between some huge snow covered Aspen trees. I pulled Mike into the back seat with me then a group of Golden, Colorado policemen, led by Officer Cox, rescued us from falling over a cliff and pulled both of us to safety."

"Oh my baby," cried Marie as she wrapped her arms around Kay and cried on her shoulder. "I was here having the time of my life while you were being murdered."

"I am fine, mother," reassured Kay. "I was worried about you and the others at Susan's birthday party. I am so glad she did not kill you."

"Ladies, ladies," said Sheriff Owens. "Please, I want to know what happened to the shooter."

"He and his family are staying in Golden, Colorado under police security until he is well and able to fly to Cortland to work for me," answered Kay. "Do you have any more questions, Sheriff?'

"Not at the moment," replied Sheriff Owens.

"I think everyone in this room wants to know where you and Officer Cox were last night and what is in these boxes?" asked Kay.

The room was as quiet as a morgue with everyone focusing their attention on Sheriff Owens and his answer.

He responded saying, "Last night, Officer Cox asked me to come get him at a local department store. He told me he needed a search warrant so he could legally enter a home that he thought might aid him in a case he was working on. It took three hours to cut through the red tape to get the warrant for him but after he made two telephone calls, one to Lieutenant Gorman and one to Lieutenant Blackshear, the judge agreed to issue the search warrant. Before we entered the house, he informed the forensic workers about Leonard's love for explosives and asked them to be very careful while walking around in the house because there might be trip wires attached to hidden explosive devices in some of the rooms. Since explosives were involved, I contacted the bomb squad."

"Were there any bombs?" asked Kay.

"No, the house was tagged clean for us to continue our search," answered Sheriff Owens. "We searched both floors and all the rooms in the house for anything that might assist in detecting Leonard's location. We were about to leave when Officer Cox asked if there was a storm cellar on the premises. The bomb squad was called out again and we had to wait another hour until they tagged the storm cellar clean to search. That man is stubborn but it paid off. We found all the information we needed to incarcerate Susan and her family."

"I see only two boxes," said Marie. "Surely she had more information on her family than what is in these two boxes."

"There were lots of boxes in that storm cellar," confessed the sheriff. "But…"

He was interrupted by Officer Cox entering the room.

"The bomb squad was tired and they got careless and missed a bomb," Officer Cox continued the story for the sheriff. "I was careful when removing the first box from the shelter. I had a feeling (he looked at Kay) or a scent in the air that told me there was a bomb hidden somewhere on the premises."

Kay knew what he was talking about when he mentioned scent. She also knew Leonard was not going to leave anything behind that would incriminate him.

"When I moved the second box, I must have ignited the bomb because as soon as I was away from the storm cellar, carrying the box to the car, the shelter exploded into flames. Fortunately, there was no one in the shelter and no one was killed. The force from the blast caused me to fall and I think that is how I tore my stitches open. Is there any food left, I am hungry."

Debbie's bedroom door opened and David ran out to greet Officer Cox. Officer Cox was embarrassed as he hugged him around the waist.

"I knew you would be all right," smiled David. "You were on my list."

"I have something for you in one of those boxes," said Officer Cox as he led the clinging eight year old to the sofa to give him a present. "I thought you might like to have one of these but you have to promise me that you will never use it on your family, friends, or animals or I will arrest you."

"What is it OC?" David said excitedly.

Officer Cox reached into the box he was carrying earlier to retrieve a sling shot. It had small rubber pebbles and some red and white paper targets to shoot at all wrapped in one package.

"This was on my list, too," smiled David.

"What list?" Kay asked as Kelly Ann and Debbie entered the door.

"What list, David?" Debbie asked her son.

"My Christmas list," replied David as he pulled a piece of paper out of his pocket. "See, I wrote OC on my list. Kay is right, mommy. You need to make a list."

Officer Cox handed the list to Kay then he asked Kelly Ann where her list was.

"I am only five years old, OC" answered Kelly Ann. "I don't know how to write."

Everyone laughed at Kelly Ann's answer which embarrassed her. Debbie picked up her daughter and carried her to the sofa to be with her brother. Officer Cox handed Kelly Ann a baby doll complete with a change of clothes.

"Thank you OC," she smiled and kissed him on the nose. "I will love you forever."

Officer Cox was embarrassed this time and everyone laughed at him.

"What is on the list, Kay?" asked Carolyn.

They all listened in humble silence as Kay read David's list. She smiled and patted David on the head.

Then Kay read the list out loud, "God, please give me a new home for OC, Mommy, Kelly Ann, and Kay to live in and a sling shot to keep them safe. That's all I want. The Christmas list was signed, 'David'."

# THE DIARY

## CHAPTER XIII

Carolyn finished her Breakfast while Officer Cox began his. The waiter served him hot bacon, pancakes, eggs, sliced tomatoes, hash brown potatoes, a bowl of fresh fruit, and several pastries. He drank three glasses of orange juice. David sat next to him and decided he would eat another pancake with syrup.

"You sure eat a lot," remarked David.

"Crime fighters need a lot of energy," spoke the waiter as he poured Officer Cox another glass of orange juice which emptied his flask. "Can I get you anything else, sir?"

"No, thank you, this was enough," smiled Officer Cox.

The sheriff, Marie, and Kay explored the two boxes on the table to see if there were any clues to where Leonard might be hiding. There were some old mementos, vacation group photos of the family and holiday pictures (some of the pictures were framed), bill receipts, letters, and a bank account ledger. At the bottom of the second box was Susan's daily diary with entries written on each page.

"Bingo," shouted Kay, holding the diary in the air. "I found the mother load. It is Susan's diary."

"Is this going to be graphic?" asked Debbie who was ready to take her children back into their room to watch television.

"I do not know," said Kay. "I have not opened it. It is locked."

Sheriff Owens pulled his monogrammed Swiss Knife out of his pocket and asked to see the diary. He cut off the material connected to the lock and returned the unlocked diary to Kay. She thumbed through the pages and read a few lines.

"This is pretty explicit, Debbie," Kay alleged. "You might not want your children to hear some of this stuff."

Debbie asked her children to follow her to their room. The waiter suggested that she take them down to the heated pool area for a swim.

"We do not know how to swim," said Kelly Ann.

"There is a wading pool with a slide," informed the waiter.

"We do not have any swimsuits," said Debbie. "We left with nothing but the clothes on our backs. I know the children will want to go swimming and it would be cruel to keep them out of the water. We will be fine watching television."

"Come with me, Debbie," requested Mr. Hughes who was not interested in Susan's memorabilia. "There are a variety of stores located in and near the hotel. We can buy those children swimsuits. This will allow us to converse on matters concerning your nuptials."

"What are nuptials?" asked Debbie.

"You have to forgive, Mr. Hughes," informed Carolyn. "He is a lawyer. A nuptial means your marriage. He wants to help you with your 'D I V O R C E'."

Carolyn spelled the word so the children would not understand what she was talking about. She did not realize that the children were more interested in the toys Officer Cox had given them.

"Come on children and put your shoes on. We are going on a walk with Mr. Hughes," directed Debbie.

Both, being obedient children, went to the room, put on their old shoes, and followed their mother with Mr. Hughes on a shopping excursion they would never forget. Officer Cox asked Officer Rue to accompany them as a safety precaution.

The waiter asked Officer Cox if he was finished so he could clear the table and take the dirty dishes to the kitchen. Officer Cox informed him, that it was important for his safety and the other guests in the hotel, not to mention anything he had seen happen in their suite.

"I have never seen any celebrities or been here when something historical happened at this hotel," confessed the maître d'. "This is the most interesting room I have ever served in my fifteen years on the job. I will keep my mouth shut if you would allow me to return and help with the investigation."

"Anyone that has tried to help us is either in the hospital recovering or dead," alleged Kay. "I would hate for anything to happen to you."

"It would be my honor to help," said the waiter. "After I saw what you did for that battered mother, I would walk a mile for you. My mother was battered and had four children. No one offered to help her and she died trying to make enough money to feed us. Please let me help."

Kay looked at Sheriff Owens and then she looked at Officer Cox and said, "It is Ok with me if it is OK with you. He might see something important that we might miss because we are tired. Like the bomb squad did."

Officer Cox tipped the waiter with a hundred dollar bill and said, "Come back if you can."

He was so excited with the tip and Officer Cox's answer that he almost dropped a handful of empty dirty plates in Officer Cox's lap. He cleared and cleaned the table, then left some of the fresh fruit for the children to snack on when they returned. He did not realize that Officer Cox would probably eat the fruit before the children ever got to see it. He excused himself from the room and was returning to the kitchen on the first floor when Carolyn ran behind him and yelled for him to stop. She was carrying the blood stained bandages in a bag from Officer Cox's bathroom.

"Will you please burn these so no one can see them?" asked Carolyn. "If anyone sees this they are going to start asking dangerous questions that we do not want to answer."

The waiter took the nasty bag and shoved it under his cart.

"I feel like a FBI agent," he smiled and continued to the kitchen.

Kay and Sheriff Owens carried the two boxes of memorabilia to the table so Officer Cox would not have to leave his seat. Carolyn, Marie, Kay, and Sheriff Owens sat in the empty seats around the table. Kay dumped all of the things Susan thought were worthy of saving from the first box, onto the table. Everyone, but Kay, grabbed something and started reading. Kay was going to read her ex-mother in law's diary.

She had not read many pages when she lowered the book and said, "Oh geez. She had three sons."

"We all ready know that Kay," Carolyn confessed. "I found a picture of Leonard and his brothers at Susan's house when I went to use the ladies' room. I put it on the table next to the birthday cake when we left the party because your mother said she did not want anything that belonged to Susan near her. Here are some more pictures of her and her sons on vacation."

"I did not see a picture near the birthday cake when we were searching the house last night," said Officer Cox. "Did you see a picture next to the cake?"

Sheriff Owens nodded his head and answered, "There were no pictures next to that chocolate cake. I did notice that one piece had been served."

"Susan never got an opportunity to cut the cake," informed Marie. "After she shot herself, everyone was asked to leave."

"No, everyone was asked to leave before she shot herself because the police did not want anyone to get hurt," politely corrected Carolyn. "But she is right, the cake was never cut."

"I saw the cake last night," disputed Officer Cox. "There was one piece of cake missing."

Kay and Marie said in unison, "Leonard."

"He must have eaten a piece of his mother's last birthday day cake while he was there," Kay said. "I am glad you did not eat any of her cake, Sheriff Owens, because Leonard has an infatuation with poisons."

Sheriff Owens tugged at his shirt collar because he was going to take a piece home for himself and his wife.

Marie was examining Susan's bank account ledger and reported, "There are hundreds of huge multi-dollar deposits listed in this ledger. Underneath each big deposit there is a large withdrawal amount with an account number next to the entry. This ledger dates back several years."

"Write down some of the dates of those deposits," Kay requested. "OC, will you see if any of these dates match any of days that those ladies, like Janet Cross' sister were murdered on. There might be a pattern we can follow that will lead us to Leonard or his brothers."

Marie wrote down the dates and handed the piece of paper to Officer Cox. He asked Carolyn to get his green notebook out of his luggage and bring it to him. Carolyn handed Officer Cox the notebook and a pencil. He began looking at the information that Lieutenant Blackshear had sent him and compared the dates. Most of the deposit dates matched the week of the murders or disappearances.

"We have to go back to Susan's home," said Kay. "Susan writes about how she and two of her sons kill a girl and bury her in the storm cellar. Listen to what she writes, 'Leonard brought his next victim to the house to meet his family. She was a shy pretty girl named Carrie Right that had lots of money. Leonard had married her that day. It was sad that the first visit to my home would be her last. We had to kill her because I was careless and left a picture of Leonard's previous marriage on the dresser in my room. I will never make that mistake again. The girl recognized the lady in the picture as one of her friends that she went to college with in Colorado named, Kaylyn Cross, who recently disappeared. Who would have thought Leonard would have married a girl in Oklahoma City that was friends with his decease wife in Colorado. She would not stop screaming after I stabbed her in the back with my favorite steel pointed fingernail file. The girl fought like a lion; scratching and kicking me. She escaped my grip and she fell down stairs. Leonard and Richard rushed to my rescue. I was afraid the neighbors might hear her screaming so Richard hit her in the face until she was unconscious. Leonard wrapped her in a shower curtain and both boys carried her to the storm cellar. It took two hours for my boys to break the concrete so we could dig a hole big enough to bury that girl. They stopped to rest for a few minutes and get a drink. That girl just would not die. She must have been faking it while the boys were digging the hole because she waited until they left the cellar to free herself from the shower curtain. She was climbing out of the storm cellar when Rosie spotted her bloody face peeking out of the cellar door. Rosie ran to the shelter and pushed the stupid girl down the steps and finished what we had started and killed Carrie by cutting off her head with the shovel. Leonard and Richard buried both pieces of Carrie along with my new shower curtain in a shallow grave in my storm cellar. I was mad because

I had just bought the last shower curtain on sale and I have not been able to find another one like it'."

Kay stopped reading and lowered the diary containing the ghastly writings of an insane woman. Marie had no idea that her high school friend was capable of killing anyone until Kay read Susan's horrendous writings from the diary. There was a knock on the door that caused Marie, Carolyn, and Sheriff Owens to scream. Kay looked out the peephole as she had done many times to see the waiter standing there. Officer Cox and Sheriff Owens had their guns in their hands, ready to shoot, in case Leonard followed the waiter into the room. The waiter entered their room pushing a cart loaded with the hotel's delicacies and pastries. When he saw the guns pointed at him, he raised his hands over his head.

Sheriff Owens and OC lowered their guns and asked the man to join them.

"You will be fine," consoled Kay. "It is stress, nothing but stress and you will get use to it."

"Since you are going to be helping us, what is your name?" asked Carolyn.

"My name is Rob Garcia," he said. "I thought you might like a snack."

"After listening to that reading, I am ready for something sweet," alleged Sheriff Owens who was still having trouble buttoning his pants after eating breakfast. "Bring that cart over here."

The sheriff was about to take one of the pastries when Kay stopped him. She could smell a familiar aroma in the air.

"Where did you get this?" She asked Rob, before she would let him serve the treats to her family. She had learned to trust her nose instead of people.

"These were made fresh today, Miss," informed Rob. "They make these fresh everyday."

"Will you eat one for me?" asked Kay.

"Sure, I love this stuff," replied Rob, selecting one of the pasties to eat.

Kay handed Rob one of the pastries she had selected. Officer Cox had his gun in his hand, under the table so no one could see it, in case there was a problem with the pastries. That would mean Leonard had discovered their location.

"I can not eat this one, Miss," refused Rob.

"Why?" asked Sheriff Owens. "Give it to me and I will eat it."

"First off, we did not order this stuff," explained Kay. "Second, the waiter was too eager to join us in our investigation. Third, there may be poison in this stuff, and finally, the name printed on this hotel uniform is John not Rob. Now, eat this or I will shove it down your throat."

Officer Cox raised his gun above the table and aimed it at Rob while Sheriff Owens fumbled for his.

"First, I can not eat this one because I am allergic to nuts and second, John is Rob in Spanish," informed the liar.

"John is Juan in Spanish," Kay angrily corrected Rob. "Yo hablo en Espaniol (I speak Spanish)."

"Kay, you are frightening me and are acting irrational," said Marie. "If he was going to poison us, he would have done it this morning when we were eating breakfast. Officer Cox please put down the gun."

"He did not meet Leonard until now," argued Kay.

"Lady your mother is right," begged Rob. "This man gave me one hundred dollars as a tip so I thought I would show my appreciation and bring you these wonderful pastries as a surprise."

Kay selected a different pastry without nuts and said, "Eat this one. It does not have any nut."

"Young lady, I tend to believe Rob, you are acting crazy," said Sheriff Owens as he grabbed a pastry and put it in his mouth.

Kay slapped the sheriff on the back causing him to spit the pastry across the table. That distraction gave Rob time to dash for the door. Officer Cox did not hesitate and shot him in the leg. Kay handed the sheriff a glass of water to wash out his mouth. Officer Cox hurried to Rob and put his foot on his back to hold him to the floor. Carolyn rushed to the telephone to call the front desk for help. Kay took her screaming mother into her bedroom to try to calm her down.

"How much did he pay you?" asked Officer Cox, aiming the gun at Rob's head.

"I don't know what you crazy people are talking about," Rob squealed like a pig. "I was trying to help."

"I will put the next bullet in your head if you do not start talking now," demanded Officer Cox as he cocked his gun, ready to fire.

Sheriff Owens put handcuffs on Rob. Carolyn said that the security people were on their way.

"You are going to spend a long time in jail if you do not talk," said Officer Cox.

"OK, I met this man in the lobby that showed me a picture of you and five hundred dollars," he confessed. "He gave me the money to bring this tray of pastries to your room. He said it was his mother's birthday present and he wanted it to be a surprise. I did not know there was poison in them."

"Then why didn't you eat one?" asked Officer Cox. "There were no nuts on that second pastry. I thought you said you wanted to help us because your mother was abused."

"I did not give him your room number, I swear," cried Rob.

"You did not have to," said Officer Cox as he pulled Rob's wallet out of his back pants' pocket. "He already knows where we are."

Carolyn opened the door to allow the hotel security people to enter and arrest Rob. Officer Cox searched his wallet for his real identity and spotted the five one hundred dollar bills. He removed one hundred dollars. He also noticed an expired green card working permit and handed the wallet to the sheriff.

"That is my money," yelled the illegal assassin.

"I did not tip you so you could come back to kill me," Officer Cox said in a low voice of authority. "Take that man to jail."

"Sir, he is bleeding and needs to go to the hospital for first aid treatment," said the hotel security guard.

"I am a nurse," alleged Carolyn. "Let me look at it."

Carolyn looked at the leg that had blood oozing from a small freshly made gun shot wound.

She said, "Yes he is bleeding so take him to jail."

Kay was able to calm her mother so that she stopped screaming. Carolyn told Kay that Officer Cox asked the policeman to take the pastries to the police department to be examined for poison.

"I am so glad those children were not here because they would have been poisoned," said Carolyn.

Kay's eyes looked wild as she could see the fear overwhelming her mother. She knew exactly what Marie was thinking. Kay hurried into the other room where Officer Cox was explaining to the duty Officer what had happened.

"The children," were the only words Kay had to say and Officer Cox knew immediately that Mr. Hughes, Debbie, and the Children were in danger. He asked the policeman to telephone the station for some back up assistance to help him search for their friends who were shopping. The Sheriff asked Officer Cox to stay with Kay and her family since Leonard knew what he looked like. He would help search for the children and the others.

"How did that murderer find us?" cried Marie.

"He must have recognized me when I was at Susan's home and followed me here," said Officer Cox. "I am sorry. I thought I was being careful."

Marie cried angrily. "Next time I tell you to shoot him, you better do it. My Evan is out there unprotected."

"He is not unprotected," said Officer Rue as he opened the door to let the happy shoppers enter.

"I saw them coming into the hotel and brought them straight up in the elevator," exclaimed Sheriff Owens.

Carolyn dropped a sofa cushion over the blood stain on the floor so the children would not notice it. The children ran to Officer Cox to tell him all about their adventure. Marie hurried to caress Evan and kissed him several times.

"I need to go shopping more often," he said, unaware of the excitement that had taken place while he was gone. "You did not need to send the Sheriff after us. I was not going to spend all my money."

"Someone dropped their candy," said Kelly Ann about to pick up the pastry that had been in Sheriff Owens' mouth.

"Do not touch that, Kelly Ann," yelled Kay. "It is nasty."

Kay rushed over to the pastry, wrapped it in a napkin, and threw it in the trash.

"I wasn't going to eat it Miss Kay," said Kelly Ann.

Officer Rue and Debbie could detect that something was amiss. Officer Rue asked to speak with Officer Cox in private and Officer Cox told the children that it was superhero business. The children took their packages to Kay so she could see what they had bought. The officers went into Officer Cox's room and he informed him of the situation. Kay asked Debbie to pack their clothes because they were leaving to a new location. Debbie did not ask any questions. She told her children it was nap time. Carolyn picked up the cushion and returned it to the sofa. Kay packed all the boxes of Susan's stuff and used Carolyn's surgical tape to fasten them together. She labeled the boxes to be sent to the Cortland Police Station to the attention of Lieutenant Gorman. Then she asked Sheriff Owens to mail it for her in two days so she would arrive in Cortland the same time the boxes arrived. Sheriff Owens thanked Kay for saving his life, then carried the boxes to his car. Marie explained to Evan why they had to pack their luggage and move to a different hotel. Officer Rue assured Officer Cox that he did not see Leonard in the shopping area.

"He does not know we are traveling with children," thought Officer Cox to himself. "That could be to our advantage. If we travel as a large family we might be able to get back to Cortland safely."

Officer Cox used his portable telephone to call Lieutenant Blackshear to ask him to reserve nine tickets using an assumed name. He knew if Leonard was watching the airport and they were flying to Cortland, they would be spotted and possibly killed. So he asked for tickets to Albuquerque, New Mexico and then he wanted tickets to fly to Cortland from there. The Lieutenant said he would call him back with confirmation numbers. After the flight plans were completed, the two officers returned to tell the others what the game plan was.

"Officer Rue will go down to your rooms and help you pack," explained Officer Cox. "Once you are ready to go, we will meet at your room then travel to the lobby together. There should be a taxi van, parked by the curb, waiting to drive us to the airport."

"Leonard will be waiting for us there," Marie cried. "The moment you ask for tickets to Cortland, he will know it is us."

"We are not going to Cortland, we will be traveling to Albuquerque, New Mexico," said Officer Cox.

"We will stay there a day then travel to Cortland. He will not know our schedule because he will not be able to follow us. There are going to be extra policemen posted at the airport near the Cortland ticket station. Three undercover officers are going to pose as Kay, Marie, and me to buy tickets to Cortland. If Leonard is at the airport, he will be watching the wrong people. I think we need to get started."

Since her body frame was tiny, Kay masqueraded as one of Debbie's children. Officer Rue pretended to be Debbie's husband. Officer Cox pretended to be Carolyn's husband. Marie and Evan did not have to pretend. Everything from the hotel to the airport went smoothly. Their flight to Albuquerque, New Mexico seemed short because they were entertained and enjoyed watching Debbie's children experience their first airplane flight. The stewardess gave each child a pilot pin to wear on their shirt and a coloring book.

Lieutenant Blackshear had taken extra safety measures to notify the Albuquerque Police Department and explained to them about Kay's situation. There was a car waiting for the nine frequent travelers to take them to their hotel. The children loved their new location and were going to get to go swimming in their new swimsuits in a covered heated pool. Kay rented the entire fifth floor at a beautiful Indian resort. Kay and Carolyn roomed together adjoining to Officer Cox's room. Officer Rue's room was next to Debbie's room that connected the newlyweds' room. The room nearest the elevator housed two Albuquerque policemen. All the other rooms on that floor were empty. Officer Cox made it clear that the connecting doors to the rooms were to remain unlocked at all times.

"I never realized when I agreed to work for you that I would be traveling across the United States in one week," smiled Carolyn.

"I never dreamt I would have the money to travel across the Untied States in one week," said Kay. "I have seen more of the United States in nine months than I have seen in my entire life. I have to say that we live in a beautiful country. Carolyn, the snow was so fabulous in Colorado. I got to see Pikes Peak for the first time and it was covered with snow. The trees out there look like they reach beyond the stars and the stars look like you could reach out and touch one. The people are very nice and there is this one handsome Lieutenant there that can make you melt when he looks in your eyes."

"Kay, what is Debbie going to do? I can tell when she talks that she does not have a good education, maybe as high as the tenth grade," confined Carolyn. "I am not trying to run your life or tell you who you can hire. She is a nice person but what is she capable of doing?"

"I am going to have you teach her the proper and professional way to answer a business telephone call and to take messages. I want to be her friend. You see, I over heard her talking to her mother. She was begging that hateful lady to let her and the children come live there but she did not want those precious children near her. You should have heard her crying on the telephone. It was heart breaking. So I would appreciate it if you would let her assist you when you are overwhelmed with work. Later, I might hire her as my secretary or give her a job at one of my companies. I own several companies and when the Christmas season is over, I am going to see who has been naughty (not doing their job) and who has been nice (working their butts off) and I am going to make some major changes," alleged Kay with authority in her voice. "I would like you to be on my team."

"I want to be on your team, too, boss," agreed Carolyn. "Besides I love working with Officer Cox. You should have been there when I removed his shirt to tend to his injury. Oh my goodness, he is beautiful, with or without blood on him."

"Carolyn, it sounds like the love bug has bitten you again," laughed Kay. "I want to go down to the swimming pool area and watch those sweet children. Do you want to come with me?"

"I am ready," smiled Carolyn.

Kay knocked on Officer Cox's door but there was no answer. She peeked inside but the light was off. She figured he was taking a nap; after all, he had been awake all night. She telephoned him from her room and left a messaged that she and Carolyn were at the pool.

At the pool, Marie and Evan were sharing a tropical drink with an umbrella in it. Officer Rue, Debbie, and the children were in the warm clear blue water of the pool. The pool was covered by glass and situated so there was a great view of the mountains from three sides. Kay glanced at a man on the diving board who was getting ready to jump into the water. It was Officer Cox. Kay yelled at him which interrupted his concentration and he fell off the board.

"You are not supposed to be in the water," yelled Carolyn. "The wound could get infected. Get out of there now."

"You are wasting your voice, Carolyn," laughed Kay. "He is going to do whatever he wants to do."

Officer Cox swam to the side of the pool where Kay and Carolyn were sitting and watching the children.

The Children kept yelling, "Watch me, watch me," then they would jump into the clean water.

"It is hard to believe that it is snowing outside and paradise in here," said Carolyn.

"Are you going to get in the water?" asked Officer Cox. "It is warm and relaxing."

"Nope, I am going to finish reading this diary," said Kay. "The more I know about this family, the easier it will be to find Leonard."

"You should not be in that water either," scolded Carolyn. "Get out of there now."

"Bring me a towel and I will get out," yielded Officer Cox.

Carolyn took a towel from a guests' towel shelf located in the back of the pool area. She unfolded it and lowered it down to Officer Cox so he could get out of the water. Instead, he grabbed the towel and pulled Carolyn into the pool, making a huge splash. Carolyn swam to the side, wet and laughing.

"You are an idiot," she yelled. "Now all my clothes are wet."

"There is a complimentary laundry room with a dryer on the first floor," laughed Officer Cox. "Your clothes will be dry in a jiffy."

"Jiffy," yelled Carolyn. "I will show you Jiffy."

She threw the towel in Officer Cox's face and pushed his head under the water. The children were laughing and splashing water on Carolyn and Officer Cox while their mother relaxed on a complimentary guest float. Officer Rue was swimming laps trying to impress Debbie with his fancy swimming techniques. Debbie could have cared less about his swimming skill. She was totally stress-free. She was getting divorced, thanks to Mr. Hughes. She was getting a new job, thanks to Kay. She would be moving to a new city away from her abusive husband and her children would be safe. It was the most tranquil and peaceful feeling she had ever experience and she was not going to let some swimming show-off policeman disturb her restful moment. Officer Cox, Carolyn, and the children played volley ball.

David asked, "Miss Kay why don't you get into the water? It is the best."

"I know David," said Kay. "I am reading something important and I did not bring my swimsuit."

"Miss Carolyn does not have a swimsuit and she is in the water," he said.

Officer Cox hit the ball in Kay's direction and it got her leg wet.

"OK big boy," Kay spouted. "You are asking for trouble."

"Will you give me the ball, ma am?" asked Officer Cox (waiting by the side of the pool).

Kay knew his intention was to pull her into the pool so she threw the ball at him. She went and sat by her mother and Mr. Hughes, out of harms way. She asked her mother to show her the wedding band. It was gold, had diamonds, and was beautiful.

"It is a beautiful ring, mother," admired Kay. "I got to see Uncle Billy's ring when I was in Colorado."

"I have a ring for you, dear," remembered Marie as she dug into her purse to find it. "Here it is, honey. I think this belongs to you."

Marie handed Kay the blue topaz and diamond ring her father had bought her when she graduated from high school. She remembered leaving it at her mother's house the night she escaped from the bomb shelter. Then it and several other pieces went missing. She never thought she would see it again and was surprised that her mother had it. She slid it onto her index finger.

"How did you get this, mother?" she asked.

"It was on Susan's finger and I asked if I could see it," answered Marie. "I knew it was your ring. I think that is when she knew I was on to her murdering ways."

"I am so very sorry I did this to you and Daddy," cried Kay. "I should have listened to you but I was brainwashed by that hypnotizing maniac. We need to pray for that family and all those people they have hurt."

"I can do that. Kay, do not take blame for the things that have happened. Everyone falls in love, even at my age." smiled Marie looking at Evan. "At least you know now what you are looking for in a man."

Kay thought her mother was the wisest woman alive and she loved her with all her heart. She taught her how to save money, play the piano, how to ride a bike, and now she is teaching her about love. Kay could not envision having a mother like Debbie's.

Kelly Ann came crying to Kay because the others would not give her the ball. Kay picked up Kelly Ann and carried her back to the pool to take care of her bullies.

"OK guys, it is time to get out of the water," yelled Kay. "Give me that ball."

"Give me one good reason why we should give you the ball," demanded Officer Cox.

"The only reason that I can think of is, that it is supper time and I am hungry," answered Kay.

"That is a good enough reason for me," smiled Officer Cox. "Here is the ball."

"Count me hungry," said Carolyn.

Kay lowered Kelly Ann to the floor and asked her to be the towel girl and bring everyone a towel.

They all went up to their rooms and dressed for supper. Carolyn applied some more medicine to Officer Cox's wound and a dry bandage.

"How does it look?" asked Officer Cox.

"Everything looks good," replied Carolyn.

In the dining room, the waiter handed out the menus and served their drinks. Most of the cuisine was spicy Mexican American food so Kay asked if she could have some extra peppers and onions on the side. David and Kelly Ann had never had Mexican food so Debbie ordered tacos for them. She did not realize their meal would include rice, beans, and two tamales.

"Officer Cox will eat anything that is left over," said Carolyn. "He is proud of his groceries and he wears them well."

Everyone laughed, enjoyed the Spanish music, and the food. Kelly Ann went to sleep in her mother's arms.

"I think it is time for bed," said Debbie as she looked at her precious daughter. "What time do you want us ready to leave?"

"Leave, we just got here," whined David.

Kay answered, "We will be leaving the hotel at nine o'clock to catch an eleven o'clock flight to Cortland."

"We will be ready, Kay," said Debbie.

Officer Rue asked if he could carry Kelly Ann to the room. Debbie gently passed Kelly Ann into his arms. Kay paid the bill and everyone went up stairs to prepare for the trip home. Kay gave her mother a good night hug and kissed Mr. Hughes.

"I will see you in the morning," she said with a yawn. "Sleep tight and don't let the bed bugs bite."

Carolyn put a clean dressing on Officer Cox's wound before she went to bed. She fell asleep as soon as her head touched the pillow. Kay took a shower and washed her hair before going to bed. She could not stop thinking about Susan's diary. She leaned on the wall in the shower stall to let the hot water wash over her body. Suddenly, a hand touched her naked back and she shrieked a loud scream and threw a bar of soap at Carolyn.

"Kay it is me, Carolyn," shouted Carolyn who thought something was wrong when Kay did not come out of the bathroom. "You fell asleep in the shower."

Officer Cox came running into the bathroom. He slipped on the bar of soap that Kay had thrown at Carolyn and slid across the bathroom floor. Kay and Carolyn screamed when Officer Cox went sailing by the bathtub in his purple pajamas. His body slammed into the toilet making a loud thump.

"Give me a towel," Kay told Carolyn. "OC do not look at me."

"I bet you tore your stitches again," Carolyn remarked as she handed Kay a towel.

Carolyn helped Officer Cox out of the bathroom so Kay could get dressed. She was inspecting his wound when there was a knock on the door. Carolyn peeked out the door to see her brother and another policeman ready to defend her honor.

"Is everything all right," he asked. "We heard screaming and a loud bumping noise."

"We are fine. Officer Cox fell in the bathroom and Kay fell asleep in the shower," answered Carolyn. "Other than that everything is fine. Go back to bed."

"How can anyone fall asleep in the shower? Was she standing up?" asked Dennis.

"Good night," Carolyn said as she closed the door.

"Why were you screaming, Kay," asked Officer Cox.

"Carolyn scared me," said Kay as she hurried to put her pajamas on. "I was thinking about Susan's diary and I must have fallen asleep. Carolyn touched my back and it scared me."

"Officer Cox where did you get those purple pajama bottoms?" laughed Carolyn as she checked his wound.

"Good night ladies," groaned Officer Cox. "It has been a long day. Put the diary away, Kay. You are going to have nightmares."

The next day was full of laughter as Officer Rue explained how he ran down the hall to rescue his sister and saw Officer Cox rubbing his butt because he had fallen in the bathroom after slipping on a bar of soap. When Officer Cox entered the dining room to have breakfast, everyone applauded him.

"OK, very funny," groaned Officer Cox.

The flight to Cortland was delayed due to snow covering the runways. The flight was rescheduled until the snow plows had cleared the snow and ice off the runways. Kay and her band of trekkers finally were able to board the airplane for home. She had brought some fruit from the hotel breakfast area for the children to eat on the flight incase they got hungry; however, the Stewardess served a hot lunch which consisted of Chicken pot pie and a brownie so no one wanted the fruit. The flight lasted for three hours, plus it arrived thirty minutes late.

Lieutenant Gorman was impatiently waiting for their flight to land so he could transport them to Mr. Hughes' home. He wanted an up dated report on the Leonard situation and he wanted to inform Kay of a development that had occurred while they were away. He had been waiting in the airport for several hours but he did not mind because he studied everyone that passed by him to see if Leonard was going to make an appearance to greet Kay when she arrived. Once they had landed, Kay introduced the Lieutenant to Debbie and her children. As they were driving to Mr. Hughes' home, both officers handed the Lieutenant a written report covering their trips. Officer Cox handed Kay several receipts from Lieutenant Blackshear so she could cover his expenses.

Debbie and her children were amazed at the size of Mr. Hughes' Southern style mansion. Kay was going to move her belongings into Carolyn's room because Marie would be sleeping in the master suite. She put the children in a room together at the end of the hall; however, Debbie did not want to leave the children by themselves. This was going to be a temporary arrangement until Kay could find a suitable home for Debbie to live in.

"Debbie could move into Mr. Blackstone's home," Kay thought. "It is a nice four bedroom home with a big fenced back yard. It would be perfect."

Kay was not going to share her plans with Debbie until she had time to move some of Mr. Blackstone's belongings out of the house and make it child safe for Debbie's family. She went down stairs to disclose her plans to Officer Cox so he could help her move Mr. Blackstone's possessions. She was comfortable with her decision until she walked into the family room to find her mother yelling at a group of grim faces.

"What is wrong?" she asked.

"Kay," started Lieutenant Gorman. "While you were in Colorado, a woman moved into Mr. Blackstone's home. She had some documents and a birth certificate that identified her as Mr. Blackstone's daughter."

"I did not know Mr. Blackstone had a daughter," confessed Kay as she sat next to her Mother on the sofa. "Since she can prove that she is his daughter, she can stay in his home."

"She is going to contest the will and sue you for degradation of character," continued Lieutenant Gorman. "She wants everything that belonged to Mr. Blackstone. She has taken out a restraining order against you until the court processing is completed."

"Well, that is not going to happen," alleged Kay. "I was going to share Mr. Blackstone's home with her, but not now. Why is she going to sue me for degradation of character? I have never humiliated or disgraced her. In fact, I do not know her or knew she even existed until now. Where has she been all these years?"

"Honey, she is not Mr. Blackstone's daughter," said Marie. "She is an impostor."

"Kay, by law, you are the sole proprietor of all Mr. Blackstone's assets and properties specified in his last will and testament. The woman has no authentication to appropriate anything from you or to dwell in any of your habitats," explained Mr. Hughes who was going to represent Kay as her attorney if this situation escalated into a court case.

"Then we need to ask her to leave the premises," said Officer Cox.

"No, OC," disagreed Kay. "I need her arrested. She is illegally trespassing on my property. Not to mention, she is breaking and entering my home while I am away."

"That is good," agreed Mr. Hughes. "That charge will stick."

"The first charge will but the second will be dropped," said Lieutenant Gorman. "I unlocked the door and let her in so she is not breaking or entering."

"I still want her arrested," ordered Kay. "The sooner we do it, the better. How long has she been in the house?"

"She arrived last night," said Lieutenant Gorman. "I know she is still there because I have a man watching the property."

"What kind of papers did she show you that convinced you to believe Mr. Blackstone had a daughter?" asked Marie.

"She had a birth certificate and some letters from her father," answered Lieutenant Gorman. "One letter stated that he wanted her to have everything and it was signed Mr. Blackstone."

"Was the letter written on blue stationary with his monogram on the bottom?" asked Marie.

"Yes, I remember seeing that. It made it official," said Lieutenant Gorman

"Arrest the witch," Marie angrily ordered. "She got that letter out of my house. Leonard must have given it to her. Mr. Blackstone wrote that letter but gave it to Eager to save for Kay. I can prove it."

Lieutenant Gorman telephoned the station to send several police cars to Mr. Blackstone's address.

"I want to be there when you arrest her," said Kay.

"You and Officer Cox can ride with me," replied Lieutenant Gorman. "Officer Rue, you stay here and wait for Officer Rodriguez. Please keep your doors locked."

Marie whispered in Officer Cox's ear, "If you see Leonard, please shoot him."

Officer Cox smiled and hurried to the car with Kay and the Lieutenant. As they were driving to Mr. Blackstone's home, Kay thought she heard someone say something to her. The voice said, "Use the key."

"What was that you said OC?" asked Kay.

"I did not say anything," said Officer Cox.

"It must be the air," alleged Kay then she felt her neck to see if the key was still there.

The officers surrounded the house and a swat team was called out in case Leonard was at Mr. Blackstone's house. They were not going to let this cop killer escape this time. Kay was asked to wear a bullet proof vest under her coat. They could see lights in the living room and a shadow on the drapes of someone moving around inside. Kay knocked on the door. The lady peered through the peephole to see who was knocking. When she opened the door, Officer Cox pushed Kay to the side and a troop of angry officers stormed into the house.

"What do you think you are doing?" yelled the imposter as Lieutenant Gorman put handcuffs on the woman.

"You are being arrested for impersonating a human being," answered Kay. "Did Leonard promise you a lot of money to come here?"

"I do not know what you are talking about," she shouted. "This is my father's house and I want you out of here?"

"Mr. Blackstone would not have a daughter like you," said Kay.

"I am going to sue," she screamed as Lieutenant Gorman led her to a police car. "You will be living on the streets when I get through with you."

"You have the right to remain silent," Lieutenant Gorman said. "So please shut up."

Officer Cox asked Kay to follow him into Mr. Blackstone's bedroom. She did not touch or move anything in the front living areas or the kitchen but there were papers thrown out of the desk covering the floor in his bedroom. She kept the bedroom doors shut so no one could see what she was doing. In her luggage, she had packed Mr. Blackstone's jewelry and old coin collection. She must have gone through everything in the house, looking for valuables she could steal.

Kay began to cry, "I would have shared everything with her if she was his daughter."

"At least, she did not get away with her plan," said Officer Cox.

"I want to talk to her," said Kay. "She might know where Leonard is hiding."

After the house was relocked and secure, they went to the police station to see the misguided child.

Lieutenant Gorman brought the woman before the Judge to set a bail amount. Mr. Hughes and Marie were driven by Officer Rodriguez to the police station to see what the Judge was going to do. The Judge asked the accused to step forward and plead her case.

She said, "My father, Mr. Blackstone died and these people are trying to steal my inheritance."

"Can you prove you are Mr. Blackstone's daughter?" asked the Judge.

"Yes, your honor," she slyly answered. "I have my birth certificate and a letter that my father wrote to me in my purse back at the house."

"This court is called to recess for one hour until this woman's information is submitted to the bailiff," ordered the Judge. "Miss Blackstone, you will be held in a holding cell until this information is present. No bail set."

Lieutenant Gorman was asked to retrieve the purse and bring it to the court. Kay once again heard a tiny whisper of a voice say, "Use the key."

Kay asked Mr. Hughes and Officer Cox to accompany her to the bank that Mr. Blackstone used which was around the corner from the police station. Marie said she would stay incase Lieutenant Gorman returned sooner than they thought and she would delay the proceeding as long as she could without being charged for contempt.

At the bank, Kay asked to have a safety deposit box pulled for her. The clerk asked for some identification and the key to the safety deposit box. She took the key off the chain from around her neck and presented it to the clerk. The clerk asked them to wait while she verified the information.

"We could do this later, Kay," complained Officer Cox. "We need to tend to this business."

"He is right," agreed Mr. Hughes. "That woman could escape if we are not in court to stop her."

"No," argued Kay. "I think I need whatever is in that safety deposit box today and now."

A banking supervisor, named Edward Reynolds, followed the clerk back to where Kay and her colleagues were waiting. He asked for more identification. Officer Cox explained that the information in the box was needed as evidence in a case that was being conducted today. The court was on recess until this evidence could be presented. Mr. Hughes

Said he could telephone one of his colleagues who could fax over any identification required to speed up the proceedings. He knew Kay had to get into the box.

Since it was a small town, it did not take Lieutenant Gorman long to return to the court house connected to the Police station. He handed the purse to the bailiff to be labeled as documents containing information for the case. Marie kept looking at her watch and the door, praying that they would return before the Judge called the court to order.

All the papers were faxed and everything was in order, so the supervisor told the clerk to give the box to her. The clerk asked Kay to sign and date a notebook. Then she was led to a security area where all the safety deposit boxes were housed. The clerk inserted her key first and then inserted Kay's. Both keys were turned and the safety deposit box was unlocked and pulled out of the enclosure. The clerk handed the box to Kay and led her to a room where she could review the contents in private.

She opened the box to reveal 30 United States Saving bonds, Mr. Blackstone's home mortgage papers, a picture of Mr. and Mrs. Blackstone when they were married dated 1942, their marriage license, and some coins he collected while overseas. She did not see anything that could possibly help with the case. She started to close the box to head back to the court house when she saw something at the bottom of the box. The aroma of PS design filled the room. Kay knew she had to see what it was. She emptied the box on the table to get to the object at the bottom of the box. It was the anniversary pen Mr. Blackstone had given her. It was attached to some adoption papers. She slowly opened the brown envelope and read the content.

The Judge returned and the bailiff called the court to order saying, "All rise for the honorable Judge Payne residing on this date for case number 2011." The Judge asked Lieutenant Gorman if he had delivered the purse to the bailiff. He answered him and the bailiff added it to the docket. The Judge asked Miss Blackstone if it was her purse.

"Yes, your honor," she answered. "The papers are inside."

The Judge asked the bailiff to examine the purse for any weapons then handed the purse to Miss Blackstone to retrieve the information that would support her case. Miss Blackstone handed the Judge her birth certificate and the letter from her father. The Judge asked that the evidence be noted and he reviewed the documents.

"This is a legal birth certificate and the letter is an original. Therefore I see no reason to doubt this young lady's credentials," said the Judge.

"NO, your honor," yelled Marie from her seat. "She is an imposter. Please let me talk."

"She is the lady that is trying to steal my inheritance," claimed the fraud. "You need to arrest her."

"Do not tell me what I need to do in my court, young lady" ordered the Judge.

"Yes, your honor," smiled the brown nosing pretender. "I was trying to help."

"Bring that woman to the bench," he told the bailiff.

Marie walked to the bench, assisted by the bailiff.

"What is your name?" the Judge asked. "I could hold you for contempt for making an outburst like that."

"My name is... Marie started to say but was interrupted when the door of the court erupted and Kay, Officer Cox, and Mr. Hughes came running in.

"THAT IS MY MOTHER," yelled Kay. "And that woman is an imposter."

Everyone was stunned and loudly talking as they ran up to the bench to prove Kay's statement.

Evan hugged Marie and said, "It is all right dear. She knows."

"ORDER in the court, order in the court," yelled Judge Payne as he hammered his gavel to the plate.

The Judge had known Mr. Hughes for years due to his law practice and asked him to explain why they caused this disruption in his court.

"Judge Payne, this lady is falsifying her identity with stolen documents acquired from Marie Lytle Hughes' home," informed Mr. Hughes. "Mr. Blackstone, which you knew well, bestowed all of his earthy possession to Miss Lytle, who is his daughter by birth. I have the adoption documents to substantiate my statement."

Kay hugged her crying mother as Mr. Hughes publicly announced that Kay was adopted at birth by Mr. and Mrs. Lytle when Mrs. Blackstone died while trying to give birth to Kay. Mr. Blackstone and

Mr. Lytle were best friends, along with Mr. Hughes, and he asked if they would adopt his daughter."

"I did not want you to know, baby," cried Marie.

"You will always be my mother, silly," smiled Kay. "I love you with all my heart."

"Arrest that young lady," ordered the Judge whose eyes were starting to tear up. "I am sorry for your loss, Kay. Mr. Blackstone was a good man."

"Thank you," said Mr. Hughes.

"Your honor," asked Kay. "Can we question that woman? The documents that she used were stolen from my mother's home by my ex-husband who is the serial killer and cop murderer, Leonard Morgan. She might have information that can aid in his capture."

The bailiff led Kay and her crusaders to a private room so they could talk to the imposter. Even the Judge attended so he could sit in on the questioning and hear what this woman was hiding. The bailiff brought the woman into the room and hand cuffed her to the table.

"Where is this man," Kay asked showing the woman several different facial photos of Leonard. "He is a murderer."

"He will come after you whether or not you tell us what we want to know," Officer Cox informed her. "He will kill you, too. We can help you with the witness protection program."

"I do not know what you are talking about," denied the liar. "I do not need any help."

"Listen to me," begged Kay. "We need to arrest this man as soon as possible. His name is Leonard Morgan and he is a cold blooded born murderer. You can yell and scream all you want until your lips bleed but he will kill you eventually, after he is through with you. He has no heart, no conscience, and no soul. He lives on the dark side manipulating innocent people like you. There is no cell that will protect you from him. He hates snitches."

"I have not told you anything," sassed the lady. "Not even my name. I am not a snitch."

"We will find out your true identity," said Officer Cox.

"We have computers that will tell us where you are from and how long you have lived there," added Lieutenant Gorman.

"Please help us to save you," said Kay.

"Drop dead," spit the woman.

No matter what they said, she would not help them. Finally the Judge said the questioning was over.

"Judge, may I ask her a question?" requested Marie who had been quietly watching the others.

"Yes, Mrs. Hughes," agreed the Judge. "You can ask her one question; then you all have to leave."

Marie patted Kay on the hand as she slowly walked towards the unidentified woman. When she was near enough to touch her; Marie punched the woman right in the mouth.

"Mother, that is not a question," exclaimed Kay as she pulled her mother away from the bleeding woman.

"Did you like that?" asked Marie. "He is going to do that to you until he kills you, whether you are a snitch or not. I do not care what happens to you because you are going to get what you deserve. If I were you, I would learn how to pray because God is the only one that can save you now."

"Did you see what that lady did," shouted the bleeding woman. "She hit me."

Everyone left the room so the screaming liar could face her hidden assassin alone.

The trip to Mr. Hughes' home was not as joyous as their flight home had been. Marie was upset about Kay finding out about the adoption. Kay was wondering if her mother's knuckles hurt.

Carolyn and Debbie had fixed dinner for them while the children were enjoying playing in Mr. Hughes' huge back yard with Officer Rue.

Officer Cox loved the home cooked meal and he ate like a horse. Kay did not feel like eating. Instead, she went into the den to have a quiet talk to Mr. Blackstone's ashes.

"Now I know why you talk to me and my father does not," whispered Kay. "You are my father. I have to tell you that you picked two wonderful people to adopt me. They kept your secret well. I must be the luckiest girl in the world because I could not have asked for two better fathers than you and my Daddy."

"Kay," Marie said in a soft voice behind her. "I wanted to tell you about Mr. Blackstone while he was in the hospital, but he insisted that

I keep his secret. He wanted to be close to you so he always lived a few blocks away from our home. He was very proud of you when you marched in the school band and when you wrote that Christmas song for your sick friend. No one could love you more than him but me."

"He still is close to me, mother," said Kay. "I need to sprinkle his ashes on his wife's grave before Christmas arrives so he can be with his wife at Christmas. I am leaving you again to go to Baltimore to honor his last request."

"I will be here waiting for you dear," smiled Marie.

"We all will be here, Kay," said Carolyn and Debbie.

"Now get in that dining room and eat something before Officer Cox commits over-eaters suicide," ordered Mr. Hughes. "I will telephone the airlines and make reservations for you and Officer Cox."

# THE FINAL REQUEST

## CHAPTER XIV

Once again it was off to the airport for another flight across the United States. Christmas was a few days away and Kay had not done any Christmas shopping. Mr. Hughes, Marie, and Officer Rue drove Kay and Officer Cox to the airport so they would not miss their flight.

"Do you have everything Kay, including Mr. Blackstone's urn?" Marie asked as she kissed her daughter on the forehead.

"Yes mother, I have everything," replied Kay. "Is there anything I can bring you from Baltimore? Any Christmas requests? "

"My Christmas request is for you and Officer Cox to come home safely for Christmas," smiled Marie. "I got my present early this year when I married Evan. So you come home to me."

"I will do that mother," alleged Kay as she followed Officer Cox into the airport for another adventure.

Kay did not realize that Mr. Hughes had reserved their seats in first class. The seats were wide, roomy, and comfortable. The flight was not long or boring because the airplane had a large movie screen which featured the most recent movie releases. Kay was not interested in watching the movie. She brought Susan's diary with her so she could read. She was still hoping to find a clue to where Leonard might be hiding. Each page she read written by this derange murderess helped her to understand their dysfunctional life style.

"Are you reading your Bible?" asked Officer Cox.

"No," Kay answered as she turned the book away from OC, because he did not approve of her reading Susan's horrendous life history.

"What are you reading?" he asked.

"Susan's diary," she said as she lowered the book.

"That book is full of hate and death," he said. "It is Christmas. The most holy time of the year and you are filling your brain with that woman's repulsive daily events. You are going to have night mares if you do not stop reading that."

"I am sorry," Kay agreed. "It is so ghastly that I can not believe anyone could live like that. I was hoping to read something that might lead us to Leonard."

"Let me see it," requested Officer Cox.

As Kay handed him the diary. He turned several pages from the back and starting reading. The clue she was looking for was on that page.

"Listen to this," he said excitedly, then read, "Our trip to Switzerland was wonderful. It was Richard's idea to transfer some of our money into a Swiss bank account. Our mountain home is quiet and peaceful. When we have enough money saved, we are going to move here to be free from the police and any gossip about my family. For now, it is a wonderful place to vacation. When Leonard kills Kay and her mother we can be safe forever."

Officer Cox closed the book and returned it to Kay.

"Now we know where he is going," he smiled. "To Switzerland, to their family mountain home. I think you have a chalet in Switzerland."

"I told you this diary would have a clue," bragged Kay. "I have never been to Switzerland. I have an idea."

"Oh no," whined Officer Cox. "I hate to ask but, what?"

"When we arrive in Baltimore, telephone Lieutenant Gorman," Kay planned. "Tell him that we think we know where Leonard is going. Ask him to contact the Police in Switzerland and fax them some face photos of Leonard. When we get there, they might have directions to Leonard's vacation mountain home."

"That sound like a good idea," agreed Officer Cox. "Wait a minute, you are not planning on going to Switzerland, are you?"

"Yes, but after Christmas," said Kay. 'It will be another adventure."

There was a man holding up a sign that read, "Gorman Family". Kay and Officer Cox knew that was for them. The driver carried their luggage to the car for them and drove them to a beautiful hotel that faced the river. Their connecting rooms were located on the sixth floor and Officer Cox unlocked the connecting door. There was a message for Officer Cox to call Lieutenant Gorman when he arrived. Kay placed Mr. Blackstone's urn on the night stand while she unpacked.

"I got a message from Lieutenant Blackshear to tell you, 'he received the check and thanks you for the thousand dollar bonus,'" reported Officer Cox.

"Is that what Lieutenant Gorman wanted to tell us?" asked Kay.

"No, Lieutenant Gorman wanted you to know that he found out the lady's name was, Sarah Kinder," answered Officer Cox.

"Her name was? What did she do; change it so Leonard could not find her?" Kay asked sarcastically.

"No she was killed in a cell fight over who was going to sleep on the top bunk," answered Officer Cox.

"Oh, I am so sorry. Lord, please forgive my short coming," she prayed. "That is awful."

"Well are you ready to sprinkle Mr. Blackstone's ashes?" asked Officer Cox.

"Will you give me a minute to use the bathroom?" replied Kay.

"Of course," said Officer Cox. "I will call downstairs for our car."

Officer Cox returned to his room. Kay went into the bathroom and knelt next to the bathtub. After he called for the car, he returned to take Kay downstairs. He noticed the bathroom door ajar and discovered Kay on her knees praying.

She prayed, "Lord, I am sorry for my unkind remark. I did not know Sarah but she had to have a family somewhere. Please, God bless them and help them through the holiday season. Also, thank you for giving us good traveling weather and getting us to Baltimore safely. Amen."

She washed her face, grabbed Mr. Blackstone's urn; then walked to

Officer Cox's room so they could leave together to get the car. Officer Cox was sitting on his bed, watching the weather report.

"Looks like more snow tonight," he said as he turned off the television.

He grabbed his portable telephone and held the door open for Kay and Mr. Blackstone.

It was a short drive from the hotel to the snow covered graveyard. Kay asked the cemetery attendant where Mrs. Blackstone's grave was located. The graveyard attendant made a map for Kay, then asked the old ground's keeper if he would show them to the grave site. The seventy-one year old man asked Kay to follow him in his dirty twenty year old pick-up truck and he would take them straight to the grave. They followed the old man around several curves and down two slippery hill sides until he reached the back of the cemetery. He parked his truck and carefully walked to Kay's car to help her walk in the snow, so she would not slip. Officer Cox stayed alert as he followed both of them to the grave site. He made sure there was no one following them or hiding behind a head stone or a tree. There were snow covered trees in the graveyard that had trunks the size of round dining room tables. Not a breeze was blowing as they solemnly walked to the grave.

"This lady has been dead a long time," informed the caretaker. "I have put flowers on this lady's grave every month for twenty-five years. This is the first time that no flowers were sent. I guess they forgot her this year."

"No, he did not forget her," Kay sadly replied. "Her husband died. I have his ashes in this urn. Thank you for taking care of my mother."

"Child, it was no problem at all," claimed the old man. "Everyone has a job to do and that was my job. What are you going to do with those ashes?"

"He wanted me to sprinkle them over her grave," answered Kay.

"Let me dig a hole for him and you can pour the ashes in the hole. If you pour him on the ground, it will turn the snow gray and look nasty," alleged the old man.

"No, I am going to honor his final request," Kay said. "But thank you."

"Do you want me to do it?" asked Officer Cox.

"No, I have to do it," she cried.

Kay opened the urn, held it over Mrs. Blackstone's grave, and gently emptied his ashes towards the ground. His ashes never touched the ground. Instead, a north wind softly blew across the cemetery and carried Mr. Blackstone's ashes into the sky. The aroma of his cologne filled the air and surrounded Kay as if to say thank you. As soon as the ashes were gone, so was the wind.

"That was strange. Did you feel that wind as it blew through here then stopped? What is that smell?" asked the caretaker.

"It is my father saying good bye," cried Kay as she lifted her hands toward the sky. "Merry Christmas Daddy Blackstone. Thank you for everything."

Kay and the caretaker returned to the car while Officer Cox slowly tagged behind them.

He said, "Merry Christmas, sir. I hope we meet again."

Kay asked Officer Cox to stop at the cemetery office again so she could thank the attendant and tell the people how much she appreciated their help. She wrote down the address of the cemetery so she could send flowers to her mother's grave side every month. She left an envelope for the caretaker with ten one hundred dollar bills in it and a note to thank him for taking care of her mother's grave.

Kay stared out the window as Officer Cox drove back to the hotel. She was sad and quiet as she reflected on her life with Mr. Blackstone and her father, Edger Lytle. She telephoned her mother when they had arrived at the hotel. She told her about the nice caretaker who had kept flowers on Mrs. Blackstone's grave until Mr. Blackstone died.

"I love you mother and will see you soon," she said as she ended their conversation.

"Good night OC," said Kay. "I will see you in the morning."

Officer Cox was eating a slice of left over pie from their supper and watching a Christmas movie.

"This is a really good movie, Kay," said Officer Cox. "It is about a man who wanted to get out of a small town but something kept happening to keep him there. He marries his high school sweet heart and they have four children, but he never gets to leave his home town."

"I have seen that movie a hundred times," admitted Kay. "I think there is an angel in that movie."

Kay sat on the bed in Officer Cox's room and watched the movie with him. She fell asleep before the movie ended. Officer Cox covered her with the blanket and slept in her room on her bed.

In the morning Kay was surprised that she was still in Officer Cox's room and had slept there all night. She found Officer Cox asleep in her room. She grabbed her over night bag and took a shower in Officer Cox's bathroom. She ordered room service and read the Bible while she waited for their breakfast to arrive. She was returning the Bible to the night stand when Officer Cox awoke. She could hear him yawning in the room connected to hers so she politely knocked on the door and asked if he was ready to eat breakfast.

"I am always ready to eat, Kay," he said.

"It will be here in a minute," she informed him.

After breakfast, Kay packed her luggage and stacked it at the door. Officer Cox was almost completely dressed when Kay told him she needed to put a clean bandage on his injury. Officer Cox protested as he removed his shirt but Kay told him that Carolyn wanted the bandage changed everyday until it was healed. He sat on the edge of the bed as Kay gently cut off the old surgical tape. She poured some hydrogen peroxide on the wound and some of the cold peroxide ran down his chest causing him to shake.

"I am sorry," apologized Kay. "Did that sting?"

"No, it was cold," whined Officer Cox.

"You big baby," Kay said as she covered the wound with a clean bandage. "There, all done."

She looked into Officer Cox's blue eyes and got a funny feeling in her stomach.

"Is something wrong?" he asked as he looked into Kay's green eyes.

Kay shook her head and said, "No, nothing is wrong. You need to get dressed so we can leave."

Kay stepped backwards away from Officer Cox and tripped on one of his shoes. He rescued her from falling to the floor.

"Who put those shoes there?" Kay scolded as she moved toward her room.

"They are my shoes so I guess I did," said Officer Cox.

There was a knocked on the door and a voice said, "Bellman. I am here for your luggage."

The bellman carried their luggage to the car, Kay tipped him, and they were driven to the airport to return home for Christmas. At the ticket counter, the attendant informed Kay that their flight would be delayed due to snow.

"As soon as it is safe for the planes, we will reschedule your flight," advised the ticket agent.

"It is Christmas eve," said Kay. "I promised that I would be home for Christmas. That was my mother's request before I left."

"You will have to wait like all these other people, Miss," said the ticket agent. "They probably want to get home for Christmas, too."

Kay and Officer Cox impatiently sat at the departing gate waiting for their flight to be rescheduled.

"OC," confessed Kay. "I have not done any Christmas shopping. Would you mind if I go shopping for a few minutes."

"Where are you going to go shopping?" asked Officer Cox. "You can not leave the airport or you will miss your flight."

"I saw some shops in the airport that are still open," said Kay. "I promise I will not take a lot of time and if I see Leonard, I will blow the whistle you gave me."

Officer Cox saw no harm in her shopping since there were a lot of people stranded at the airport and since the security officers had increased in number due to the holiday. Kay had a great time last minute Christmas shopping for her family. Kay bought Carolyn and Debbie some diamond earrings. She bought Mr. Hughes a history book about the Indians and their cultures in the Eastern states. She bought her mother a crystal cornucopia and a diamond cross necklace. She bought Debbie's children several small electric hand held games for traveling. She bought Officer Rodriguez and Officer Rue a gift card and put two hundred dollars in each of them. For Officer Cox, she bought a pair of purple and black polka dotted pajamas that had a pocket on the shirt and a pull string on the bottoms so he would not have to wear his belt to bed. She also bought everyone a small pocket cross to carry with them wherever they traveled. The sales clerk quickly and beautifully wrapped all the packages in gold paper, topped with a red bow. She returned content and pleased with all of her purchases.

The ticket agent announced that their flight was rescheduled to leave at seven o'clock and would arrive in Cortland at mid-night.

Kay and Officer Cox slept on the return flight home. Kay used Officer Cox's shoulder as a pillow. The plane landed at eleven thirty which gave them thirty minutes to get their luggage and drive to Mr. Hughes home in time for Christmas.

"I have never ran through an airport that fast in my life," Kay laughed exhaustedly.

Officer Cox flagged down a taxi to take them home. Kay tipped the driver one hundred dollars if he would speed and get them home safely.

"Lady," complained the driver. "I need the money but I do not want to get a ticket at Christmas time."

"I am a policeman," Officer Cox informed the driver as he showed him his badge. "If someone stops you, I will take all the blame and pay the ticket."

The taxi driver ran every red light between the airport and Mr. Hughes' home. They arrived at the house at eleven forty five. Kay gave the driver his tip and thanked him for getting them there safely.

They carried their luggage to the front door. They could hear everyone inside playing the piano and singing her song, "For all I want is time, to spend with this family of mine."

Kay rang the door bell.

"They are singing your song," said Officer Cox. "Merry Christmas, Kay."

Then he kissed her.

Officer Rodriguez looked out the window and saw their luggage on the front porch.

"It is Kay and Officer Cox," he yelled as he unlocked the door.

"Merry Christmas," greeted everyone as Officer Rodriguez opened the door.

"Merry Christmas, baby," yelled Marie. "Welcome home."

"Merry Christmas," Kay said as she hugged her mother. "I told you I would be home."

"Did you bring us something?" asked David.

"Yes, I did," smiled Kay as she handed the packages to Carolyn and Mr. Hughes to distribute.

Kelly Ann had a new baby doll in her right hand and her arms wrapped around Kay's legs as she said, "This is the best Christmas I ever had, Miss Kay."

Kay watched everyone opening their gifts and laughing at Officer Cox's polka dotted pajamas and she agreed, "It is the best Christmas I ever had, too."

## IN MEMORY OF DONNA REYNOLDS

## FRIENDS FOREVER

.